Djibouti

ALSO BY ELMORE LEONARD

FICTION

Road Dogs

Comfort to the Enemy

Up in Honey's Room

The Hot Kid

Mr. Paradise

The Complete Western
   Stories of Elmore Leonard

When the Women
   Come Out to Dance

Tishomingo Blues

Pagan Babies

Be Cool

The Tonto Woman & Other
   Western Stories

Cuba Libre

Out of Sight

Riding the Rap

Pronto

Rum Punch

Maximum Bob

Get Shorty

Killshot

Freaky Deaky

Touch

Bandits

Glitz

LaBrava

Stick

Cat Chaser

Split Images

City Primeval

Gold Coast

Gunsights

The Switch

The Hunted

Unknown Man No. 89

Swag

Fifty-two Pickup

Mr. Majestyk

Forty Lashes Less One

Valdez is Coming

The Moonshine War

The Big Bounce

Hombre

Last Stand at Saber River

Escape from Five Shadows

The Law at Randado

The Bounty Hunters

NON-FICTION

Elmore Leonard's 10 Rules
   of Writing

Djibouti

ELMORE LEONARD

Weidenfeld & Nicolson
LONDON

First published in Great Britain in 2011 by
Weidenfeld & Nicolson
An imprint of The Orion Publishing Group Ltd
Orion House, 5 Upper Saint Martin's Lane
London WC2H 9EA

An Hachette UK Company

1 3 5 7 9 10 8 6 4 2

Copyright © Elmore Leonard 2010

First published in the USA by William Morrow,
an imprint of HarperCollins USA

The moral right of Elmore Leonard to be identified as the
author of this work has been asserted in accordance with
the Copyright, Designs and Patents Act of 1988.

A CIP catalogue record for this book is
available from the British Library.

ISBN 978 0 297 85672 6

Printed and bound in Great Britain by Clays Ltd, St Ives plc

The Orion Publishing Group's policy is to use papers that
are natural, renewable and recyclable products and made
from wood grown in sustainable forests. The logging and
manufacturing processes are expected to conform to the
environmental regulations of the country of origin.

Djibouti

For Mike Lupica

CHAPTER ONE

XAVIER WATCHED TWO LEGIONNAIRES stroll out from the
terminal to wait for the flight: dude soldiers in round white
kepis straight on their heads, red epaulets on their shoulders,
a wide blue sash around their waist, looking like they from some
old-time regiment except for the short pants and assault rifles.
Standing there waiting for Air France arriving from Paris, due in
Djibouti at 8 A.M.

From the terminal Xavier watched an air force cargo plane
land and taxi to the end of the strip where a line of Blackhawk
helicopters were parked. By 8:30 the once-a-week Air France was
in, the stairway wheeled up and a gang of Arabs and Dara Barr
coming off, the Foreign Legion checking out the passengers,
seeing could they tell a terrorist they saw one.

Now Dara was coming along talking to an Arab-looking
guy, nodding, getting along, maybe sat next to each other on the
flight. The man wore a tan suit and striped tie, had a trim Arab
beard but looked citified, not the kind rode camels. Now Dara

was putting on her shades. She'd be saying how hot it was this early.

Xavier crossed the lobby to wait as they came through customs, Dara taking some time to get her visa; it allowed her to stay six months if she wanted. She'd tell them no, she planned to cruise around and shoot pirates for a film. Now Dara was coming out with the Arab gentleman, saw Xavier and ran into the arms of her six-foot-six black assistant, slim in his faded jeans and T-shirt, Xavier seventy-two, twice Dara's age, Dara squirming, glad to see him, Xavier kissing the crown of her blond hair saying, "You the best thing I've smelled all week," and raised his eyes to the Arab gentleman watching.

The man smiling now. "Dara's told me about you."

This Arab with a Brit sound to his voice.

"I understand you've been through the gulf countless times as a seafarer. Now you come as Miss Barr's cameraman."

"More her grip," Xavier said.

Dara got them shaking hands, introducing Xavier LeBo from New Orleans to Ari Ahmed Sheikh Bakar. "Known as Harry in England," Dara said. "Harry's with IMO, the International Maritime Organization, investigating—you ready?—piracy in the Gulf of Aden."

"Actually," Harry said, "my role is with the Djibouti Code of Conduct people, under the auspices of the IMO."

Dara said, "Tell Xavier what you do."

"Quite simply, I speak to pirates directly, the leaders, about the hopelessness of their venture. They're bringing the navies of the world down on them in their outboard skiffs. I try to convince them there's simply no future in piracy."

"Harry," Dara said, "is the spokesman for what is proper in this African world, or what can be gotten away with, and what is outright improper, hijacking ships and holding them for ransom."

"Dara, as you know," Harry said, "actually sympathizes with the pirates." Harry getting a look of amazement in his smile. He turned to Dara to say it was great fun traveling with her and learning about her films, actually stimulating. "I love your stories," Harry said to her. "You'll call me as soon as you have time, all right? Promise? And I'll introduce you to an actual pirate, sort of a gentleman rogue. Or that's the way he sees himself."

XAVIER WATCHED HARRY GIVE Dara a peck on the cheek and hurry out to step into a Bentley, shining dark green in the morning sun.

"He does all right, huh?"

"He went to Oxford."

"Learn to talk like that?"

"His mother's English, his dad's Saudi. They keep an apartment in London on Sloane Square. He says his mom's hip, at one time ran with the Sloane Rangers. She stayed there on and off while he was at Oxford."

"He's for real? The man talks to pirates?"

"We're meeting him in two weeks at a place called Eyl, a pirate stronghold on the Somali coast."

"He call it that, a stronghold?"

"It's a beach town where they're holding eight hijacked ships. I said in two weeks they might be gone. He said, 'Or there might be more.' They've had an oil tanker there for three months. There are always ships, Harry said, being held for ransom. Harry plays the patient, understanding good-guy role. You heard him, he called it his *role* with the Djibouti Code of Conduct. Seventeen countries that agree piracy must be stopped. Once in a while they meet in Djibouti. Harry lives in the European quarter, a

Saudi working for the improvement of Somalia. If that's what he's doing."

"But you like him," Xavier said. "Thinkin, Hmmmm, I never had an A-rab boyfriend."

"When could I?" Dara said. "Come on, I want to see our boat."

THEY PICKED UP DARA's luggage and equipment cases and put them in the rental, a black Toyota sedan, Xavier asking if she'd like to stop at the hotel first and freshen up.

"Have my hair done?"

"You could."

"Have I ever had my hair done?"

"Once I know of, when we got the Oscar. That's the best-lookin you ever been."

"*We* got the Oscar? You told Harry you were a grip."

"Bein humble in the presence of the Brit sheikh. You want me to be a grip, I'm your grip. You want me to shoot somethin, I'll shoot it. And you'll like my work. I been shootin shrimpers, gettin 'em to act up. I believe I could do the same with these Somali gangbangers, shoot 'em pullin off their acts of piracy, the first big-time acts in three hundred years, believin they got the stuff to do all they want. They cocky. You say you want to put 'em in a movie they gonna wet their pants."

"I'm counting on them," Dara said. "But I want to see the boat. How big is it?"

"A thirty-foot trawler. All cleaned up and painted it looks like a boat for gay sailors, a cute little fat-ass boat. Has a beam on her can ride most seas. Or put paravanes on her, stick out to the sides, you want to keep her from rollin too much."

"She's ready to go?"

"Stores comin later on. I made a deal with a man supplies hotels. We stockin French table wines and Heinekens, the only beer I could find around here. The Heineken man must have people workin for him carry machine guns. You can't drink the water. You might even be puttin yourself at risk takin a bath." Xavier said, "You mention shootin here when we get back—lemme show you what you have, you might not want to shoot it. This Djibouti's a nasty place. Hot, full of open sewers, has rats, dirty kinds of bugs, like that beetle rolls up bat shit bigger'n he is?"

They were following a fairly straight road along the east coast of the city.

"But if you gonna shoot some now"—he paused—"get a feel of what to look for when we back? Fine. But don't shoot people lookin at you."

Dara took an HD camcorder, a small one, out of her cotton shoulder bag.

"They want to be paid?"

"Some even refuse the bribe. Spit in front of you and walk away. I don't know it's their religion the reason. They mostly Sunnis here. The pirates, I hear they somethin else. Okay, we go over a few blocks now and head back south."

Dara lowered her window. "You're starting with the slums?"

"Girl, this is the upscale part of town, where the Europeans live."

Dara, shooting now, said, "Sort of like our French Quarter."

"I was gonna ask if it reminds you."

"It does, a little. Vieux Carré with Moorish doorways and windows."

"Old-time French Colonial built by Arabs. I been through the gulf thirty-seven times. Mostly comin west we'd put in here to refuel."

"You always went ashore?"

"I could be a tour guide, keep you from steppin in the sewers. You don't see none here but you will, we get to the African quarter. Look way over left. That's the U.S. Embassy. How'd you like to be the ambassador to Djibouti? His wife ask him, 'What you gonna do today, dear?' Ambassador say to her, 'You know, I wouldn't mind tryin some of that khat. Suppose to make you feel cool while you doin time in this ghetto.'"

Dara said, "I hear khat is big in San Diego, all the Somalis living there. But why San Diego?"

"See if they any retired pirates there. Now we comin to the Central Market, biggest one in town, the mosque standin over it. Rows and rows of stalls sellin shit—clothes, chickens, all kind of fruit and vegetables. Look at the outfits, the colors on the women. Lookit over here, the table of meat."

Dara was shooting it.

"It's moving."

"That's the flies on the piece of goat loin, all movin around to get a bite. Look at the girl there, holdin branches of leaves, cellophane around the bunch. She sellin khat. Only good two days so you keep it out of the air." Xavier reached over to touch Dara shooting the rows of stalls, the women sitting under umbrellas. "Look at those guys, the wads in their jaws. Suckin on khat, known as the flower of paradise. All day they be chewin and suckin. They fly it in from Ethiopia, deliver ten eleven tons of chew every morning. Keep the men happy."

"The women don't use it?"

"What they can sneak. You in the Muslim world. Women get seconds maybe."

"I got some of that in Bosnia," Dara said.

"Your best one. You know how to shoot women, get in their souls, how you do them. Hey, but you good with men, way you let 'em be theirselves thinkin they hot shit. Listen, you gonna get a chance tonight, see the bad boys up from Somalia in the big city."

"You're sure they come here?"

"Buy a suit of clothes . . . buy cars and they hardly have any roads down where they live. They come here lookin for French pussy and settle for Ethiopian chicks. They not bad, or the chicks down from Eritrea, they special, have that fine bone structure in their faces. You gonna see the bad boys out clubbin, the first time in their poor-ass lives in the big city cuttin up."

"How do you know they're pirates?"

"They tell you. Let the chicks know they loaded from hi-jackin ships, makin good pay from it. I talk to a party lady after the boys left or passed out, had some English. She say these Somali desert boys are more fun than the Frenchies. Love to get all the way drunk. And they rich, finally livin their lives."

Dara got out a cigarette and lighter from her shirt pocket, a faded blue work shirt loose and comfortable on her. She said, "They go out in skiffs, take down huge cargo ships and tankers, and make at least a million or so each time." She snapped her lighter but didn't hold the flame. "I wonder if they're getting help. Tipped off, told what ships look good, easy to board."

"They gone after a hundred or so and score forty-two times," Xavier said. "That's like battin over four hundred."

"Somebody," Dara said, "could be giving them information for a piece of the action."

"Who you think's doin it?"

She said, "Maybe we'll find out. I want to see my boat," and snapped the lighter again.

CHAPTER TWO

XAVIER POINTED TO THE commercial port off to the west, fuel tanks and cranes standing against a glare of sky. They were loading container ships from a framework of steel girders. Dara saw a cruise ship in port, a navy supply ship at anchor in the stream. Xavier said, "The warships must be out tryin to catch pirates. I told a sailor the other night, 'Go to the bars, man, the pirates all in there spendin the loot.'" Xavier drove out a road past land development and across a causeway to follow the pier straight out to a jog, the pier jutting out on an angle to become a wide concrete dock where pleasure boats took on fuel and provisions.

"You see it yet?"

"Not that sailboat."

They were approaching a motor-sailer tied up on their left. "That's *Pegaso,*" Xavier said. "Sixty-two feet bow to stern, enclosed wheelhouse. She's made for comfort, but she'll move in a wind."

"What is it, a yawl?"

"A ketch. Like a yawl but with a big mizzen aft, stepped forward some. She'll raise four sheets of canvas in a friendly sea, jib to mizzen."

Dara saw a guy with a girl in a bikini on the stern, the man raising a glass to them as the Toyota rolled past. The girl's hair was red, kind of wild.

"The guy's takin his girl," Xavier said, waving to them, "on a trip round the world. Givin her the test. She don't complain or get seasick he'll think about marryin her."

"You're kidding. The girl agreed to it?"

"Guy's wealthy, has his rules."

"I don't believe it."

"They started out in Nice, a cold wind, a mistral, come blowin down from the Alps. He figured, she become seasick he'd drop her off in Monte Carlo, not have to take her all the way round the world. But she made that part of the trip fine. They come down through the Suez, the Red Sea, now they gettin ready for the Indian Ocean."

"He told you that?"

"The man's chatty. Said his boat will run you thirty-five thousand a foot you want one like it. Full of electronics and power, so he don't have to lift nothin."

"How does he make his money?"

"As I understand, it's in the family, goin way back. It don't sound like he works any."

"Not an overnight millionaire."

"The man likes to talk is all. You ask him about his boat, he tells you. They stayin at the Kempinski, Billy Wynn and Helene. He's close to fifty. I'd put Helene at twentysomethin."

"And a knockout."

"It's how she has the ticket to ride. I been runnin into them different places. Had drinks with Mr. Wynn at the hotel, loves champagne. He said call him Billy."

They were coming to their boat now at the end of the dock.
"I told you a trawler," Xavier said. "This one all cleaned up and
painted pure white with a pretty orange trim. Lookin gay don't
mean she ain't seaworthy."

Xavier pulled up even with the trawler, Dara looking past
him at the white hull, the orange trim along the gunnels and
around the top of the wheelhouse. She said, "You're right, it's
kind of cute, isn't it?"

They stepped aboard, moved from the deck to the wheelhouse to go below, from the galley to the head and a double mattress wedged into the bow. Behind her Xavier said, "That's yours.
I got a nine-foot hammock gonna hang from the foremast to the
wheelhouse, while you sweatin below."

"Or I put the mattress under the hammock and stare at your
butt till I fall asleep."

"You can take the hammock you want," Xavier said.

"We'll work it out," Dara said. "We've got a fridge, a shower
. . . kind of a bunk in the galley. We get aboard we'll find places
that suit us. How much wine did you get?"

"Five cases of red we don't have to chill."

"What if we have company?"

"Muslims don't drink, but I'll get us another case."

"Store them in the head, we'll look like that German U-boat,
Das Boot. This one have a name?"

"*Buster.*"

"You're kidding."

"They call it *Buster 30*, goin by its length, but chubby. The
tank's topped off. Saab marine diesel below, but only fifty-six
horsepower at twenty-eight hundred rpms, and that's it. We
gonna be out cruisin the gulf at six knots. The boat manager
called this a power cruiser."

"How much?"

"Man said he wanted two thousand a week, eight for the

month. I showed him your piece with the write-ups and pictures. This a Frenchman leases us the boat. I tell him ordinarily the transportation is loaned to us no charge, since we show his company name in the film. I tell him he can even be standin by the sign says DJIBOUTI MARINE DESIGNS—LUXURY ON THE WATER. I tell the man, 'But you not the Salvation Army, you in business, so I'm payin you,' and put a wad of forty hundred-dollar bills in his hand. Now he's holdin the money, can feel it. He says, 'All right.' Says, 'Okay. You come back here in four weeks.'"

Dara said, "I have to put him in the film?"

"The man's savin you four grand. Course you put him in the film."

She paused, in the galley again. "Who cooks?"

"I take the helm and keep track of where we at, you do the fish."

"Are we forgetting anything?"

"The food service man's seein about gettin me a gun."

Dara stared at him, not saying a word.

It got Xavier to smile. "I do whatever you tell me. Still, situations can rise up you never been in before. We out there among the bad boys with AKs and weapons fire rockets. They drinkin, chewin khat, so they feelin good they go hijack a ship. I said to one of 'em I'm talkin to in a club last night, 'You always high you out to sea?' The man say, 'If we not drunk, what are we doin in a skiff and think we can seize an oil tanker?' They on the sauce gettin millions for their ransom notes. It's funny long as they don't have eyes for *Buster*."

Xavier would drop Dara off at the Kempinski and come back to see the stores put aboard. Get *Buster* loaded, ready to leave in the morning, 0600. This time, driving past the sailboat, there was no sign of anyone aboard.

"Mercedes came and picked 'em up," Xavier said. "You didn't see it? Billy Wynn has a man drives 'em around, he don't have to mess with traffic. He has a driver, you have me, and a suite at the hotel, price of a deluxe room, 'cause you a famous American filmmaker."

"Do I have to shoot the hotel?"

"It won't hurt you. Use Billy you need a model. I bet a dollar he's waitin for you."

"With his girlfriend?"

"I can't speak for Helene, but I know he's dyin to meet you. I told him what we up to."

AT THE DESK SHE said, "Dara Barr. I have a reservation," and turned to look at the Kempinski Palace's five-star Arabian lobby, the fountain outside the entrance, while the desk clerk pressed keys and stared at the screen. Dara told him to look for it under Xavier LeBo, and the Somali's face brightened.

"Yes, of course, Mr. LeBo. You must be his companion."

"I'm his boss," Dara said. "We don't bunk together." She was given the card to open the door and was told her luggage would follow immediately.

The room was nice, sort of French, a settee and a couple of chairs with arms, a carafe of what looked like sherry on the glass table. Dara got a bottle of ice-cold water from the bar compartment and drank it looking out at the swimming pool that seemed to extend into the sea. She saw one, no, two women in lounge chairs, but not together, lying in the African sun and Dara thought, Not today. Check on the cameras before you do anything. She called the desk to say she was still waiting for her luggage. Got "Yes, madam, immediately," and went in the bathroom to wash her hands and fool with her hair for a few minutes, trying to give it some life. The phone rang.

She said, "Yes?" expecting it to be the desk clerk.

"Miss Barr, this is Billy Wynn. I met your cameraman, Xavier LeBo? We got along great talkin about seafarin . . . I had seen you on YouTube being interviewed and showing clips from your films—I couldn't believe you're *here*. The only one of yours I've seen the whole thing of is *Katrina*. I downloaded it and watched it last night. Dara, you nailed that hurricane. Thirty thousand people in New Orleans taken off their roofs?" Telling this with an East Texas sound, not much, but Dara heard it, Billy Wynn delivering his lines in no particular hurry, serious, sure of himself, a playboy—if that was still the word—taking his girlfriend for a ride around the world in his two-million-dollar sailboat.

What he said was, "If you're not too tired, why don't we meet downstairs for a drink?"

"I don't have my luggage," Dara said. "I've been waiting, I called the desk . . ."

"If I don't have it in your room," Billy said, "in five minutes, I'll owe you a bottle of champagne."

Dara set out two champagne flutes from the bar cabinet and went back to the bathroom to wake up her hair, rubbed it for a while with a towel, gave up and tied a bandana around her natural blond hair, leaving the ends curling out. She stared at herself in the bathroom mirror. Now she slipped on her sunglasses.

That was better.

But why bother if his girlfriend's with him?

And thought, Why not?

He came to the suite with the bottle of champagne and a bellman pushing a luggage rack. Billy Wynn said, "Damn, but I'm a couple minutes late," and held up the champagne.

"I put the glasses out for you," Dara said, not bothering to watch his reaction. She dug a ring of keys from her jeans and turned to the bellman. "You can leave the trunk and cases here on the floor. The hanging bag goes in the bedroom." She went down on one knee to open the locker and got to her feet as she raised the lid and looked down at her cameras and battery packs snugged in foam inserts. She said, "It's all there."

Billy looked over as he opened the champagne: a tall guy with a noticeable belly hanging over his low-slung white shorts.

"You worried it wouldn't be?"

His hair was kind of a mess, long and uncombed, but seemed to go with his rich-beachcomber look.

"I don't worry about it," Dara said. "You met Xavier? He brought a camera and the rest of the equipment."

"I asked him"—Billy coming over to hand Dara a glass of champagne—" 'What're your people, Watusis?' I'm six foot and have to look up at him." Billy said, "Why don't we sit down while we visit?"

He paid the bellman and came over to take a chair, Dara already on the settee, an ashtray on the end table next to her. Now she lifted a pack of Virginia Slims from her shirt pocket and lighted one and offered the pack to Billy Wynn.

He shook his head. "I smoke cigars."

"It doesn't bother Helene?" Dara stepping right in.

"I only smoke 'em at sea." He grinned at her. "You been talking to Xavier, haven't you?"

"He mentioned you had your girlfriend along."

"And if she likes sailing as much as I do, it could mean we're compatible. We take it from there."

"Were you ever married?"

"Almost, a couple of times."

"They got seasick?"

He was grinning at her again.

"Let me explain it to you. I spend a good half the year at sea, sailing all over the world. Do I want to leave my good-looking wife at home for that long if she doesn't care to sail? Helene says okay, she'll give it a try."

"What does she do?"

"You mean does she work? Helene's a fashion model. I met her in Paris, she's working a show for one of the houses. I'd watch her come down the runway with her bored-model look, red hair afire, her swarm of freckles subdued . . . She'd glance in my direction, sitting a couple rows back, and smile."

"She knew who you were."

"No. She told me after, she pretends to see people she knows and gives them a quick smile. Show she's not aloof."

Dara hesitated. She said, "If you're out in your boat half the year . . ."

"You want to know do I work. My family's had oil leases in Oklahoma for a hundred years. It was my granddad put us in the shipping business, oil tankers going back and forth between Nigeria and East Texas. This trip, I'm looking into doing business with the Saudis, see how they're dealing with the pirates"—grinning now—"and I find out you're making a pirate movie, a documentary, the real stuff. Xavier said you're gonna sail out to the gulf and talk to 'em, get interviews."

"I hope to."

"You think the Somali government's behind them?"

"I doubt it," Dara said. "It's been almost twenty years since they've had a government, one that works. The Islamists in Somalia, the straight-arrow Muslims, say they're against piracy, but who knows."

"They're all Muslims," Billy Wynn said.

"Some more than others," Dara said. "You know the Somalis hijacked a Saudi tanker."

"Months ago, the *Sirius Star*," Billy said. "The last I heard they're still trying to work out a ransom. I was wondering," he said now, "if it might be an outfit like al Qaeda financing the pirates. Where'd these fishermen get their guns, AK-47s, RPGs . . . ? I've heard they come from Yemen. The government selling weapons is making money while the people go hungry." He said, "Well, the UN's taking serious action, finally. You'll see warships out'n that Gulf of Aden but, man, it's a mean piece of water."

Dara listened, sipping her champagne and smoking her cigarette.

"They catch some of the pirates," Billy said, "what do they do with them? Kenya will take some, throw 'em in prison. But whose laws have they broken? Who tries them?"

"I don't know," Dara said.

He turned on his grin.

"But you can sure get people to talk in your movies. I admire that."

"You like documentaries?"

"I do. Good ones always reveal the truth," Billy said. "I can't wait to hear what the pirates tell you."

CHAPTER THREE

Y OU WENT TO A fashion show in Paris to look for a girlfriend," Dara said. "Is that right?"

"I remember what one it was, Chanel. The guy who runs the house wears the stiff collar and shades? He was there, came out at the end."

Billy the Kid started to grin.

"I was there to look over the girls. See if I might pick one out. They tend to be skinny, but that's okay, they all in pretty good shape."

"Ask her if she wants to go sailing?"

"Not right away. I see a girl for forty-eight hours. In two days you find out all you need to know. She acts intelligent, but she's busting her ass to pick the right words, uses *I* when she means *me*, and reads the wrong books, if she reads. I don't want to sound heartless, but we'll be doing a lot of reading aboard, talking about books. I ask if she's ever shared a tiny flat with another girl and thrown things at her. Nine out of ten say, 'No, but I sure wanted to.'"

"She fails the test?"

"Becomes a forty-eighter. I start with looks, get that out of the way. Then brains and personality. I'll be with this girl a good four months in fairly tight quarters. Now if she's funny *and* smart, that's a combination made in heaven."

"Helene's funny?"

"Helene's the goods."

DARA TOLD XAVIER SHE wanted to have dinner out of the hotel. She'd looked up the Blue Nile on rue d'Éthiopie, a five-star restaurant and it sounded just right.

Xavier said, "Who gave it the five stars, the owner? You want to have a girl wash your right hand? Pours water over your fingers and catches it in a bowl? Then you take a towel off her arm? What if you left-handed?"

"We're going," Dara said.

"You want the girl shovin some kind of stew on your Ethiopian flatbread? They call it *injera,* so you know what the girl's tellin you. Or maybe you go for the *sega wat,* the diced lamb all cut up. These fine women make a show of servin us. Say no to the Queen of Sheba salad. We don't eat salad in Djibouti. Or get out of the Blue Nile in less than three hours. We be finishin off three different wines at one-fifty a bottle, and that's house wine."

"We're not going," Dara said.

They went out for the evening with no plan other than meet Billy and Helene later at a club, Dara planning to shoot Djibouti nightlife. Prowl around with her hand on the camera in her bag. Billy had asked them to dinner, but Dara said they'd be working most of the evening. See you later on. He'd told

Xavier the name of the club. She would love to find out what he was up to, the generous rich guy interested in her work; once in a while with a hint of East Texas country boy looking for Saudi crude. After a few glasses of wine she might ask him, "Billy, what are you up to out here in your sailboat? What's your game?" He'd laugh at her and she wouldn't have time to get him to talk. This evening she was sneak-shooting Djibouti. She wouldn't mind using it as the title of her documentary. *Djibouti*. She loved saying it.

XAVIER TOOK HER TO the Chez Chalumeau restaurant on the rue de Paris. They sat down at the table and Dara put on her sunglasses wondering why it was so bright in here. Xavier said, "So you can see what they put in front of you. They cook French mostly. The side dishes could be Arab, but good here. Go with the lamb, you won't get in trouble."

Dara said to her menu, "Which one's fish?"

"Their tuna they call a Somali name. They got shark, the fin, octopus they fix in its ink, oysters. The crabs are good if they fresh. Or they can fry up some squid's tasty." Xavier said, "Remember, we gonna be eatin fish all the next month."

They ordered lamb, no salad, and a bottle of red. Xavier ordered another bottle as the floor show came on: four Somali girls shaking their bums to a drum and a guy singing or making sounds, the four dressed in long pink pongee gowns with panels, scarves they swished around their hips as they kept their bums rolling, spinning, bumping . . . Dara said, "The Blue Nile doesn't have cooch dancers, does it?"

"I don't believe they have."

"I want to know how they do it."

"Practice," Xavier said. "We get out on the boat, I'll beat on something and you try and get your ass up to Somali speed."

THEY FOLLOWED THE RUE de Paris to the Place Ménélik to sit at a street café. "Have a cup of coffee and watch Djibouti night-life," Xavier said. "Cup of coffee and sip some cognac. Watch the tourists cuttin up. Off a cruise ship come down through the Suez. They sayin, 'Ain't Africa *fun*?' They could be in Marseilles doin the same thing." Dara busy working her camcorder over Ménélik Square. "You gettin the Foreign Legionnaires. French boys never seen anything like these slim black chicks givin 'em eyes. Got epaulets on their shoulders, with fringe, and a sash around their waist. Man, this is where to get stationed, if you can stand the heat. Go in the clubs, see the girls rubbin against the boys. You notice they don't wear that flap off the back of their kepis no more, like Beau Geste? You gettin the action?" Dara was shooting with the camera in plain sight. "What you don't see, too many American military hangin out. They been warned about the girls. You see some sailors, some Shore Patrol. Look over there. Keep 'em from bringin home any kind of African dose," Xavier said. "Café Las Vegas, run by a Corsican. That's where we meetin Billy and the model."

BILLY SAID, "I CAN'T believe we're in a French joint on the rue de Paris and they don't have Perrier-Jouët, Blanc de Blanc '99?"

Xavier said, "I can't either. Let's go talk to the man, see if he has something like it. I never had a beverage cost nine hundred dollars a bottle."

They left Dara and Helene alone at the table, Dara's blond

hair washed and fluffed out, Helene's red hair—no stylist in sight—tied back. She said to Dara, "I can feel my face shining."

Dara said, "You look good." She hadn't spoken more than a few words to Helene with Billy Wynn at the table. Now she said, "I can't imagine sailing all the way around the world," and waited.

Helene said, "You mean on a boat or with Billy?"

The girls by themselves now, Billy and Xavier checking the wine list at the bar.

Helene said, "I'm actually going to powder my nose," and got up from the table. After a moment Dara got up and followed her into the restroom.

"I'll see what I can fix," Dara said.

Helene was at a mirror brushing something on her cheeks. Dara moved in to look at herself in part of the mirror and Helene edged over a few inches. Dara took out her lipstick.

"I don't use any unless It's some kind of occasion." She looked at Helene in the mirror. "You have a wonderful tan. It brings out your freckles. Makes you look like a kid."

"I'm thirty-four. Billy thinks I'm in my twenties and I let him."

Now Helene was staring at Dara's reflection.

"You know what I keep thinking about, constantly? Going out on that fucking boat again."

"For four months," Dara said.

"Or longer. 'Take in the mains'l. Lay down to the galley and put on some chow.' 'Aye, aye, Skipper.' I sound like an idiot."

"You don't get seasick?"

"I get bored."

"You don't have to go."

Helene said, "You don't know what's at stake. Billy's almost twenty years older than I am. We marry and he ever passes away? I'd be something like the thirtieth-richest woman in America."

"He told you that?"

"An inducement, giving me a goal."

"It could be a long wait," Dara said. "He seems in good health. He doesn't smoke."

"Cigars," Helene said. "You think I'm out of my mind?"

"You must like him—"

"I *do*. He's kind . . . he's thoughtful . . . He's funny sometimes. He calls Obama 'that spear-chucker we got in the White House,' but Billy likes him, I can tell." She looked at Dara's reflection again.

"You married?"

"I've been too busy," Dara said, "to think about it."

"But you're not, are you, a lesbian? Some of the girls I work with are. They're nice, not especially bitchy. Sometimes I'll tell a guy I'm one to shut him down."

Dara said, "I like guys. But I like whatever I'm doing right now, whatever I want, more. I lived with a lawyer once—he didn't want to get married either. He'd tell me why we were better off single living together and go through a, b, c, once in a while, d. He'd thought of another reason."

"What's c, having sex anytime he wants?"

"He talked constantly. He'd say things he thought were funny. He'd start telling me a fact, anything, about world populations and go on and on. One time I asked him a question about the Supreme Court he could've almost answered yes or no. He started talking and I wanted to shoot myself."

"You were fucked, and you did it to yourself," Helene said. "Billy tells long stories about investigations—I guess for the government—and makes it sound like he's in it. Billy goes, 'Me? No.' Takes a swig of champagne. 'But I know things.' He's either a lovable jerkoff or, I don't know, maybe some kind of CIA guy. But you know what's weird? Wherever we are, I know somehow he's going to hand me a glass of champagne."

"He turns you down, you're still a runway star with the hair and the body."

"If I ever get in shape again. You're the first person I've felt I can talk to. You know why I'd marry him, all the bullshit aside, because he's a fucking honest-to-God billionaire. I knew you'd smile. He doesn't have to be funny. He can talk all he wants. But why is he always handing me a glass of champagne?"

"I wouldn't think to get you drunk and seduce you."

"I'm practically bare-ass on the boat. No top, ever, out of sight of land. He doesn't want some sneak with binoculars seeing what he's got."

Dara said, "What's the problem?"

"I don't know how long I can last."

"If you want to quit, go out in the boat tomorrow and throw up."

"I don't get seasick."

"Put your finger down your throat. Or, stay with it and write a book. Tell what happens going around the world with a billionaire. And maybe around and around. You could get an advance, I think at least a million, and a pro to write it for you. What's the difference?"

"If he turns me down, I write the book in my own words. And if I marry him I don't have to write the book."

Dara said, "I'm gonna stop worrying about you."

They got back to the table as Xavier and Billy Wynn were coming with a Somali in a white suit, the shirt open, a yellow scarf looped about his shoulders. Xavier calling, "Dara, we got us a pirate."

FIVE OF THEM SAT around the table with bottles of Blanc de Blanc Billy brought from the bar he said for openers, Xavier anxious to introduce his pirate.

"Dara, like you to meet Idris Mohammed."

Idris rose to his feet and bowed.

"Commander of a gang of swashbucklers run out in the gulf and hijack whatever ships look good. Idris say he's never lost a man or killed any crew on the ships."

"I can't tell you," Dara said, "how happy I am to meet you. May I call you Idris?" It got a look from Xavier.

Her pirate had those Somali cheekbones in a thin face, a good-looking guy with a neat beard and white teeth smiling at her. He said, "Yes, Idris, of course," with an African accent.

Dara asked him, not wasting a moment, if he thought of himself as a pirate, or had a more acceptable name for what he did. Idris smiled.

"I think of us as the Coast Guard giving fines to ships that contaminate our seas, thousands of them leaving their waste in the waters we once fished."

"You were a fisherman?"

"My family."

"You speak English so well—did you ever live in America?"

"You detect that, uh? Yes, Miami University in the state of Ohio for part of several years."

"Wow," Dara said. "What did you study?"

"It was my understanding you don't study too much there."

Dara smiled and then Idris smiled.

"You're my first pirate," Dara said. "Did Xavier tell you what we're doing?"

"Making a movie, yes, about pirates. If I can help you I will. My home is in Eyl, in Somalia, but I'm here at least a week each month. I have a residence in the French Quarter and a car to get me around, a Mercedes-Benz drophead. It's black, completely black, with dark windows to keep out the sun."

Sounding proud of it.

"You drive to Eyl?"

"Once in a while. Or I travel with a friend who has a Bentley and a driver."

"That wouldn't be Ari the Sheikh Bakar, would it? Known to his chums in England as Harry?"

"Ah, you are the one he met on the plane from Paris. Of course, Dara Barr, the filmmaker. I saw him briefly this afternoon. Yes, he said he met you, but you haven't called him."

"I did, but there was no answer."

"Harry keeps busy. He runs around being the good guy."

"He said his job is to talk to pirates."

"Yes, he does that, tries to convince us there is no future in piracy. I tell him, who needs the future? We can make enough now to improve our lives. There is nothing dishonorable in what we do. The sea is our life."

"Ask him," Billy Wynn said, "how much he thinks he'll get for that Saudi tanker?"

Idris said, "It's taking months, isn't it?" a pleasant sound to his voice. "That one isn't mine, so I don't know if progress is being made in negotiating a payment."

"They started out wanting twenty-five million," Billy said, "the ship and its load of crude worth ten times that."

"Well," Idris said, "they could settle for only two or three million, it would still be profitable."

"You know," Dara said, "there are warships hunting you. The American navy, the French, German, Greek, even the Chinese."

"Yes, I think I saw one or two warships," Idris said. "I believe they're painted gray?"

Having fun with her.

"You and Harry," Dara said, "are sworn enemies, but it sounds like you're friends."

"Dear, we met in this club two years ago, and had a good laugh we find out I'm the bad guy and he's the good guy. I tried to get him to quit acting respectable and become a pirate.

You know what he said, 'I don't need to make money that way. Mother sends me an allowance. Whatever I need.'"

"He sounds like a cool guy," Billy said. "I should talk to him."

Then Idris asked Dara if she'd like to go for a drive. Dara hesitated a few seconds before she asked him to swear in the name of Allah he was a pirate and not putting her on. He swore he was a man of honor from Miami University in Ohio.

Xavier said, "Girl, we leavin town oh-six-hundred. That's A.M."

Too late. Dara was walking out with Idris.

Xavier settled back, thinking, Now you worried about her goin out with an African pirate, after puttin up with Bosnian thugs and white supremacy assholes makin her pictures? She's gonna shoot him in his Mercedes and fit it in someplace.

CHAPTER FOUR

THE FIRST DOCUMENTARY FILM Dara Barr shot on her own was called *Women of Bosnia* and it won an award at Cannes. Dara stayed on the women, no men in the picture identified, only the women after the men had used them.

She made *Whites Only* intercutting neo-Nazi white supremacists with Klansmen wearing robes of different shades. It won Best Documentary at Sundance: skinheads and coneheads exposing their racism to Dara's camera.

She walked out of her studio on Chartres in the Quarter and shot Katrina ripping through New Orleans, flooding much of the city, and her two sisters, divorced, left town together for Hot Springs, Arkansas. Her mother and dad, retired, living on St. Charles Avenue, thought of having their home repaired for the third time, sold the property and moved to Sea Island, Georgia. In the lull that followed the hurricane Dara's camera stayed on people who couldn't leave, homeless now, waiting for help that never came. Dara said she shot Katrina because there it was, outside. It won an Oscar.

The awards came during her first ten years making factual films, showing people's lives, getting them to talk about who they were. Dara was thirty-five at the time she began thinking about her next one.

Nuns? She found them in a convent, sisters who had taught her in grade school, a gathering of Brides of Christ, pressing their rosaries through withered fingers. Some still wore their habits. Not one Audrey Hepburn among them.

Try the other direction: a call girl talking about love for sale as she dresses to meet a john at one of the better hotels. She moves around the bedroom with her exposed breasts beginning to sag, telling Dara, "What do I do after, run a house? In New York it's a three-bedroom apartment on the West Side. Sit in the living room talking to the john waiting for the high-energy black girl. He's looking at *Playboy*. I was in *Playboy* when I was eighteen, before you had to shave your cooze and come off looking like a fucking statue. Is that what you want to make, a movie about me bitching?"

An idea came along from a guy who sold restaurant supplies in a town devoted to restaurants. Gerard, a nasty drunk before he found his Higher Power in AA and cleaned himself up. Gerard's idea—he'd even finance it—shoot AA meetings, the drunkalogues, a man or woman standing in the front of the room telling about harrowing situations inspired by booze. "I look up, I'm driving into traffic coming at me on the freeway, fast, nine o'clock Friday evening."

Dara had doubts, but listened to stories at meetings, heard recovering alcoholics being contrite, heard others tell their drunkalogues like they were doing stand-up. "I go out to wash the car, I'm in my bathing suit, and I come in the house smashed." One after another. "In two years I had three DUIs and did thirty days for driving without a license."

"Everything is told," Dara said. "These people are telling the film instead of showing it. They're doing monologues. Albert Maysles knew how to set a mood. He was seventy-eight when he made *In Transit,* got passengers on a train talking about intimate moments in their lives. But while they're telling, they're showing who they are. He got as close to his subjects as possible and seldom asked a question, never ever foreground himself in his scenes."

Gerard said, "So you don't want to shoot drunkalogues."

Dara became fixed on the pirates reading a three-column headline in the *Times-Picayune:*

SOMALI PIRATES ARE
HEROES TO VILLAGERS

She read the piece that began: "Somalia's increasingly brazen pirates are building sprawling stone houses, cruising in luxury cars—even hiring caterers to prepare Western-style food for the hostages."

Down to: "In northern coastal towns the pirate economy is thriving thanks to the money pouring in from ransomed ships, which has reached thirty million so far this year."

Dara pulled stories off the Internet and read about Somali pirates for the next few hours, accounts of what they were up to, some stories with photographs:

The Saudi oil tanker carrying a hundred million dollars of crude, hijacked, boarded by pirates in less than fifteen minutes.

The MV *Faina,* a Ukrainian cargo ship, being held for ransom since September, thirty-three Russian tanks and assault rifles aboard.

Photographs of Somali speedboats skimming over the water with six or seven pirates aboard, each boat armed with AK-47s and rocket-propelled grenade launchers.

Another photo, a trawler and its crew of Somalis wearing

casually wrapped kaffiyehs and T-shirts, and a sign on the trawler's wheelhouse that read SOMALI COAST GUARD.

She began to realize these guys were doing their own style of piracy, nothing like the old-time cutthroats. The Somalis were having a good time getting rich. She thought of Xavier who lived around the corner on St. Philip, and phoned him.

Xavier's voice came on asking Dara, "What you up to this hour?"

She said, "You've been through the Gulf of Aden, haven't you?"

XAVIER LEBO, SIX-SIX STRAIGHT up in his bare feet, seventy-two years old, a black man with a gold ring in his ear, some gray in his hair and white teeth he showed smiling at Dara. Xavier had gone to sea when he was sixteen. He told Dara he'd been through the Gulf of Aden thirty, forty times counting both ways. He said, "You know how many ships pass through?"

"All I'm sure of," Dara said, "it's on the east coast of Africa."

"Twenty thousand merchant ships and oil tankers a year," Xavier said. "The ones headin west go up through the Red Sea to Suez, where the Egyptians try to shake you down. The other way you go all the way to China. You interested in the pirates, huh, rippin off all the ships go by."

"I wouldn't mind talking to some of them."

"They gone after a hundred ships and caught maybe forty of 'em. Take money from the safe and what they want from the galley. Or they run the ship down to Eyl and hold it there for ransom. Ask a couple million for a Greek cargo ship and get it. You know what they want for the *Sirius Star*, the Saudi oil tanker? Twenty-five million. The Saudis say they won't give 'em shit. All right, they'll take seventeen million. They'll get *some-thin* and buy new cars. You know what their favorite is? Black Toyota SUV with black windows. I hear some of the pirates are dressin up. They put on a suit and tie, drive up to Djibouti to get laid and marry a fine-lookin woman. Be his Djibouti wife."

Dara heard him flick his Ronson to light a cigarette.

"You know where to find the best-lookin girls in Africa? Eritrea, on the Red Sea, above Ethiopia. But now I think about it, they some fine-lookin Ethiopian women I've seen. Smart-lookin thin ladies with the cheekbones, some black as coal, their race not tampered with much through the ages." He said, "Hang on a minute, I got to take a leak, relieve my worn-out bladder."

He came back on and Dara said, "I'm thinking about doing one on the pirates. Interview some of them . . . Does that make sense?"

Xavier said, "Yeah, but they take one look at you, gonna hold you for ransom."

"Really?" Dara said. "What do you think I'd be worth?"

THEY MET THE FIRST time two days before Katrina, knowing it was coming, Dara waiting for a table at Felix's, the manager telling her, "Just a few minutes, Dara."

Xavier got up from his table and waved her over.

"Come on sit here. They lyin to you, 'just a few minutes.'" He pulled out a chair at his table, a dozen oysters and a bottle of beer waiting. "You don't mind, I like to ask you about a movie you made." He started to smile a little. "The one you called *Whites Only*? You surprise me. Nice-lookin woman associatin with those freaks. They try and mess with you?"

"At first," Dara said, seated now with Xavier. "I told them I'm too busy to fall in love, okay? I asked what they've got against African Americans. Got them saying nasty things and started shooting."

"Shoulda used a shotgun."

Dara had a dozen oysters, then another while Xavier was on his third plate, Xavier telling her he'd been going to sea on and off most of fifty years. "Me and three hundred thousand Filipinos. I don't know where they go. I always come back to New Orleans."

They had a couple of cognacs and coffee after.

"You gonna shoot the hurricane's on its way?"

"I may as well."

"Bringin the Gulf of Mexico up the river. You gonna need a tall man to hump equipment, keep it dry."

"And a second cameraman," Dara said.

By the time they were shooting what was left of the Ninth Ward, Xavier was aiming a shoulder-mounted Sony at people sitting on top their homes, Xavier seeing their despair and hoping to catch it on film. Later on he sat in on the editing of these scenes and watched Dara give it her touch, eliminating his smash close-up of a woman's face to treat her more gently, the woman on her roof holding a child. Xavier would look at Dara's cut and see what it was like to be that woman.

He went to Hollywood with Dara for the Oscar show.

She even brought him onstage to stand next to her in his tux Dara borrowed from one of the Lakers, Xavier looking down at the top of her blond hair, done to slant across the corner of her eye. He thought Dara looked like a movie star. Even had on makeup. Dara in a black gown pasted on her slim body. She looked to Xavier like she was supposed to look. It seemed natural to her, like the hot chick was inside the documentary film shooter waiting to make her move. She held up Oscar, raised him over her head as she thanked her sponsors. Then brought Oscar down and thanked her cameraman Xavier LeBo, saying his name in a slow way as she looked up at him. "Xavier kept talking to me, asking if I was quick enough to shoot a hundred-and-fifty-mile-an-hour hurricane going by." Dara said, holding up Oscar again, "Xavier deserves some of this award."

Xavier said, walking off with Dara, "You right that time."

DARA MADE UP HER mind they were going to East Africa to get the real stuff, pirates in action boarding merchant ships. "And talk to them," Dara said, "get their side, the entire shipping world against them. We'll head south along the Somali coast to—wherever they're holding the ships."

"Eyl," Xavier said, "on the Indian Ocean. Gonna need a trawler, a deep-sea fishin boat cleaned up, can take any kind of sea. I get it ready, stock provisions—for how long?"

"A month at least. Where do we get the boat?"

"Djibouti, at the crossroads of us and the Arabs. Leave Djibouti, you in the Gulf of Aden lookin for pirates. Us and warships from around the world, all out there like we know what we doin."

"You've read about the pirates?"

"You say we goin to Somaliland I read everything's been written about pirates. The past few months the Internet's heavy with pirate shit and the different navies after 'em."

"I'll print out the latest stuff and read it on the plane," Dara said. "I imagine we go to Paris first."

"Connect there to Djibouti. Air France or Daallo, you want to travel with the natives. You have a name for the movie?"

Modern-Day Pirates.

"About stock and bond salesmen?"

"You like *Djibouti*?"

"That has a sound to it, yeah. I'll give you one, *The Evil Solution.*"

"You're kidding."

"One of the pirates called it that. Man name of Shamun, head of the gang that took the Saudi tanker—seven times bigger than the *Titanic.* He said when evil is the only solution . . . No, he said they have to get Somalia to settle down first, with a gover'ment can go after the pirates when they ashore. He said get rid of the foreign boats fishin these waters and you rid of the foreign navies watchin over them. He said if they busy with fishin boats they can't protect the ships haulin goods. Shamun said, 'So they become our fish.'"

"It's not a bad line," Dara said.

"You want to hear what else he said? 'What we doin might be evil, hijackin their ships. But if evil's the only solution'—where I stole the title—'then we do evil.' This is a man in the middle of all this shit goin down, calls it The Evil Solution."

"It only works," Dara said, "if the audience knows whose point of view it is. Otherwise it sounds like a Sherlock Holmes title."

"All right, you come up with the name of your picture," Xavier said. "I won't worry my head about it."

"Are you packed?"

"Leavin tomorrow." He said, "How about *Dara Barr's African Adventure*? Have natives bangin on tribal drums."

"I was thinking of laying in drums," Dara said.

"Good, you gettin yourself in the mood," Xavier said. "I'll see you next week in Djibouti."

CHAPTER FIVE

D ARA WAS OUT ON the *Buster* twenty-seven days.

She caught a ride on a supply plane off the carrier *Dwight D. Eisenhower* and was back in Djibouti three days before Xavier arrived on the *Buster*. It gave her time to put together a rough cut with the beginning of an idea, a theme.

SHE WAS IN HER suite at the Kempinski Palace again looking at happy-pirate footage on her seventeen-inch MacBook Pro. She had Idris Mohammed in his Mercedes trailing dust in the moonlight. She had Idris at the tiller of a Yahama-powered skiff trailing a high wake; Idris in sunglasses, a yellow scarf around his head; Idris and his Coast Guard boys going out to hijack a ship.

She liked the rhythm of the edit: pirate skiffs getting a beat going with quick cuts to faces she thought of as rimshots coming in a flow of action and gone. She cut much of the shipping footage: cargo ships and tankers in extreme long shots, too far away to tell if they were moving. She kept most of the navy ships and helicopters, the few she had: a dozen countries out patrolling the Gulf of Aden, but try to find them. She did have the light plane attempting to drop bags of ransom on the deck of an oil tanker, and missing. Several pirates drowned trying to retrieve the loot. One washed ashore with $153,000 tied in his shirt. There were clips that had too much lead she'd trim to get in and get out. An excess of scenery to cut: long shots of villages on the Somali coast. She'd keep Eyl, Eyl was the stuff, drama developing that she hadn't expected.

Dara thought of a place for the cooch dancers shaking their pongee bums at blinding speed. If she were to take them out of the Djibouti sequence, show pirate faces in a moving skiff, eyes half-closed in the wind, a wad of khat in their jaws, and cut to the cooch dancers?

She thought, Aren't you clever? Lose the poetic fucking around and keep the girls where they belong, in Djibouti.

Xavier had brought several bouquets of khat aboard in dry ice. He told her it was *ghat* in Yemen, *jaad* sometimes in Somalia, Kenya shipping twenty tons of khat to Somalia every day. In a population of seven or eight million—women and children not chewing or getting much of a chance—that left a million males with wads in their cheeks. How much was that, two pounds a day each? Ask Xavier.

She had questioned his bringing a pistol aboard. She said, "None of the freighters are armed. It's international law."

"But if they had guns," Xavier said, "they wouldn't get hi-jacked, would they? Nobody's gonna take the *Buster* from us."

She worked at a dining table the hotel brought in and watched the entire twelve hours of footage on her laptop while she waited for Xavier. She would edit it down to their first two weeks at sea: to Idris's party at his home in Eyl; the fun-loving pirates turning against them, not so loving anymore; and finally, meeting Jama, the African American al Qaeda Muslim who becomes a one-man gang. Most of Jama would come later.

By the time she finished editing, still not sure now what the documentary was about, she had a feeling she could make it work. It was alive, it was about what was going on right now in the Middle East. She would look at footage with Xavier and hear his ideas, what he thought could be the theme. He'd say it looked like two different stories. What did she have to hold the whole thing together? What was it about?

She had spent four weeks with Xavier in a thirty-foot boat. Apart only three days and she couldn't wait to see him again; he'd become part of her life. If he were thirty-seven years younger she might even be in love with him. Maybe. She thought about a young version of Xavier.

When the hotel phone rang she picked up and said, "Xavier?"

"Miss Dara? Yeah, this is Xavier. How you doin?"

"Not bad," Dara said. "Yeah, I remember you now, the tall colored man? Why don't you stop by for a drink?"

"I could do that," Xavier said, "it don't put you out none."

"Where are you?"

"Still at the dock. A man's been waitin here to search *Buster*. Now he wants me to go to the U.S. Embassy with him. I could be a while."

"Tell them whatever he wants to know," Dara said. "I did. I worked three whole days, got through all twelve hours and now I'm taking the rest of the day off, drinking champagne in my underwear."

"Do I get to see that?"

She said, "It's too bad you're an old man."

"You either cheeky or horny," Xavier said, "talkin to me like that. I get to the hotel, you want to make a bet on what happens?"

◆ ◆ ◆

XAVIER ARRIVED WITH EVERYTHING they had on the boat. They talked, having fun getting back together. Once they got around to sitting next to each other, the laptop on the dining table, Dara in her bra and shorts, they watched *Buster* leaving Djibouti on the way to the gulf. Dara had shot this from the concrete pier.

"For now, this is how we open."

"You got the boys swimmin for the loot drowned?"

"It comes later."

"Wouldn't be a bad way to open. Droppin the money bags and missin the deck. You got your audience glued to the screen."

"We could open on the cooch dancers," Dara said, "you want to get creative. We see it as we shot it, leaving Djibouti, and decide how to move scenes around."

Now they were watching Dara aboard, shooting straight ahead from the deck, *Buster*'s bow in the foreground rising as the sea rolled beneath her to come down in the trough.

"The first couple of days," Dara said, "I expected the next wave would swamp us."

"You didn't get sick."

"You saw how I looked."

"Till you learned *Buster*'s ways. Lookit how you held the camera steady." Xavier said, "Where's Billy Wynn? You kept him in the picture, didn't you?"

"He's coming up abaft. Here, *Pegaso* blowing past us, a hundred yards off our port bow."

"Man, you the little sailor, ain't you?"

They watched the sailboat on the screen coursing past them.

"You don't have him comin about, goin back to Djibouti?"

"We don't see Helene," Dara said. "We thought he'd left her."

"Then changed his mind," Xavier said, "and was goin back to get her."

"I could speculate in voice-over why he turned around," Dara said, "but Billy's not what this is about. Or Helene."

"You mean what you thought at the time," Xavier said. "We don't see them again till comin on two weeks."

"Ten days," Dara said. "Billy with his elephant gun."

"Man, he put on a show, didn't he?"

"That's when Idris joined us on the *Buster*."

"I like all that," Xavier said. "Things happenin."

"We leave Billy flying past—"

"We don't see him come about?"

"Forget Billy, he's somewhere ahead of us now. I'll say *Pegaso* is vulnerable in a hostile sea and we hope to run into Billy again sometime soon."

"I see Billy comin on as star of the movie."

"What about Jama?"

"He's good, but he's the bad guy."

"Jama shot five people at one time, but I don't have it on film. None of the things he did."

"Girl, he's still the bad guy."

"I don't know how I'm going to work that."

"We see the bodies comin out of the house," Xavier said. "Then cut to us in our deck chairs sippin wine and chewin on khat. I noticed you favor it."

"I'd like it a lot better," Dara said, "if there was another way to do it. Chewing leaves to get a buzz—"

"Fucked with your sensibilities, didn't it? You been thinkin, what if you crumbled up the leaves and smoked it. Would that work?"

"Would it?" Dara said.

◆ ◆ ◆

THE FOOTAGE ON THE screen showed pinpoints of light dotting the Somali coast. Dusk now, a lamp hung from the foremast to throw a dreary light on the open deck, the *Buster* plowing ahead.

"What you gonna talk about here?"

"Hoping we run into pirates. I'll list the countries with warships out here hoping the same thing, and cut to . . . Here it is, the guided missile cruiser, CG-66, coming up on us with that blinding spotlight."

"Like it's gonna eat us up," Xavier said, "or want to board us. Man, it's big. All that gray metal risin over us. You tell who you are and ask 'em over for a drink."

"First I got on the bullhorn," Dara said, "and told them to identify themselves."

"They got a kick out of that, the *Buster* givin 'em orders. You tell who you are and the captain knows you from your films. He called them 'docs.' A word you never use."

"I don't care for 'docs.' I think we were delaying the ship from being somewhere. I like the clip, though, tracking over the sailors looking down at us."

"Close on six hundred feet of cruiser slidin alongside. They want to know what we doin," Xavier said. "You tell 'em through the bullhorn, 'We makin a movie about pirates.' What you think we doin. I thought the PA voice would say somethin about the task force out here in harm's way to protect shipping and run off the pirates. They love to use 'harm's way.' You see the steward mates? They wonderin what's this tall-ass nigga doin with that hot white chick? Out in the middle of the ocean. I bet they still talkin about it. 'Man, he's got the deal.' "

◆ ◆ ◆

XAVIER WOULD PLAY WITH the Sony, the big camcorder, the days nothing they wanted appeared on the sea, the *Buster* still bearing east, Xavier shooting life aboard the *Buster*. Dara frying fish would look up to see Xavier with the Sony on her. He'd say for home movies he'd watch on his TV. Dara on deck in a canvas chair against the wheelhouse, the boat drifting, it didn't matter, Dara looking fine in her shorts and T-shirt that said *Laissez les bons temps rouler* across the front. Blond hair curling out of her do-rag, a cowboy bandana. She'd look up at him through her shades and shake her head.

He said, "You documentin pirates—we ever see any—and I'm documentin Dara Barr makin herself famous. They gonna say, 'Why, this Dara Barr's just a girl,' I show anybody my footage. I shoot you starin at me and lookin away. Certain times." Xavier sitting with his back against the foremast, long brown legs stretching out of his trunks, no supporter, sometimes seeing the shape of his donkey lying beneath shiny green satin. Xavier LeBo believed was he ten years younger, they'd be letting good times roll all over this boat. See if they could manage in the hammock.

They watched themselves on the *Buster* now.

"Four-hour watches," Xavier said, "means the one on deck can look at the hammock but not get in it. You can't see all the way around the way the hammock curls up on you." Xavier slept on deck during her watch to see if she stayed awake. Dara would say to him—Xavier sneaking over to see if her eyes were open— "Jesus, will you go to sleep."

So Xavier tried sleeping below when he was off and would lie awake waiting to hear Dara scream at a shape coming out of the dark. When she did yell into the hatch, "Boats coming up on us . . ."

Xavier, in the bow, jumped up ducking his head.

"They in sight?"

"Not yet. I hear them, three boats."

WHEN XAVIER WOULD WATCH *Women of Bosnia* with Dara and look over to see her staring at her work on the screen, she'd be chewing gum in time to the women speaking. On the beat. No hurry. Waiting and picking it up again. She said one time, after, still in her seat, "Fuck."

"What's wrong?"

"I stayed too long on their hands. Like I've never seen hands before."

Xavier, working on *Katrina,* would try all kinds of weird angles, shooting down on a scene, or zoom in for a smash close-up, his favorite. Dara would say to him, "We're telling a story: the way hurricanes leave people and what they do. That's drama enough."

Xavier would hear her quiet voice in his head. This nice woman he kept thinking was a fox. Dara keeping some other part of her under wraps.

This time she told him she heard three boats coming.

THEY WATCHED TWO OF the pirate boats swerve in close to cut their speed and have a look at them on the *Buster* before veering off after the first boat, going for a cargo ship in the distance, Dara waving and yelling to them, "Stop by on your way back," as loud as she could.

Xavier remembered shooting Dara but didn't see her in the footage on the screen.

"They comin like wild dogs and you cut it?"

"I like 'coming like dogs,'" Dara said, "but we don't need that girl showing off, that 'Stop on your way back.' Did you see Idris?"

"Those Arabs tend to look alike to me."

"He was in the lead boat, the guy in the yellow kaffiyeh. We're meeting him tomorrow," Dara said. "Today he's occupied."

"Takin care of business," Xavier said. "You guessed there were three boats comin." He waited and said, "Didn't you?"

"At first I thought there were four," Dara said. "It turns out Idris had two Yamahas on his."

Was this nice girl having fun with him? Xavier could never be sure.

CHAPTER SIX

T HEY WERE CLOSER NOW to the cargo ships and tankers on the screen, Dara using a Super Telephoto lens, the big Sony mounted on sticks to keep the camera steady while she brought the ships even closer: as many as five or six spread over the screen at one time, merchant ships and now and then a warship riding shotgun.

"Most of this was filmed during our third week," Dara said. "I slipped it in here to get something going."

"You know how many times I shot you punchin up news stories on your Mac? Where's that footage?"

"I'm using the information."

"But you don't show how you gettin it way out here, waitin for somethin to happen."

"I'm showing what the news story's about. Here, the U.S. missile cruiser . . ."

"What I don't see," Xavier said, "is any documentary stuff goin on. Where the people this is about, the poor Somalis havin to hijack ships. The only one I've seen was drivin a tricked-out Mercedes."

"It's coming up," Dara said. "The logline is they've gone after a hundred and eleven ships, hijacked forty-two and collected fines that come to over thirty million, for trespassing."

"You can say that with a straight face, huh?"

Dara said, "Shut up, please, and watch." She said, "Eight ships are still in the hands of the hijackers. They're negotiating. What we want to find out is who all's involved."

Now they were looking at the guided missile cruiser USS *Vella Gulf* on the screen. "Flagship," Dara said, "of Combined Task Force 151. A search and seizure crew from the cruiser—the guys in the inflatable boat—are rounding up the pirates in their skiff. I'll say something about the seven guys with their hands in the air."

"No match for the U.S. Navy."

"I'll say they're being taken to the cruiser, where they'll be identified by the crew from *Polaris,* a ship registered in the Marshall Islands. I'll say the Somali rights activists have been thwarted in their attempt to seize the *Polaris* and levy a fine. Cut to the cruiser's Seahawk helicopter firing at them. Or I might call it the cruiser's gunship."

"I like 'thwarted,'" Xavier said. "You make the cruiser the bad guy."

"All that U.S. Navy firepower against seven guys in a skiff with an outboard motor."

"Seven guys with machine guns, RPGs, and twin Yamahas."

Dara said, "I requested permission to come aboard to interview the suspects—"

"I know—where is it?"

"I trashed it. My request denied over the PA system. We're

having no luck with our navy. I find out on the Internet the *Vella Gulf* transferred the prisoners to the *Lewis and Clark,* a navy supply ship. Now they're being held down in the cargo hold, where we used to chain slaves."

"You makin the *Lewis and Clark* a slave ship?"

"You know what I mean. In the hold, guarded by marines."

"I know how you makin it sound."

"Here," Dara said, "a different boatload of nine freedom fighters, hands in the air. I got this from CNN. Caught in the act by a French frigate. I'll say, 'The French navy is said to have taken fifty-seven pirates in seven patrol operations.' I think the frigate's name is *Le Floreal.*"

"What'd they do with them, the nine guys?"

"Watch. We cut to the Italian destroyer. You remember the name?"

"Luigi Durand de la Penne."

"Named for an Italian officer during the second war, served as a demolition team member. I don't like that. What is he?"

"He's an underwater demolition man."

"Responsible for blowing up two British warships in Egypt. I guess Cairo. Here they are. The reason the crew's laughing, they thought I was English, and Luigi was blowing up English ships."

"I got it," Xavier said.

"It's a good clip. We learned it's helicopters that make the difference. They can fly five times beyond the ships' radar and—CNN said—'deter pirates.' Captain Fabrizio Simoncini of the *Penne* said, 'My priority is to protect merchant shipping, not give chase to pirates.' Voice-over will say you chase them down and then what? Free them? Let them escape? Or hand these poor men to Kenya for trial?"

"By poor you don't mean they broke."

"CNN calls it a game of maritime cat and mouse. The

mouse getting bolder, more sophisticated. While the cat, well-intentioned but largely declawed, isn't nearly as scary as he was imagined."

"You gonna tell it like that?"

"I'm not sure I'll keep the Italian captain, or get into what happens to the pirates. No, I don't have to use the CNN stuff. But now here comes a spokesman for the U.S. Navy I got off CNN."

The man on the screen—a navy commander in uniform—is saying, "We're making headway against the robbers. With the agreement of the countries that have ships in harm's way—"

"There, he said it. I knew somebody would."

"The ships' owners have agreed to bring these criminals to trial, then put them in a prison in the country of the owner or ship them off to Kenya."

Dara said, "They've made thirty million hijacking ships, but lost out on a three-hundred-million-dollar market when they had to stop fishing. Toxic waste dumped in their seas, while foreign fishing companies have come from as far away as Japan. And the commander says, 'If everybody else can make a living fishing here, why can't the Somalis?'"

She said to Xavier, "I don't have an answer to that."

"Girl, they don't care about fishin. They stumble onto piracy," Xavier said, "and can't believe it. They havin fun and gettin rich. They flyin out to take a ship, one of 'em stands up to piss over the side, bottle of Heineken in his hand, drunk as he wants to be—it's part of bein a pirate—drunk and mellowed some by the khat in his jaw, the man dreamin of Ethiopian pussy. Who's gonna stop him? This what you want to film, what these guys are doin? They enjoyin every minute of it. Gonna keep takin ships till it gets dangerous. A bunch of 'em will quit. The ones stick it out become as dangerous as the gunboats after 'em. Be more navies out here. Won't be long the pirates will come out shootin and your gunboats'll blow 'em out of the sea. I expect some will keep comin, not knowin anything else."

Dara was quiet lighting a cigarette, thinking of what she'd say.

"I want to show why the Somalis became pirates."

"To get rich," Xavier said. "You stuck with the idea these rascals are good guys. It's like you made a picture called *Men of Bosnia* and left out all the women they raped. How they had children from guys, a line waitin to have their turn. The woman never knows which one's the father."

"The pirates aren't vicious," Dara said. "They don't rape and kill."

"That you know of. *Katrina* you show guys bustin into stores, comin out with TV sets. 'Cause they poor and can't afford to buy one? No, 'cause they bad dudes, they breakin the law and you say it, tell how it was. The pirates haven't taken and raped any women 'cause there no women on the ships they hijack. Maybe an old Filipina in the galley. They hit a cruise ship you gonna see what happens. Find some good-lookin young women among the old people they settle for robbin? Why these cruise ships are puttin their passengers off at Djibouti, fly 'em to Dubai and pick 'em up again. They gonna do it till they start goin broke."

On the computer screen now they were looking at *Le Ponant,* a 290-foot, three-masted sailing cruise ship.

Dara said, "You remember *Le Ponant*? Hijacked in the gulf on its way to the Mediterranean for summer cruises. No passengers aboard, but a crew of thirty young people, seven of them women. You remember that?" Dara said, "I read it to you off the computer."

"Now I do, yeah. The women hid."

"In a forward storage area for most of two days," Dara said. "All they had to eat were nuts and raisins, and helped themselves to the wine stored there. The seven ladies had to go to the bathroom in a metal bucket. The rest of the crew, meanwhile, were allowed to have meals prepared by their chef. The pirates brought their own food, spaghetti," Dara said. "The women finally came out of the storage locker—for all they knew the rest of the crew were dead. Three of the women's boyfriends were crew members, so they were worried sick. They had no idea the crew was treated quite well. The women came out and the pirate leader, Ahmed, asked the captain, 'Why did you hide them?' Very indignant. 'You thought my men would take them to bed?' "

Xavier said, "Was more like, 'You thought we gonna get some ass off these women? Shame on you.' Was his tone."

"The point is," Dara said, "Ahmed addressed the captain with indignation for thinking he had to protect the women."

"His khat-suckin guys grinnin at the girls, not even mindin all the warships layin out around them."

"Look," Dara said, "as long as the pirates were underdogs and behaved themselves, didn't shoot anybody, they're the good guys. All they're doing is getting back at the shipping companies, and 'getting back' seems acceptable in their world."

"You gonna explain that in your voice-over?"

"Or," Dara said, "we show the pirates are being used by un-scrupulous middlemen in London, in Dubai, Nairobi—this was on the BBC—who contact the shipping companies, work out ransom negotiations and take their cut."

"I'll ask you again," Xavier said, "you gonna explain all that in the movie?"

"If I have to."

Xavier said, "You gettin into somethin over your head. Where the dudes climbed up on the *Buster,* boarded us on the high seas? You trash that episode?"

"It's next," Dara said. "I'm still thinking of a way to use it."

CHAPTER SEVEN

Now they were watching on the screen a ship stacked to the bow with trailer-size containers that would be dropped onto railroad freight cars or hooked to eighteen-wheelers in a few weeks, the ship coming west to the Red Sea and Europe.

A bottle of French Pinot Noir stood on the table between them. "This wine," Xavier said, "cost twelve bucks, a store on Magazine. Djibouti wholesale we pay fifty and think we drinkin pretty good wine."

Dara said she was never sure why a good wine was good. She liked this one, but never got much of a taste holding the wine in her mouth. Xavier said, "You any good you can even tell where it's from. Catch a scent of maybe smoke, you sniff it, or has a taste of wood." Xavier said, "I have a friend name of Christopher in Tucson, Arizona, could take a sip of this wine, roll it over his taste buds, tell you where it's from and what the taste is, Christopher detectin a hint of tobacco juice musta been spit in the barrel."

The container ship was passing within a mile and a half of the *Buster,* Dara on it with the Sony. She said, "You hear what I hear?"

"I see 'em," Xavier said, "comin top speed. Two pirate boats, six in one, three in the other. Goin for the aft end of the ship like hyenas gonna nip at her fantail, the lowest freeboard and no containers in the way. Yeah, I remember this. The crew puttin fire hoses on the pirates. Hittin 'em good and the boats veer off."

"Now they're firing at the ship," Dara said.

"Can't get close enough to hit anybody. They veer off a ways and Niag'ra Falls comes down on the pirate boats, the hoses reachin out to them."

"They're giving it up," Dara said. "Who wants to board a ship soaking wet?"

They watched the boats heading for shore, more than a mile from the *Buster.* "Here's where the one spots us," Dara said, "and falls back. The boat with all the guys continues heading in. If they'd seen us we'd be facing nine instead of three."

Xavier said, "*Facin?* You they mama, one of their biggest fans. You love pirates."

"I should've asked if they want to be in a movie," Dara said. "It might've given them pause. I remember I told you to use the Sony and shoot as long as we can. I had the Canon peeking through the hole in my bag."

"I remember I said they try and snatch it from you," Xavier said, "lemme have it."

THE SCREEN SHOWED ONE Somali in the boat, holding it against the *Buster;* the other two coming up over the side, both swinging AKs from their shoulders while Xavier was shooting the closer one looking right at him, Xavier filming until the hand spread open in front of the lens. The pirate put his hand on the camera to take it and Xavier held on. He said, "You want to put me out of business?" and looked over at Dara and the other pirate—a young guy with a skullcap of short hair.

Xavier saw him snatch at Dara's bag hanging from her shoulder. Dara took his hand around the wrist and started talking to him in what sounded like a kindly way, speaking Cajun French to him, and now the young pirate was nodding as Dara glanced at Xavier.

"He said yes, he would love to be in a movie."

Now she was speaking French to the pirate looking up at Xavier standing over him, translating to Cajun what Xavier was saying. "You won't be in the film you don't return my boss's camera. She'll be all over my ass. Understand what I'm sayin?" Dara at the same time shooting him through the hole in her cotton bag.

Xavier's pirate said something to his buddy in Somali, yanked the Sony from Xavier's hands and went into the wheelhouse, this fella with a don't-fuck-with-me attitude.

Dara slipped the bag off her shoulder, handed it to Xavier and followed the one with the Sony through the wheelhouse and the hatch to go below.

Now Xavier faced the younger pirate holding the AK.

He said, "How things goin, Dog?"

The boy looked nervous, not knowing how to answer this English coming at him.

Xavier said, "Why don't you hand me your gun," moving a step toward him. "So I don't have to take it from you and heave your ass over the side. You comprende 'heave your ass'?" Xavier smiling to show the pirate he was offering this suggestion as a friend. Now he motioned to the young man to step over here, closer to him, Xavier saying, "We got Pirates at home playin baseball for Pittsburgh. Only time I saw 'em was in '79, they playin the Orioles for the World Series and won it. I was seein a woman in Baltimore and she got the tickets. Willie Stargell, my hero at the time, thirty years ago when I was prime, was named the Series MVP. Hit four hundred with seven extra-base hits. I think it mighta been a record. I won money bettin the Pirates, but this woman got mad and quit doin right by me."

Xavier was ready to take the AK from the boy, but heard Dara's voice again speaking French, Dara coming out of the wheelhouse now with the other guy, Dara holding Xavier's Beretta in her hand, the gun loaded, thirteen in the magazine, one in the throat.

"Kwame," Dara said, "will return the Sony if we give him your pistol. But you have to say it's okay."

"They neither one speak English?"

"Hardly a word."

"Tell Kwame," Xavier said, "he don't give you the camera, I'm gonna shoot him between the eyes with this gun and pitch his ass in the sea."

Dara told the Somali in her Cajun French, "Kwame, my associate says yes, he'll let you have the pistol, if you prefer it, to the camera."

Said all this handing Xavier the Sony and said, "Start shooting," as she handed Kwame Xavier's Beretta and the deal was done.

Xavier said, "You know what you doin?"

Dara said, "We'll have to use subtitles on my lines."

"You giving this man our only protection?"

"We'll get it back," Dara said.

CHAPTER EIGHT

DARA, THE NEXT MORNING, came out of the wheelhouse to see Xavier on deck scoping the shoreline through binoculars.

"I woke up thinking about a picture I love, but can't remember its name."

Xavier lowered the glasses to his chest but didn't turn to her.

"A wine lover takes his buddy to Napa to sample wines. Paul Giamatti's the one who knows wines. Can't stand Merlot, it's so common. I'll think of the buddy's name in a minute. He's a likable lout. He's getting married the next week, but keeps jumping in bed with a girl he meets. Actually he does her standing up."

"*Sideways*," Xavier said, raising his glasses. "You hear the boats comin out this time?"

She said, "That's why I came up," looking at the shore now, about three miles from them.

"We're meetin the Sheik of Araby in a few minutes," Xavier said. "You anxious to see Idris?"

She said what was on her mind. "Use the little camcorder but keep it under wraps. He might not want to be filmed. I'll decide later if we show him the footage."

"I asked are you anxious to see him."

"Well, he ain't bad."

"For a Arab or a hijacker?" Xavier said. "You don't mind gettin close with a black guy?"

"If I were nuts about him, why not?"

"You sayin that for my benefit."

"You aren't bad either," Dara said, "No, what I like about Idris, he comes off as a free spirit. But is he for real or is he putting us on? Billy Wynn comes off the same way."

"Won't be long we be seein Billy," Xavier said. "And cool Helene."

"Really. You think she's cool?"

"I do, and I haven't even spoken to her."

THE CLIP PROJECTED ON the screen showed three boats coming out, their sound rising to a hard whine. Dara said, "They're called skiffs in most of the reports, but they're twenty-four feet long and they're deep." She said, "They sound angry, don't they?"

"Pissed off," Xavier said, "haulin ass for these African muggers."

They watched the boats on the screen reduce speed, creeping toward the *Buster* now, the Yamahas rumbling.

Or grumbling, Dara thought, and liked it for the voice-over, if it worked. Now she was explaining to someone, anyone: *Now I'm laying in a voice-over for my documentary,* Djibouti. *It's an interesting title, isn't it?* Djibouti. *I feel lucky I found it. I'm humbled by it.*

What does that mean, you're humbled? You've never been humble in your life. But leave it, it might work.

I've only made three documentaries.

But worked my ass off for other people. *Cajun* was one, a disaster. Limp. Folksy. You should do your own. Maybe call them "docs." It won't hurt you.

I've only made three docs in my life and all three happened to win major awards. Heck.

Try saying *shit.* You're being humble again.

I've produced three docs that won awards and I'm determined to make a name for myself.

Boring. Who cares? Just say:

There is nothing I'd rather do in the entire fucking world than make documentaries.

Delete *fucking*?

Just get rid of the docs.

"COMING LIKE WILD DOGS," Dara said. "How about 'Coming like wolves'?"

"It's the same thing. But 'dogs' sounds meaner."

They watched Idris Mohammed standing in the lead boat, his yellow scarf around his head and looped under his chin, a long Arab-looking shirt open, and sunglasses. Pirate chic. The first thing she'd say to him. *You didn't stop on your way back yesterday. Maybe you didn't hear my invitation. I know it was a bit windy.*

Not the invitation, the fucking wind blowing.

But when his boat bumped alongside the *Buster,* the pirate chief looking up at her in his yellow scarf, Idris said, "It comes as my pleasure to see you again. Forgive me for not stopping yesterday. I knew if I did I would stay with you and my Coast Guard boys would have no one to instruct them."

He called them that, his Coast Guard boys.

Idris was maybe a quarter black, a quadroon? She remembered a scene in *True Romance,* the one where Dennis Hopper knows he's going to be shot and tells Christopher Walken, a Sicilian gangster, his great-great-grandma was fucked by a nigger. Meaning a Muslim from Africa like Idris.

What she kept wondering, How did Idris get started? Who gave him machine guns so he could hijack ships and make enough to buy whatever he wants? Who was backing this fun-loving pirate?

He said, "Yesterday we had trouble boarding the ship, so we let that one go. What difference does it make, there are so many ships come through our sea. Today," Idris said, "is an easy one. These boys are not mine, they from another clan, with experience. They won't need anyone telling them what to do."

"Good," Dara said. "I'd love to see you in action, but I'll settle for an interview."

He said, "Yes, a chance to be with you. Perhaps make plans for sometime we not doing nothing so important as being together."

He had turned and was speaking Somali to his Coast Guard boys, all armed with AKs, gesturing now for them to get going. He said to Dara, "There is a sailing yacht out there you can't see. It's maybe two miles from here."

Xavier shooting all this with the Canon, recording Idris's voice.

"Two persons aboard. Maybe we know them."

Dara said, "Billy?"

"It could be, yes, I'm hoping so."

"You'd hijack Billy's yacht?"

"Worth two million dollars he told me," Idris said. "How much you think he'd pay to keep it?" Idris grinning now. "I'm kidding with you. We frighten Billy, that's all, as a joke. Show we have a sense of humor. People don't think we have things to laugh at, but we do. Funny things happen to us."

"Climb aboard," Dara said, "we'll go rescue the poor guy."

She turned to Xavier as Idris stepped aboard.

"You get all that?"

"The whole thing," Xavier said.

CHAPTER NINE

BILLY WYNN WAS WEARING a canvas shooting vest with cartridge loops on both sides of his chest, eight loops, four empty. He threw his lines to Xavier and Xavier pulled the *Pegaso* alongside to tie on to *Buster,* the boat sitting a hundred or so yards from Eyl's beach of white sand and shelves of rocks.

He said to Idris, "Hey, it's good seeing you again, buddy." He told Dara and Xavier he must've looked like money-money-money sitting out there like a brain-dead Republican, no idea there were pirates about. He said to Dara, "I *know* you never vote their ticket, you're too with-it. You know things." He said, "I saw the boats coming out toward us, I thought sounding mean—I told Helene, 'Hon, go on below while I take care of business.'" He didn't mention what Helene asked him, if this was part of the test. Wild Arabs bearing down on them. Was she being funny? He questioned times he wasn't sure. His feeling for Helene was love, the tender kind, till she drew him to the king-size bed he called their love bunk.

"The first thing I did was check my elephant gun I keep up

here in the cockpit when we're under way. Every morning I bring it topside and fire both loads. Get use to the kick."

Dara saw Idris about to step from *Buster* to the *Pegaso* and said, "Wait." And handed Idris a mike to aim at his buddy. "You'll be doing me a huge favor."

"But I can't show my face," Idris said, "I'm a bandit to people who can persecute me."

"We're only shooting Billy while I talk to him, for the film. You won't be seen."

Xavier shot Idris stepping to the sailboat, Billy offering a hand, Xavier hearing, "Man, but it's a treat to see you again," while they shook hands. And Idris's voice: "You had trouble with my men? They went by us towing one of the boats and drinking champagne. I said, 'What is going on?'"

Xavier nudged Dara. "You gonna love it."

Dara called to Billy, "What did the pirates want?"

"Hold me for ransom, what those people do."

"Where's Helene?"

"I told her stay below while I run 'em off." He looked around. "She's still there."

"Two weeks ago," Dara said, "we saw you leaving Djibouti. You flew past us and turned around to go back."

"I took off," Billy said, "not realizing I was short of stores."

"Champagne?" Dara said.

"Among other goods. These guys now," Billy was saying, "they're making a wide circle to come around and run past me from about fifty meters." He said to Dara, "Why, you think I drink too much?"

Dara said, "How would I know?"

"Helene says getting ripped seems to calm me down. I become serious for some reason. Helene says I make pronouncements."

Idris had to wait before saying, "You wave something at my boys, show you're a friend?"

"Like what, a white flag? I'm out of the cockpit holding a double-barrel rifle fires six-hundred-caliber Nitro Express rounds. They're coming past me now, ducks in a row. I fire and blow the Yamaha off the first one. The second boat I fire a speck wide, hit the outboard but took a chunk out of the stern. The boat sank in five minutes opened up like it was. I see the guys swimming to the first boat drifting away. Dumb guys don't bring any oars. They look like they're in a panic, the ones in the water, till they got pulled aboard the third boat. I reloaded, my shoulder sore as hell. You talk about a kick—I've seen that Holland & Holland knock people right off their feet. There's a trick to not getting injured by the recoil."

Dara said, "What about the third boat?"

"They sat out there two hundred meters looking at me. I wanted, I could've hit two of 'em before they pulled away."

Dara said, "Why didn't you?"

"For what? 'Cause they want to get rich? I thought of telling Helene to put her bra on and come topside. Show these Moham-medans what they're missing. You know my elephant gun set me back a hundred and thirty-five thousand? I'll tell you for a fact, it's good to have the means."

Dara said, "The third boat left?"

"No, I finally motioned 'em over. Put the rifle down and held up a bottle of champagne in each hand." He said to Idris, "Those were your guys want to hijack me?"

"They want to greet you," Idris said, "as a friend of mine come to visit. But you shoot at them?"

"At the boats, not knowing their intention," Billy said. "I was to shoot *at* them, they'd be floaters."

Dara watched Idris on the screen shrug and then smile. He said, "I apologize for the misunderstanding." She watched him turn now to gaze toward the coast. "And would like you to be my guests"—the camera moving toward a scattering of low buildings along the beach, one much larger on the slope above, dominating the scene—"at my home in Eyl."

DARA CLOSED THE LID of the laptop.

Xavier said, "You went on the sailboat so you could speak to Helene."

"I got Billy to invite me. He said, 'You want to learn how to sail?' I told him I had to use the head and went below. Helene was sitting at the table in the salon with a bottle of champagne. She said, 'Get a glass. That fucking gunfire—my ears are still ringing. He wants me to fire it, get knocked on my ass.'"

"Champagne helps now?"

"It can't hurt. I find if I stay ripped it's easier to follow instructions. 'Aye, aye, Captain.' He's teaching me how to sail, in the fucking ocean. I don't know how many times I thought of sticking a finger down my throat."

"But you hung in."

"Still his little sailor. I have to actually mop the fucking deck."

"Part of the trial, eh?"

"I guess. I'm not sure it's worth it."

"Outside of that, you still like him?"

"He's weird. Always looking for pirates, his elephant gun handy."

"But he doesn't try to shoot them."

"He sunk their boat. If they happen to drown, tough shit."

"What's he talk about?"

"The rules of the sea. How to tack, come about. How much money he has. Arabs. He doesn't care for Arabs, I found that out. He said, 'The Mohammedans scored with 9/11'"—Helene trying to sound like Billy from East Texas—"'now they'll try for a bigger bang.'"

"Does he mean al Qaeda? Bin Laden and his people?"

"Billy doesn't say. I think he's dreaming, trying to think of a role he can play. And I happen to be with him, I'm his gang."

"He isn't CIA, is he? You mentioned that once."

"He hinted at it, sounding like he's some kind of government agent, but he's not. I came right out and asked him and he smiled, very condescending, and patted my cheek. Like what do you expect from a chick works fashion shows. He said why should he get tied up in rules and red tape when he's got the way to get answers on his own. He means he's got enough money to bribe anyone who can help him. He believes terrorists are playing a part in this, letting the pirates have thirty million, less than half of what's been paid so far."

"That much in ransoms?"

"At least More than sixty ships have been hijacked—the latest number he told me this morning—ransomed off or still being held."

"How does he know that?"

"He makes phone calls. To Billy, the bad guys are the lawyers and Mohammedan terrorists. He always calls them that, Mohammedans. At first he thought it was al Shabaab, the strict Muslim gunmen. They're supposed to be against piracy, but Billy says bullshit, they're taking a cut like everybody else. He told me al Shabaab means 'young guys' and calls them 'the lads.' He got that from the BBC."

"But if Idris and his guys are doing all the work—"

"Billy says Idris is afraid to complain."

Dara shook her head. "He doesn't know Idris."

"Billy says they'll shoot him and get somebody else."

"But Idris is having a ball hijacking ships." Dara paused.

"There *was* something on the Internet about middlemen, lawyers handling the ransom negotiations from Nairobi, even London. Billy thinks the lawyers represent terrorists?"

"Or they don't know who they represent, or care. Billy can be terribly boring, but he's not dumb."

"Maybe melodramatic?"

"Serious," Helene said. "Sometimes he's so fucking serious it's scary."

"The money's delivered directly to the pirates," Dara said, "by boat or dropped from a plane. I've seen it."

"Billy says they get only part of it that way, for show. It keeps the lawyers out of the news."

"Idris," Dara said, "has never even hinted at someone telling him what to do."

"Ask him about it. Maybe Billy's full of shit."

"I don't know—Idris has always seemed straight with me," Dara said. "It's why I like him."

"I do too," Helene said and took a sip of champagne. "The other night at that club in Djibouti, Las Vegas, he asked me to go for a ride. You'd already left, I didn't know if he wanted to show me the sights or jump me."

"He made a move when I was with him," Dara said. "I told him I don't do it in cars, even a Mercedes."

Helene raised her hand to slap Dara's.

"So you went for a ride with him?" Dara said.

"No, because Ari Ahmed Sheikh Bakar walked in and we started talking. Billy was still after Idris, asking him about his pirates, if they were high when they boarded ships, making it sound like a guy-thing. Idris—he's so fucking cool—said, 'They do what pleases them.' So Harry and I went for a stroll."

"I flew in from Paris with him," Dara said.

"I know, he told me. The two of you talked all night. So you know more about him than I do."

"To me," Dara said, "Harry's one of the good guys, if there are any."

"That's what I told Billy after we left the club. Billy said, 'There is no way to tell who's good and who's bad in this fucked-up Mohammedan world.'"

"He may be right," Dara said.

CHAPTER TEN

NOW THE LAPTOP SCREEN showed cargo ships and the massive Saudi tanker *Sirius Star* lying at anchor a mile or so off the coast of Eyl, Dara's camera coming on to them from the sea.

"Waiting to be ransomed," Dara said. "I have the names of the ships and where they're from. The voice-over will say the going rate for ransom payments is between three hundred thousand and three million. For the Saudi tanker, hijacked three months ago with a hundred million dollars of crude oil, the pirates started out asking twenty-five million, but have come down considerably. We'll have to find out what they're after now." Dara said, "There's the *Blue Star,* an Egyptian ship and . . . I think the one straight ahead is the *Biscaglia*. Pirates attacked the ship and the paid security guards jumped over the side."

"You not armed," Xavier said, "you don't hang around." He said, "Now here's one of those planes nobody in it."

"Drones," Dara said. "Unmanned Aerial Vehicles. They fly over at night and take pictures of the hijacked ships."

"If they know the ships are here," Xavier said, "send in some special forces people and take 'em back."

"I'd like to show here if we get the chance, ransom money being air-dropped."

"We seen them miss once."

"Helene said Billy thinks the airdrop is for show. Proof the ships are being hijacked for money. But people behind the pirates—Billy says lawyers and warlords, clan elders—are all getting a cut."

"How's Billy know that?"

"Helene says he makes phone calls. I'd love to shoot another money drop," Dara said. "The ransom's always paid in hundred-dollar bills, none printed before 2000. Somali shopkeepers don't trust older bills."

"And we cut to Eyl," Xavier said, "to Sayyid Ali Yaro in front of his shop full of expensive men's attire. Also watches, canned goods, automatic weapons and, down the street, Ali Yaro's car lot, full of black Toyotas."

"He's saying in Somali," Dara said, "It's true, pirates are his best customers, they don't bother to bargain. They buy high-priced outfits and aftershave. Beautiful women come here to meet our pirates."

A Somali on the street appeared on the screen. He's speaking English, taking his time to be clear, saying, "It surprise me the sea robbers don't fight among themselves. They know how much each one is paid according to his importance. They don't harm captives, the crew of the ships. We know this, because we see no bodies wash up on our shore."

Dara said, "Next, an open-air barbecue where the restaurant is preparing meals for the hijacked crews. Goat, on a spit."

"Goat wouldn't be bad," Xavier said, "they called it something else."

The screen showed Eyl from the beach and streets of flat, tin-roof structures, some framed from scrap lumber, doors open to show the entire store, and rubble in all the streets, a junkyard, houses rebuilt over crumbling remains; but a human feeling in the colors, a cement house painted yellow, another blue. The camera moved up a street of hovels and beyond, to homes among palm trees.

"The upper end," Dara said, "Idris Mohammed's digs, a tan brick California bungalow that goes on and on, with a patio. The sound of the generators must drive him nuts."

"The man has enough power," Xavier said, "to light New Orleans. Look at the big TV dish up there."

"Idris said, 'Shake a leg with your shooting so you have time to come to my home, please.' He always says please."

"You sound like him," Xavier said. "You gonna shoot the man in his house?"

"You are," Dara said, handing Xavier her cotton bag. "Get the cars in the drive, a Mercedes and a Bentley—Harry must be here—four, no five Toyotas, all of them black."

A Somali with an AK slung from his shoulder stood close to the open doorway. He stared at Xavier. Then at Dara. Then at Xavier again, looking up at him as he stepped aside.

Watching the picture on the screen, Dara said, "Remember this guy?"

"Everybody starin at us like we movie stars."

They watched Dara enter the house, the camera holding on her as Xavier followed to sweep the room in a pan, close to dark in here, low-watt bulbs in the ceiling fixtures. Daylight from the open doorway helped.

"I shot those blue walls tryin to make out the pictures hangin there. I think they were bare-naked ladies, but it was hard to tell."

"I thought they were landscapes," Dara said.

IDRIS AND HARRY BAKAR were watching an Al Jazeera news-cast on the flat screen across the room, the boys having a scotch, smoking cigarettes and sucking khat, the bottle, the bouquet and a bowl of ice on the stone coffee table between them. They knew Dara was in the room.

Dara knew it.

But they stood up to watch the news for several moments before Idris muted the Arabic words with the remote and came for Dara grinning, telling her she made him so happy to see her, took hold of her and kissed both cheeks. He said, "Look who I have, your travel companion, Harry Bakar."

Harry was grinning too. He took her hands but kissed only one cheek. He smelled of cologne.

In the suite watching the computer screen she said to Xavier, "The big grins. Was it the news or were they glad to see me?"

"I think it was the herb."

"Did you talk to Harry much?"

"Just enough to think he's okay."

"We have to work on the audio, try to clean it up."

"I can bring it up. But for now . . ." Xavier reached over and turned off the sound.

"I liked Harry's kaffiyeh," Dara said, "the way he does desert wear, draped over his hair and around his shoulders, a casual British look with the bush jacket."

"Has that way about him."

"You think he puts it on?"

"Takes it to the edge any more he's over the line."

Dara said, " 'Call me Harry, if you will.' "

"You got him down, Mr. Harry Baker from Oxford."

"I said to him, 'Isn't it pleasant to relax with a scotch while you make a pitch to end piracy?' "

On the screen Harry was smiling. So was Idris. Idris glancing at Harry.

"I had the feeling," Dara said, "there was something between them they were dying to tell me. But Harry surprised me, started talking about a new president of Somalia, elected by the legislature meeting in Djibouti."

"Get into all that, you gonna lose your audience."

"I know, but I want to quote Harry saying the new president will bring peace, once the foreign fishing companies leave the gulf. I said, 'That's the stipulation? You'll have pirates until the fishing boats go home?' He said, 'Unfortunately, yes.' "

Xavier said, "What you want with that?"

"Show how the Somalis see it. Their only way to make a buck is hijacking ships."

"Or they starve? Come on, you gonna tell your moviegoers that?"

She said after a moment, "You don't think it'll work."

"Not the way you pitchin it. Do it straight. Make a picture about guys committin armed robbery at sea. What's wrong with that? They fun-lovin 'cause they found a way to get rich, but they still criminals . . . only with some class."

"Change the tone," Dara said.

"The one you have in your head. Shoot what you see, not what you want to see."

"I know what I'm doing, but I sound dumb."

"You are dumb," Xavier said, "and you know better."

◆ ◆ ◆

"YOU MIGHT'VE NOTICED," DARA said, "the two buddies making remarks to each other in Arabic, then raising their eyebrows, interested in what I'm gonna say. 'Did you know we have an aircraft carrier in the gulf?' 'Really? When did it arrive?' I tell them, 'Yesterday, the nuclear-powered *Dwight D. Eisenhower*.' Harry goes, 'Good show.' Idris says, 'You need a giant ship with jet planes to chase my little skiffs?'

"I said to Idris, 'Is there an Islamic group like al Shabaab behind pirate activities?'

"Idris said, 'Al Sha*baab*, are you kidding me? They're children playing like it's olden times. They're very serious.' I told Idris I've heard hijacking has cost the owners much more than thirty million. He said, 'Yes, perhaps as much as forty million. More coming in as we speak.' I said to Harry, 'Is that right, according to your estimates?' Harry said, 'He might be a bit low.'"

Dara said she asked Harry while Idris was out of the room how they met. He said he heard Idris might be interested in a sporting rifle he had for sale. "Over a few drinks we agreed on the price." Harry smiled. "And from that meeting on we're mates."

Dara said, "I'm not sure why, maybe because we were in the Middle East, I asked him, 'How many rifles did you sell Idris?' Harry stared at me rather deadpan before he said, 'Four hundred.' He said, 'Uzis I promoted off a chap in Tel Aviv,' giving his tone a hint of cockney, like Michael Caine, and kept staring at me until I smiled." Dara said, "You know why he told me? He wanted me to know he's half British but is still part of the Arab world. I said, 'And now you're promoting a solution to end piracy?' Harry said, 'You might call it that, yes.'"

"You ever ask Idris what he did with the Uzis?"

"I'm guessing he found buyers in Somalia. Warlords always need guns." Dara watched the screen. "This is where Harry's saying to Idris, 'Will you please tell her.'"

"I remember," Xavier said, "both watchin TV and grinnin when we come in. Now I shoot Idris changin the channel from Al Jazeera to CNN and we see a container ship flyin the Stars and Stripes. The *Maersk Alabama,* the first American ship, captain and crew, taken by the Somalis."

"The first American ship boarded," Dara said, watching the screen, "in more than two hundred years."

"This crew wouldn't stand for it," Xavier said. "Took the ship back and ran off the pirates. Only they had the captain a hostage by then."

"He gave himself up," Dara said, "so they wouldn't harm the crew. Richard Phillips, fifty-three, from Underhill, Vermont. They put him in the *Alabama*'s deluxe lifeboat, tried to slip off to Somalia three hundred miles away and ran out of gas. Here's the lifeboat."

One like the *Alabama*'s was on the screen now: an enclosed twenty-eight-foot orange fiberglass boat designed for thirty-four passengers with food and water for ten days.

"No toilet," Dara said. "It doesn't look big enough for that many people. The *Bainbridge,* the destroyer on the scene, tied onto the lifeboat to keep it from drifting off. Talks began now by satellite phone, between clan elders in the pirates' home port and I think navy brass and a hostage negotiator from the FBI. The elders wanted two million for Captain Phillips. The navy wanted the four pirates to surrender and stand trial, the only agreement they'd consider. The pirate spokesmen said if you don't pay the ransom or try to rescue the captain, this will end in disaster. Words to that effect. The navy took it as a threat to Captain Phillips's life."

Dara was looking at the screen. "This is Sunday. Idris and Harry were watching Friday—why they were grinning. I wanted to ask Harry what he was so happy about, but I didn't get around to it."

Xavier said, "So they got SEALs for the job."

"Three Navy SEALs were dropped on the *Bainbridge* with sniper rifles and set up undercover on the fantail. The lifeboat on the tow rope was less than a hundred feet away, like point-blank range for snipers. But waves were tossing the lifeboat, making it hard to get a target that wasn't moving. They could barely make out the pirates through the boat's windshield, and it was getting dark. Word came down from the White House. President Obama said, 'If the captain's life is in danger, take action.' The SEALs watched one of the pirates put a gun to Captain Phillips's head and they were given the word. Each fired one shot and the three pirates were taken out."

Xavier said, "Wasn't there four of 'em?"

"Four when they started out," Dara said. "The *Bainbridge* sent a rubber boat to see if Phillips and the pirates needed anything, food, medicine. The fourth pirate jumped ship, went back to the *Bainbridge* in the rubber boat and gave himself up."

"Had enough of bein a pirate."

"He was sixteen," Dara said. "I'm not sure how old the captain's son is. On TV the captain's wife, Andrea, sent a message after he was rescued that said 'Your family is saving a chocolate Easter egg for you, unless your son eats it first.' "

"Lemme see do I understand your meaning," Xavier said. "What you sayin, Somali boys don't have chocolate Easter eggs, they get shot?"

Dara didn't answer him. She thought of something else and said, "The *Alabama* was bringing four thousand tons of corn-soya to malnourished refugees in Somalia while Somali pirates were holding the captain for two million dollars. It was also carrying three hundred and twenty tons of vegetable oil for refugees in Rwanda."

"You have reasons now," Xavier said, "not to feel sorry for the pirates."

"After the three in the lifeboat were killed," Dara said, "bloggers all over the Internet were saying, 'Don't fuck with Americans.'"

"How'd that leave you?"

"It made sense. We have a problem, we don't pay our way out, we go after it." She said, "You know what I've learned since? It's likely the rifles were mounted in gyroscopes and the snipers wore night-vision goggles and took aim through scopes on their rifles. Put red dots on the Somalis and they're off to where Allah gives them all those hot-looking chicks. I thought, Shot by cool guys who know what they're doing. I reacted like everybody else."

She said, "Remember in Eyl I told you what I wanted to do? Get Idris to let us visit a ship he's holding for ransom. Get back to work. Talk only to members of the crew, no pirates."

"I believe I asked why would he let you? You said 'cause CNN's put him in a good mood and you know how to talk to him."

"I told Idris the afternoon we visited," Dara said, "the world must wonder how you treat your hostages. I'll ask the ship's crew and they'll say the Somali pirates are decent," Dara said, "a couple of Saudis among fifteen Filipinos. And the first officer was Saudi. I mentioned it to Idris and Harry and Idris asked me how I knew about the crew. No, first he asked why I picked the *Aphrodite* with all the ships anchored out there. I said I was curious about it, an LNG tanker. I told him I looked at the crew list to get the names and nationalities and saw two Arabs among all the Filipinos.

"Harry asked if I happened to know what the vessel was carrying. I said, 'I just told you, liquefied natural gas.' Harry said, 'Isn't that highly combustible?'"

"Playin dumb," Xavier said.

"Then Idris told him don't worry, the ship will be gone in a day or two."

"I remember we went aboard," Xavier said, "we're told we could speak to the crew all we wanted, as long as we know Tagalog. Idris havin fun with us. Idris said it wasn't his ship, but he'd come along and watch over us. Said he'd tell the pirates aboard to duck if they saw me aimin the camera at them. Meanwhile you shootin away with your tiny spy pen while Idris is watchin me with the Sony."

Dara brought the video spy camera out of her jacket and clipped it in the breast pocket, the top inch of the pen, its pin-hole lens showing. "A pen if you didn't know better."

Xavier said, "I thought it *was* a pen."

"It is. Anyone who stares at it," Dara said, "I slip it out of the pocket, stop shooting and start taking notes."

"Whyn't you use it at Idris's house?"

"Too dark in there. This one does need a lot of light. Push the button on top and I'm the camera. I did manage to get the two Saudis while they're ducking away from you." She said, "If there's some kind of plot . . . You know what I mean, to use a highly combustible ship? I don't think Idris would be in on it."

"But you act like you suspect somethin's goin on. Way you start lookin over your shoulder."

"It was later," Dara said. "After I found out Billy's watching the gas ship and knows more about it than we do."

CHAPTER ELEVEN

Billy was driving Helene nuts. He'd say, "You don't mind living on the boat?" Helene would tell him she loved *Pegaso*, loved sailing.

Billy said, "I'm glad you go for champagne."

"Love it." Stay half in the bag it was easier to take the boring mind games he played.

"Champagne or coffee," Billy said, "why stock beverages we don't need."

He was starting to sound weird. He said to her while they were moored off Eyl, seeing only a few lights ashore but hearing the generator from up on the slope, "You don't feel cooped up?"

She wanted to hit him with something. The fire extinguisher.

"All I said was why don't we go ashore and take a walk?"

"No, you said why don't we go ashore and stretch our legs. Like they're cramped from being stuck aboard a couple of weeks."

Helene took a moment before saying, "Whether I said let's

go for a walk or let's stretch our legs, I swear they both mean the same thing to me. I'm happy to be here, but I'd also like to fucking go for a walk. Okay?"

Billy liked it when she talked like that. He grinned saying, "I was teasing you. See if you'd hold your ground or start crying. Say it again."

"What?" Helene said.

"You'd like to fucking go for a walk. Most girls use the word, it doesn't sound right. You give it meaning. Let's hear you use it in a sentence."

The guy was unreal.

"You want me to say *fuck* or *fucking*?"

"Either one."

Helene said, "You want to take a walk or fuck?"

"Lemme think," Billy said, grinning at her.

"Two hundred years ago," Billy said, "the last time a U.S. ship was attacked by African pirates, a young naval officer by the name of Bainbridge skippered a ship that took part in the action. Today the USS *Bainbridge*, named for that young officer, in naval combat off the coast of Tripoli, is again confronting African pirates. You realize that?"

"You sound like the guy on CNN."

They were in the *Pegaso*'s salon watching the coverage on television.

"This time the wogs picked on an American ship with an American captain and crew, the *Maersk Alabama*. Maersk is the owner, he's Danish, but everybody aboard is a Yank. It's a seventeen-thousand-ton container ship. This time the wogs bit off more'n they can chew."

"But they have the captain."

"The hero of this action. Giving himself up so the wogs won't fuck with his men. Leave 'em alone. Captain Richie Phillips, they put him in that motorized lifeboat and thought they could sail off with him and ran out of gas."

"And the guy who should've kept the gas tank full," Helene said, "is thinking he's fucked, he's gonna get fired or go to prison for not doing his job. I wonder if anybody's thought of him."

"Hon, this has nothing to do with some oiler's misfortune. This is about the captain of the *Alabama,* now a hostage of the wogs. Four kids with automatic rifles have put Captain Richie Phillips in the most potentially heroic position of his life."

"If he wants to be a hero."

"One that could win him the Congressional Medal of Honor. Or whatever they award if you're not military. That's the chance, what puts him in the right place. Get him pictured on the cover of *Time* or *Newsweek.*"

"Or both. Sometimes they do the same stories."

"This one about an American looking his fate in the eye. The wogs want two million for him." Billy paused. "They aren't Kafirs, Kafirs are Hindus, and they aren't gooks. Wogs are in a huge area from the Middle to the Far East. I'm thinking there must be a special name for these guys."

"Towelheads."

"That's crude. I'll stick with wogs, or Mohammedans. Four of them are holding the captain for ransom. They don't get two million for him he's a dead man."

"They said that?"

"Not in those words. This is a standoff between armed wogs who want money and the government of the United States represented by Captain Phillips. If we give in to their demand and pay the ransom, we're pussy. We're turning our back to what's most precious to us, the ideals of a free people."

She thought he was going to say "our precious bodily fluids."

Helene, on the settee, put her glass down and looked at Billy. He was serious. He was the guy Sterling Hayden played in *Dr. Strangelove,* General Jack D. Ripper. *How I Learned to Stop Worrying and Love the Bomb,* the subtitle. Sterling Hayden was so serious he was weird. Calm, talking about the Communist conspiracy to put fluoridation in our drinking water to fuck up our precious bodily fluids. They watched the picture twice while they were still in the Mediterranean. Billy said he'd watched it six or seven times at least and thought Jack D. Ripper was a martyr, giving his life for the sake of our precious bodily fluids. That's who Billy sounded like at times, Sterling Hayden.

Billy said, "I'd be willing to bet Richie Phillips somehow got on the horn with the commander of the *Bainbridge* and told him, 'Don't pay them. Not one dime. Threaten to send a missile up their ass if they don't surrender. Tell them how it works, you get caught you stand trial. Give 'em one minute to make up their minds, with a ticking clock next to the phone the wogs can hear. I bet anything the commander gave them a time limit. The wogs tell him, 'But we have Captain Phillips, he will be killed too.' The commander tells them, 'Richie Phillips is willing to give his life for his country and what he believes. Are you?'"

Helene listened to the CNN report and said, "Well, it isn't gonna happen tonight."

She needed to get straight in her mind which guy was the real Billy Wynn. Serious enough when he was sailing the boat, but weird when they anchored and he sounded like Sterling Hayden. She wondered what he'd be like at home, if he wore a cowboy hat. Sooner or later she'd have to meet his friends down in East Texas. Have people over for a cookout and square dance in their cowboy boots. She thought, No. Wait a minute. Billy didn't listen to country, he liked—what was the guy's name he played almost every day? His friends would come to the cook-outs in raggedy straw hats and move their shoulders in time to Jimmy Buffett's "Margaritaville." Jesus.

WHAT BILLY DID MOST of the day, anchored off Eyl, was listen to CNN and study the ships held for ransom, creeping over every inch of them with his huge binoculars. He'd get the names of the ships and look up their registry and then make a few satellite calls to his informants in Djibouti and Qatar, Billy lounging in the *Pegaso*'s salon.

Helene heard him say, "Well, it's the *Aphrodite* now, a thousand-foot LNG tanker. I can see five tanks sticking out of the deck." Billy said, "What I want to know is where it's going," and hung up.

He said to Helene, "They changed the name of the ship from *Heureka* to *Aphrodite*."

"Yeah . . . ? They sound like cool guys."

"Originally it was out of Piraeus with a Greek master and crew. The owner now is from Dubai in the United Arab Emir-ates but lives in London. I said to my informant, 'You sure the owner isn't living in a cave up in Pakistan?' If they don't find that fucker soon I'm gonna get on it. We're offering twenty-five mil to learn his whereabouts and nobody's stepped up. You know why? We're offering too much. What's a former goat herdsman who delivers milk to him gonna do with twenty-five million bucks? Buy a car?"

Helene said, "Are you talking about whoever fingers Ben Laden?"

"Hon, it's bin, Osama *bin* Laden with a small *b*. No matter who my informant tells me owns the ship, I think it could belong to bin Laden. I wonder if anybody calls him that? 'Hey, bin, how you been?' It was on the History Channel all the ships he owns. You ever watch it?"

"I love the History Channel."

"You never saw it in your life."

"I've heard of it."

"Their shows are great. The world's worst natural disasters, Krakatoa, tsunamis, the Johnstown flood, the attempt to assassinate Hitler. They show him for what he really was, a homasexual dictator."

"Hitler was gay?"

"You ever see him at play up at his mountain retreat? Acting like a girl, slapping Eva Braun on the ass? I'm of the opinion Eva was a tough broad. She loved Adolf and wanted to straighten him out. You understand Eva was his cover."

"I don't think it's possible to turn," Helene said, "or they don't want to. Guys you can tell are gay—ones I'd meet—are always having fun, and they're smart. I don't know about the ones you can't tell if they are or not."

Billy said, "We finally got a lead on something that's bigger than these Mohammedans playing they're pirates. We'll keep tabs on the *Aphrodite* when she's released, not let her get too far away. I think she'll have to put in at Djibouti to take on stores."

Billy popped open a bottle of champagne.

"I told you I saw Dara and her bearer going out to the ship with Idris. How would she know, without my kind of sources? You know how many paid insiders I have on this now? Six. How could she know *Aphrodite*'s gonna blow up a U.S. port?"

"How do *you* know?"

"Hon, al Qaeda's got a huge hard-on for the U.S. It's been eight years since 9/11, al Qaeda's thinking up its next move against us. It's got to be a good one, something different but showy. Dara might not suspect what's going down, but something's on her mind. I bet her a bottle of champagne I'd have her luggage in her room inside of five minutes. I intended to come with the bottle, a cool way to meet her. Miss Smarty's already got the flutes out. The girl's aware, has a keen sense of things."

He sounded just like Sterling Hayden.

"Are you gonna tell her what you think?" Helene said.

"I've only thought of one scenario. I may need a couple more people on this. There's an ex-SEAL I hire. I tell Buck what I want to find out and he delivers. Won't take any pay till he does the job, then holds me up. The man has style. Buck Bethards. He could be anywhere, but I'll give him a call. Buck'll drop whatever he's doing to work for me."

Billy was pouring champagne now, telling Helene, "When you're not too busy, google the ports in the U.S. that allow delivery of liquid natural gas. I'll bet there's no more'n a half dozen, all of them inland a ways." He raised his flute to touch Helene's.

"I notice you and Dara seemed to hit it off. Why don't you talk to her girl to girl, see if you can find out what she's up to." Billy said, "Hon, I'd appreciate it."

THEY WERE TOPSIDE NOW, early evening, the sun sliding around before falling like a stone behind the hijacked ships. Or it was the fucking wine. Helene said, "You're still looking at them?"

Through his huge binoculars. "I'm trying to locate the three Saudis, one of 'em's first officer."

"What's the captain?"

"Egyptian. His name's Wassef."

"I got what you want. The *Times* did a story about dreading the day an LNG tanker is used by terrorists. You're not the only one smells a plot. There are five ports in the U.S. for this kind of tanker, all inland. Everett, Mass., near Boston. Cove Point, Maryland. Elba Island, Georgia, and Lake Charles, Louisiana."

"That's four. Where's the fifth one?"

"A hundred and sixteen miles out in the Gulf of Mexico, the Gateway Energy Bridge."

Billy said, "Want to walk on the beach?"

Helene stared at him, the glasses against his face.

"Stretch our legs?"

"Slip the raft over the side, lock the hatch and turn on the Mean Dog tape."

"Idris asked us to stop by. He's throwing a party."

"For his Mohammedan buddies?"

"For Harry, he's still here."

Billy lowered the glasses. "I wouldn't mind talking to Harry. See if I can find out what side he's on."

CHAPTER TWELVE

THE NIGHT OF HIS party Idris presented a bonus to a half dozen of his mates: brown oxfords from Tricker's on Jermyn Street, London. Now they were showing the inscription inside the shoes: *By Appointment to His Royal Highness Prince of Wales. R. E. Tricker, Shoe Manufacturers Ltd.* Now they were throwing away their sandals.

Dara and Xavier were in her hotel suite watching footage.

"About when we got there, the boys lookin down at their kicks, grinnin," Xavier said, "pokin each other. 'Look at mine.' They all wearin the same brown wingtips. How'd Idris know their sizes?"

"I don't know if he asked them or took a guess. I'm using the spy pen at the party," Dara said, "only the second time for a film, after I shot the guys aboard the gas ship. I still wasn't sure it would give me what I want."

"You said long as you facin what you shootin."

"I know, but I still try to be so casual about it. What I got of the two Saudis looks great."

"They kept duckin out on me. Did not want to be in a movie."

"And I got them at the party."

Xavier said, "Where are they?" looking at the laptop.

"They're coming up."

"You got Idris and Harry in their white suits."

"I've got tons of Idris and Harry."

"I liked those dogs," Xavier said. "They puttin it on 'cause they can do it, spend their lives misbehavin. I ask Idris, 'You get along with the al Shabaabs? Understand where they comin from?' Idris shrugs his shoulders like he don't care, says to me, 'Some like it jihad.' Like it's something cool Arabs say."

"Maybe it's an Arab expression."

"I don't know—it's the first time I thought a Arab said somethin funny."

"Look at the color," Dara said. "High def and you don't even see the camera."

"You like the torches?"

"I love the torches. Exotic lighting and mood in the same prop. A gang of Arab pirates, a goat turning on a spit, the pool lit. Music. Several ass shakers. Here they are, the two Saudis, always together, always smoking Marlboros." Dara lighted a cigarette. "I'm trying to figure out why Idris brought the Saudis and not the rest of the crew. The captain and the first officer stayed in the house most of the party."

"Passed on the roast goat," Xavier said.

"The two we thought were both Saudis ate but didn't drink. I kept shooting with the spy pen as I talked to them. 'Hey, didn't I see you guys on the *Aphrodite*?' The younger one said, 'You making a movie, uh? Want me to star?' There's no way he's anything but African American."

"Boy visitin his homeland," Xavier said.

"I told Idris and he said, 'Oh, is he?' Idris said Harry invited those two. Harry didn't think the Filipinos would fit in and feel comfortable. Like the captain was having a ball staying in the house."

Dara said, "And there's the guy you gave your gun to, Kwame. Putting on his new shoes."

The pirates lounged on the floor around a cocktail table eating and drinking, were still admiring their new shoes.

"I didn't give him my heat, you did."

"Tell Idris you were showing Kwame the gun and he thought you were giving it to him," Dara said. "Remember?"

"I'm showin my piece to a man was robbin us?"

"I didn't see you had to go into that. You told Idris Kwame took your gun by mistake. Idris got it from him and gave it to you."

"I don't see it in the movie."

"I didn't use it. Too much to explain. I told you we'd get it back, and we did."

BILLY BROUGHT HELENE THROUGH the Eyl people squatting in the dark at the edge of the yard, the locals watching the dinner party on the patio: most of the guests eating with their fingers from bowls they shared. The watchers murmured to one another licking their lips.

"Mmmmm, roast goat," Billy said. "You ever have it?"

"Love it," Helene said.

He brought her among the diners in camp chairs and on fat cushions, to the ones lounging on the brick floor around the cocktail table.

"You like the music?"

"Love it."

Billy started toward Dara in the crowd talking to her bearer,

Xavier, Billy believed born of Watusi stock. "Eating with his fingers seems natural to him, doesn't it? And look at Dara sucking her fingers, enjoying the Arabian cookout."

Helene thought of "Margaritaville."

Billy was saying, "Mohammedans are a unique people, aren't they? Like to sit on the floor eating goat. We see chickens in the yards, but goat seems to be their dish." He said to the table, the Somali nearest him about to take a drink, "Tell Allah you'll be back on the Islam wagon tomorrow."

The Somali stared at Billy, his mates jabbing Arabic words at him until he said, "You sink one of my boats, you leave the other one with no use in it. I believe you should pay me for their destruction."

Helene saw Harry and Idris coming in their white suits. New York, they'd start a trend, guys in white suits with different color scarves. She waited for Billy to make a thing out of the Somali's demand so he could talk for a while.

Billy said to the pirate, "What's your name, amigo?"

The Somali said, "My name is Booyah."

Billy said, "You putting me on?"

Idris stepped in. "No, Booyah Abdulahi is his name. Booyah's an honorable man."

"Well, I want to pay him what I owe," Billy said. "I hit his boats with six-hundred-caliber Nitro Express rounds. Firing the gun will knock a normal person on his or her ass. I've been trying to get my companion to fire the rifle, a Holland & Holland, but she won't take my dare."

Helene rolled her eyes looking at Dara.

"I put one of the boats under," Billy said, "and the other's beached for good. I'll pay what they're worth."

"And the motors?" Idris said.

"Yeah, and any personal effects."

"The weapons they lost," Idris said, "and the gasoline, in

five-gallon containers, several of them in each boat?" He turned to Harry Bakar. "What is petrol selling for now, eight dollars?"

"Look," Billy said, "I'll pay for all that. I'm curious about those ships anchored out there"—talking to the table now—"that tanker especially. You weren't afraid to board it?"

"No smoking," Booyah said. "No lighter, no matches."

Harry said, "Excuse me," to Billy, "but this afternoon the owners of the *Sirius Star* agreed to pay Mr. Abdulahi three million dollars for its release. I believe within the next few days."

"Three million, huh, that's all?" Billy said. "How much you asking for that LNG tanker? I wouldn't touch it you paid me ten million dollars. I bet you could get that much too. Ten mil or you'll blow her up. I understand you have to keep the gas cool once you convert it to liquid. I read if any leaks out and turns to vapor and becomes a cloud and you ignite it . . . ?"

Helene looked at Harry listening to every word.

"The heat will melt steel at twelve hundred feet. I read that if terrorists had a gas tanker and blew it up, you'd have thousands dead and injured on your hands."

Helene said, "I'm going to the loo, okay?"

Idris watched Dara say something to Xavier and follow after Helene. He thought it was curious how women always go to latrines together. He heard Billy say:

"Anybody ever ask the crew if they worry about getting blown up?"

HELENE SAID AT THE mirror, "With my tan I could lose three pounds and do bikinis."

Dara said, "What's it like being a companion?"

"It's the same as 'lady.' Or, 'the lady.' Once in a while 'old lady.' He tries so hard to impress me."

"You're a possession."

"Yeah, but he's in love with me. He tells me whenever he's high. That's when he's the nicest, if you've ever heard of that. He's never mean, he's just so fucking boring."

"I'll bet you don't marry him," Dara said, "if he ever asks you. You decide the money isn't worth it."

"He promised to put ten mil in my account the day of the wedding."

"He's buying you."

"So what, he loves me. He grins when I say 'fuck.'"

"How do you say it?"

"Like, 'This fucking boat is driving me out of my fucking mind.' The regular way, but I wouldn't say that."

"Why's he so interested in the gas tanker?"

"You heard him, he thinks bin Laden's gonna blow it up."

"Where?"

"He's trying to figure that out. Or they'll run a ship into it."

"The crew's part of it?"

"Billy says not the gooks. He says if they don't change the crew again, like at Djibouti, then it's the two Saudis will blow it up at some American port."

Helene was using a comb now trying to untangle her hair, saying to Dara, "You went on board to talk to the crew?"

"Tried to communicate. We didn't get much."

"Billy wonders if you have pictures of the Saudis."

Dara said, "Tell him I got them aboard the gas ship and this evening, a little earlier."

"Billy said if you have the Saudis on film"—Helene working on her hair—"he can tell if they're terrorists or not. He has head shots of all the bad guys."

CHAPTER THIRTEEN

THE PARTY COMING TO an end reminded Xavier of a stage
once the show was over and the houselights were turned up,
the pirate chiefs walking off in their new shoes with leftover
dinner wrapped in newspaper, for the women who had to stay
home. Xavier was waiting for Dara to finish talking to Idris and
Harry Bakar, Dara still digging for information.

Telling them she read that the people running the pirate business were wealthy Somalis living other places now, in England
and Saudi Arabia. Harry said he heard gangsters were running
the show, the Italian Mafia telling the pirates what ships to look
for coming through Djibouti on their way everywhere, information they got from secret agents, spies. Harry smiling, saying to
Dara, "Did you know you were making a thriller?"

Dara said she wasn't sure what she was making.

Xavier said to her, "You ready?"

And Idris said, "Harry doesn't know what he's talking about.
Do you think I work for criminals?" He took time to name the

seven pirate clans boarding ships for the honor of the Somali people, making it sound as if they were Arab Robin Hoods.

Dara seemed to have eyes for Harry Baker, the reason they stood there thinking up things to say, Harry and Idris too polite to end it.

Xavier said, "We gonna make our train, we better get movin."

No smiles or chuckles, only Dara got it. She said, "Well, it was quite a party."

Sitting in the hotel suite with her, Xavier said, "You had trouble tearin yourself from their company."

"I was trying to think of a way to mention the gas tanker," Dara said. "Tell them why Billy thought it was a bomb. But if I was serious about it they'd say I was imagining things."

"And if you made fun of Billy's idea—"

"We'd all be grinning and I'd feel stupid. I wouldn't have learned anything."

"You coulda asked what happen to the Saudis at the party? They disappeared on us. They go back to that gas ship? Then you in it, you wonderin about it."

"Why didn't you ask them?"

"I just thought of it," Xavier said. "You know at that time, hijackin an American ship was the best thing they'd done, the Somalis still proud of theirselves but tired of talkin about it, tired watchin Al Jazeera, nothin new happenin. That was Thursday, the night of the party. The SEALs didn't shoot the three pirates till Sunday. After that it was death to Americans, but we didn't know about it yet."

"I've got a lot of that I can use," Dara said, "if it goes with my story. 'Somali Pirates Threaten to Target Americans,' in the news. 'Pirates want revenge, not ransom.'"

"That time, it was gettin hot, wasn't it?"

"It was turning into a movie," Dara said, "a real one."

◆ ◆ ◆

IDRIS AND HARRY WALKED across the front of Idris's California ranch toward rooms off the four-car garage, Harry saying, "You tell them you don't work for criminals. What difference does it make? Dara leaves and we never see her again. You like her," Harry said, "because you aren't used to a woman being herself, and also intelligent."

"I like her and would like to know her better," Idris said and looked at Harry. "Are you ready?" Opened the door and walked ahead of Harry into a room without furniture, the walls and floor unpainted concrete. Harry followed bringing a Walther PPK from inside his white suit.

The three Saudis were on the floor, backs against a wall, the first officer in his uniform slumped, his chin resting on his chest.

"Bored," Harry said, and then in a louder voice, "Duad Dahir Suliman, are you bored?"

The first officer's head came up, eyes open, confused. Now he was getting his legs under him to rise.

Harry said, "Stay as you are."

The first officer was now upright on his knees. He said, "Yes?" He said, "Please tell me why we wait in this place. Are we your guests or not?"

The two sitting against the wall had not moved. The one with the wrap of white cloth around his head was black, about thirty, with a beard and hair to his shoulders. They sat watching Harry Bakar with little interest. Idris had already put them both down as al Qaeda. Harry believed it too. He said to the younger one, "You must be Jama Raisuli. Is that correct? Tell us who gave you your name. It sounds Berber to me."

Jama, looking up at Harry, said, "The party must be over," in English, with no hint of a Middle East accent.

Harry said, "It certainly is. Tell us, is the first officer one of you?"

"I don't know him," Jama said.

Harry turned to Idris. "You hear him? This Jama Raisuli is American. What we hear about him must be correct. He turned to Islam for the love of Allah and protection while in prison." He said to Jama, "What prison were you in?"

The man sitting with Jama turned his head to say a few words against his shoulder. An Arab with short hair, the bones of his face showing in his skin.

"Qasim al Salah wants you to keep your mouth shut," Harry said. "I'll bet you prefer Jama Raisuli to being called 'boy' or 'nigger.' Isn't that correct?" Harry waited, got no response and said, "There are others like you, still citizens of America. You can return whenever you want as a traitor and be tried in court. Tell us why you came here."

"You're nada to me," Jama said, "and I tell you nada."

Qasim put his face to his shoulder again and spoke to him.

"I turn to a true life," Jama said.

"Good for you," Harry said. "Tell me about your shipmate Qasim al Salah, who hasn't said a bloody word. He's one of you?"

"He and I are one in Allah."

"With little room for the first officer," Harry said and turned to the young Saudi still upright on his knees. "So we don't need you, do we?" Harry extended the Walther and shot Duad Dahir Suliman straight off in the center of his forehead, Harry stepping back as the first officer fell toward him, the young man's eyes still open.

The two against the wall stared at Harry without expression, Idris turning to him stunned. "You had to *shoot* him?"

"He's of no use to us," Harry said. "We inform the master of the *Aphrodite* his first mate disappeared. Ran off with these two and the cooch dancers in one of your Toyotas." Harry grinned. "A jolly group. The Egyptian can believe it or not, it makes no difference." He looked at the two sitting against the wall. "This Jama the Amriki is thinking how he can persuade me not to shoot him. Qasim al Salah has faced death many times before. He's tired of it, so he gives himself to his fate, still refusing to speak. I'd like to know what's in his head."

"He doesn't have to speak," Idris said. "Allah put these two on the gas tanker and sent it to us."

Harry said, "Why didn't you take it yourself?"

"I smoke too much to board a tanker. Three packs a day— I'm going to climb on a gas ship? I chew a bit of khat so I don't smoke so much," Idris said. He watched Jama the black American take a cigarette from his pack of Marlboros and light it with a match, Idris saying, "Let me have one of those if you will, please."

Harry watched Jama, not bothering to look at Idris, slip the cigarettes into his shirt pocket again, Harry smiling.

"As the Americans like to say, 'Fuck you.'"

Idris said, "I thought Americans were generous."

"Some are, some not," Harry said. "They have the world's nationalities in America, blacks from the time they were used as slaves. It should be enough to make blacks disposed to Islam if not al Qaeda." He said to Jama, "You should go home and tell the darkies how much fun you're having as a terrorist."

"You have to insult us," Jama said, "before you shoot us?"

"Shoot you," Harry said, "where did you get that notion? Tomorrow you will be riding in a procession of cars under armed guard. Shackled and blindfolded if you give us the least trouble. Late the second day the caravan arrives in Djibouti. We phone the American embassy and speak to the person in charge of their

Rewards for Justice program, a way they've planned to stop your atrocities."

"They have a list of the ones," Idris said, "known to be al Qaeda. Both of you are on the list."

"With photographs," Harry said. "We hand you over to the American State Department's Bureau of Diplomatic Security"— Harry had to grin—"and guess what they give us for you naughty boys. Six million U.S. dollars. Five for Qasim and one for Jama."

"You didn't spread enough terror," Idris said to Jama, "to get your numbers up."

CHAPTER FOURTEEN

THEY WERE AT WORK again in Dara's hotel suite, looking at the rough cut on her seventeen-inch screen, a bottle of red on the table. They watched:

Xavier coming out to the *Buster* in a pirate skiff, a young Somali at the tiller. "Sixteen years old," Xavier said, "dyin to hijack some ships. I told the boy it wasn't for my age I'd be a dedicated pirate myself. They give us all these stores, stalk of green bananas, liter bottles of water wrapped in plastic, the meat—"

"I smelled it," Dara said, "and threw it over the side."

"That's what happen to it. I wondered how those sharks got diarrhea. The boy was no help to me till he picked up the bunch of khat I promoted for us." Watching the screen, Xavier said, "Good, you got me relievin him of the bouquets. The boy startin to chew on a bunch."

"This was Friday," Dara said, "the natives still friendly. They've got the captain of the *Alabama* in a lifeboat and want two million for his release. Sunday, the SEALs took out the pirates and the standoff was over."

"And all hell broke loose," Xavier said. "You ever use that expression?"

"It broke loose shooting Katrina but I restrained myself."

"You ask me did I see Idris and Harry Baker that morning. I found out from the khat-chewer runs the coffee stand, they left at six A.M. in five Toyota SUVs, armed, gun barrels stickin out the windows. Want people to see they mean business. I ask the khat-chewer where they headed, to Djibouti? He say, 'Where else?' They have water and gasoline strapped on top the vehicles."

Dara said, "Idris and Harry and two guys in handcuffs with hoods over their heads."

"In separate SUVs," Xavier said, "in the middle of the parade, one with Idris, one with Harry Baker."

"Did we know at that time who they were?"

"We knew they had to be the two guys off the gas tanker, one Saudi, one American. That got us wonderin about the ship, full of liquid natural gas. You not thinkin and light a cigarette, the port where you sittin could go up in flames. But these two and another one from the ship, the first mate, were at Idris's cookout. We don't know what happened to the mate. Where did he go?"

"And the Egyptian captain," Dara said.

"I told you I served under him one time?" Xavier said. "Captain Wassef. That trip, the captain picked me out to be a helmsman and we'd talk some when he was on the bridge. He was the only captain I ever served under was friendly."

"That's right," Dara said, "you ran into him."

"Still ashore the mornin after the party. Upset," Xavier said, "chain-smokin Turkish cigarettes and drinkin coffee. It's when he tells me his first officer's missin and two from the crew."

"The two with hoods over their heads," Dara said, "put in the SUVs."

"See, Captain Wassef didn't know nothin about them,"

Xavier said. "The *Aphrodite* stopped at Balhaf in Yemen, the LNG terminal there, took on their load of liquid gas and was escorted out of the port by the local Coast Guard. Then out a ways—they in international waters now—another gunboat, he believes from Yemen, stops the ship to inspect the load. This is when the two al Qaeda guys come aboard."

"The captain told you that?"

"He don't know they al Qaeda. *We* find it out later on."

Dara said, "This is when the explosives were planted."

"Must've been," Xavier said. "Steel-cuttin shape charges planted round the containers of frozen gas. Captain Wassef don't know nothin about it and we don't either at the time. But the captain's suspicious. He phones Emirates Transport in Dubai wantin to know what's goin on. Who are these desert-lookin boys he don't know joinin his crew? The transport company tells him to calm down, stay on course and keep his mouth shut. Captain Wassef thinks okay, now he's goin to Lake Charles, Lou'siana, no more trouble. Only the next day out of Yemen the ship's hijacked by pirates and *Aphrodite* ends up in Eyl."

"Where the two al Qaedas who joined the crew," Dara said, "are shanghaied by Idris and Harry and taken to Djibouti."

"We don't know what's goin on at the time," Xavier said. "But the pirates must've found out al Qaeda wants the ship. Emirates Transport offers the pirates a half mil for a thousand-foot tanker worth a quarter of a billion dollars, not even countin the payload, and they accept it right away. Like they can't wait for the ship to leave Eyl. Want to get it out of their hands fast."

"You didn't seem worried," Dara said.

"I don't make decisions. You see a movie in it, you tell me what we gonna do."

"You went swimming," Dara said, "bare-ass."

"That evenin, yeah. I remember you waitin to see me pull myself aboard."

"You looked young," Dara said. "I could see you years ago attracting curious girls with your slim body, the girls wondering what a man six and a half feet tall looks like naked."

"You mean they curious how a man that tall is hung," Xavier said. "I was good-lookin too."

It was a bottle of 'Neuf du Pape on the hotel table now. Dara filled their glasses halfway thinking of him yesterday evening on the *Buster,* the hijacked ships a mile off, their solemn lights showing, the ships waiting for their release. She said, "I wanted to shoot the ransom drop, remember? Do it from aboard the gas tanker."

"Shoot the money comin down," Xavier said, "watch it don't hit you on the head."

"But there was no ransom drop that time."

"We don't know they were ever paid the half mil."

"We waited too long," Dara said. "We should've left the morning after the party."

"Wouldn't matter," Xavier said. "Come Sunday, anywhere in the gulf, we the game. Hear the Yamahas gettin louder, pretty soon we see the pirates skiffin out toward us."

BILLY HAD *PEGASO* OUT among the hijacked ships spread over a mile, Billy with his high-powered glasses on the LNG tanker, waiting for it to, goddamn it, move out.

"Man, that's an ugly ship. Round shape of five steel pods showing topside, the other half below, the superstructure hanging off the fantail. She rides low, easy to board. But who'd want to?"

"Not me," Helene said. She lounged topless in the cockpit holding Billy's bottle of champagne. He'd said a while before, hell, why didn't she take her panties off too? She told him it would fuck up her tan lines. "You get a real even tan, the white parts of you look sexier." She said, "How long have we been out, hon?"

"Thirty-four days."

"How much longer will we be . . . aboard?"

"A hundred and twenty days, give or take."

"But that's"—she paused to get her tone under control—"four more months. Didn't you say it was about a four-month cruise from Marseilles?"

"I don't count doing surveillance or going to parties as sailing. It isn't my fault we have to sit and wait on the gas ship."

"So it's going to take longer than four months, huh? Starting from right now."

"It could take longer we run into pirates in the Malacca Straits we ever get there. I'm told they got it under control, so I'm not gonna worry about it. I doubt I would even if they weren't."

"What?"

"Under control."

Jesus Christ, Helene was thinking, we haven't even started yet.

"We're at the party," Billy said, "you meet the captain of that gas ship?"

"The Egyptian? For a minute. I told him I love the pyramids. We did a layout on top the Aswan Dam one time for *Bazaar*. You know there aren't any regular bathrooms in that entire fucking country? There's a hole in the floor you have to hit. Go in a souk crowded with Egyptians, there's no place to have a whiz."

"What'd you do?"

"Wet my pants."

For two days they sailed among the hijacked ships keeping an eye on *Aphrodite*. Sunday CNN announced the rescue of Captain Phillips from the lifeboat, the three pirates killed by Navy SEALs. Billy listened to the news grinning. "Bing bing bing, a shot apiece and the captain's free." He said, "Well, the wogs had to learn the hard way."

"Don't fuck with Americans," Helene said. "Right?"

Monday morning she heard *Pegaso*'s engine start up, loud, Jesus, almost underneath her. She came topside in a sweatshirt to see Billy taking in the sails. Helene said, "What's up, Skipper?" Now he was in the cockpit steering toward a little white boat a mile or so off.

"Why, isn't that *Buster?*" Helene said, being cool. "We gonna visit?"

"Look toward the beach," Billy said. "There's the one coming to visit, with AKs and a grenade launcher."

She could hear the high whine now of the pirate skiff, streaking dead ahead toward the *Buster*.

Billy raised his glasses to see the pirates unroll a bedsheet and hold it taut, bow to stern, Arabic words painted on it in black Billy picked up his satellite phone and dialed a number. He said, "Mustaf? This is Mr. Wynn," and read him the words on the banner. *"Al Mout Li Amrikas.* What's it mean?" He listened and said, "You shittin me? We were all good friends the other day." He listened and said, "No, I'll take care of it," and turned off the phone.

Helene said, "Well . . . ?"

"It means 'Death to Americans,' " Billy said, putting on his shooting vest.

XAVIER SAID TO DARA, "You can look it up in the book"— watching the skiff cut its motors to leave a hundred feet between them—"but I know it don't mean 'Welcome to Somalia.' "

"I'll have to talk to them," Dara said, "explain why they were shot."

Billy pulled up on *Buster*'s port side, tied on and stepped aboard with his Holland & Holland double-barrel rifle in one hand and a bottle of champagne in the other.

He said, "I'll confuse them a little first," and held up the rifle, the one he used to destroy two of their boats, saying, "See?" and shaking his head. Touched his chest and said, "Me?" and shook his head again. "I'm not gonna fire this expensive rifle. You are," and gave them time to talk among themselves. Now he waved them to come toward him. One of them started the motor and let the skiff rumble in closer. Billy said, "I know you're sore at us for the way the SEALs took out your boys with only three rounds, a single shot each," Billy sounding sincere. "Come on, I want you all to try this sporting rifle. Tie on here and listen to what I'm gonna tell you. In honor of your dead boys I'm offering this rifle as a tribute. The four of you—that boy driving isn't old enough. You have to be eighteen. The four of you each take a shot at a target we set up." Billy held up the bottle of champagne. "This is the target. If you'd like to have some, my lovely assistant will serve you. You each take a shot at the bottle. Whoever hits it wins the rifle."

One of them said, "What happen we all hit it?"

"Kwame," Billy said, "is that you? How you doin, man? Anybody hits a bottle, we put another one up. Now I want you to step aboard. You're gonna be shooting on the *Buster,* ten meters bow to stern. You stand here behind the wheelhouse and take aim at the target my lovely assistant Ginger will hang on that lanyard comes down from the mast to the bow. Seven or eight meters from your rifle barrel, that's all. Who wants to be first? Kwame?"

KWAME TOOK THE RIFLE, hefted it, aimed at the sky to the west, lowered the front sight to the bottle hanging from the lanyard, set himself, cheek against fine wood and gunmetal, squeezed the trigger and was kicked back to hit the table wedged against the curved bench, in the stern, hit the hard edge before he knew what was happening and dropped to the deck. Kwame pushed himself up saying to Billy, "You don't give us a trial shot to know what we shooting."

Billy said, "Let's see how the other boys do first. Then you can take another shot if you want," injecting another six-hundred-caliber Nitro Express round into the breech.

The next Somali hefted the rifle, aimed it, lowered it, aimed, then hefted it again feeling the weight of the gun, pressed his face against the smell of oiled wood, squeezed the trigger and was kicked back to land on the table and lay there laughing. Now the others were laughing, three of them with the boy on the table. Kwame wasn't laughing. The boy came off the table rubbing his shoulder and arm, telling the next boy how to hold this rifle. The next boy did as he was told, fired, twisted away from the kick and went over the side, the Indian Ocean swallowing him.

Billy said, "The boy know how to swim? He don't he better learn. Somebody fish him out if you will, please. Who's next?"

"You are," Kwame said. "You shoot, let me see you don't move. You show us with this gun."

Billy slipped in a load. He stood back of the wheelhouse, aimed, fired, shattered the bottle and held on to the kick, the barrels coming up, muscled it and barely moved. He slipped another round in the breech looking at Kwame. "Want to try it again?"

Xavier, his ears ringing, filmed the scene from the off side of the wheelhouse with the Sony as Dara was telling Billy there was still another shooter. Billy handed the boy the rifle saying he hoped it didn't tear his shoulder off, reaching to it and feeling bones.

The boy didn't hold the rifle in a tight grip or press his cheek against it. He fired and the kick sent him back six feet against the curved bench. It stunned him, he lay there until the other boys started laughing. Billy watched the lad getting to his feet, trying to make himself laugh. Everybody but Kwame.

Billy slipped another round into the throat of his double-barrel beast, asking Kwame, "You want to try again? Help yourself," and offered the rifle.

Dara watched Kwame reach to take it, but then let his hand drop.

"Who won this game?"

"I told you, the one hits the bottle," Billy said. "I'm the only one did, so I keep the rifle." He said, "Tough luck, my friend," put his hand on Kwame's shoulder and said, "*I'm* sorry," when Kwame winced.

"Amazing," Dara said.

Xavier heard her. He said, "Yeah, but they still on the boat."

BILLY, HIS HAND ON Kwame, moved him to the rail where the skiff was tied. Billy said, "*Al Mout Li Amrikas*? You must be thinking of some other Americans. You got your new shoes on? I told Idris Mohammed—he's going to London—where to get 'em for you boys. They comfortable?"

Kwame looked down at the shoes, nodding his head.

"Try not to get 'em wet out here," Billy said, "that's an expensive pair of footwear."

Now he was telling Kwame to get his boys home and ice those shoulders before they stiffened up on them. Telling Kwame he had some personal business to take care of and asked him, "You know anything about that gas tanker?" Nodding to the thousand-foot *Aphrodite* with the five tanks coming out of the deck. "You know the one owns it?"

"You don't smoke on the ship," Kwame said. "Is very dangerous."

"I'll remember that," Billy said. Christ, able to read NO SMOK-ING from a mile away. "You know where she's going?"

"To America someplace."

"You get your shoulder iced," Billy said. "You hear? It was a pleasure seeing you, Kwame. Maybe we can do it again sometime."

CHAPTER FIFTEEN

T HEY WATCHED THE SKIFF heading back to Eyl, a boatload
of pirates holding their shoulders. Dara was out on deck now
with Helene; Billy stood at the bow watching Xavier sweep
broken glass into the sea, talking to him.

Dara saying Billy surprised her; he was so cool the way he
pulled it off, putting the rifle in Kwame's hands.

"I never know who he's gonna be," Helene said. "Sometimes
he's Sterling Hayden with his precious bodily fluids."

"Kubrick's *Dr. Strangelove*," Dara said. "I thought it was a
terrific picture when I first saw it. It's still good, but you can see
everybody playing their parts."

"Ones they don't usually play," Helene said. "They're having
fun and don't care if you know it. It's easy to fake things."

"What does he know about *Aphrodite*?"

"Everything. Like there are only five ports in the United States
that take that kind of ship. I looked it up for him. You have to sit
out in the water a long time before they let you tie up. Then you

have to hook up lines to take the gas off the ship to wherever they store it. Any leaks out and hits the ground you're fucked."

"He's waiting for the gas ship," Dara said, "to get its release, and then what, follow it? Kwame said it's going to the U.S."

"He keeps watching it through his glasses," Helene said, "telling the ship to move out, goddamn it. When Billy wants to do something and has to wait, he drives you crazy."

"Well, you're not going around the world," Dara said, "unless the gas ship does."

"I've been thinking," Helene said, "if we actually follow the ship, are we going home? But I don't want to put any hope in it."

Dara said, "Or think of it blowing up a city in the U.S."

"Right. But I don't know—Billy's always changing his mind."

Dara said, "Where are the ports in the U.S.?"

"Boston. Near there," Helene said. "Two more on the East Coast in Maryland and Georgia, and one in the Gulf, near Lake Charles."

"Louisiana," Dara said, "not far from New Orleans."

THEY SAW BILLY TURN to look at them from the bow and Helene said, "He wants to know why you're interested in the gas ship."

"I guess the same reason he is," Dara said, and watched Billy pause to say something to Xavier.

"He wants to see the pictures of the two guys," Helene said, "you took at the party."

"I got them on the ship too," Dara said.

Billy came over to them now and Helene said, "She'll show you the pictures if you want."

Billy said, "The two wogs?"

"I think one's African American," Dara said. "I got him at the party blowing smoke at me."

"I bet anything it's Jama Raisuli," Billy said. "Don't move, I'll be right back," and left them, stepped over to *Pegaso* and went below.

"He'll get his Arab pictures," Helene said, "so you can pick out the two guys."

"How's it going otherwise?"

"I drink, I smoke."

"And listen," Dara said. "What's he want to do about the gas ship?"

"I told you, he wants to follow it."

"But what's his game? Find out where the ship's going, and then what?"

"I'm not sure," Helene said, "you'll have to ask him."

Billy came back with a stack of 8 x 10 photographs he began to lay out on the roof of the wheelhouse.

"From what I remember of them at the party I'd say it's . . . this guy," laying down a shot of Jama, white teeth showing in his beard, hair to his shoulders, "and this guy I call Mr. Bones, Qasim al Salah."

"You're right," Dara said, "Jama and Qasim."

"All those wogs look alike," Billy said, "but Qasim's got that bony look you tend to remember. And the scar across his chin, like somebody cut him one time. Always wears those gray kid gloves. This colored guy who turned wog, Jama Raisuli, has a familiar name but I can't seem to place him."

"Sean Connery," Dara said, "played an Arab chieftain named Raisuli in *The Wind and the Lion*. He rides off with Candy Bergen bitching at him. I have the DVD. Brian Keith plays Teddy Roosevelt."

"Billy has it too," Helene said.

"I do, don't I?" Billy said, looking at Dara now. "You keep on amazing me, a young lady who doesn't use her head just to grow lovely hair. Yeah, Connery playing an Arab with his Scotch accent, he still made us believe he was a Mohammedan. Now this colored guy we think turned Arab on us, saw the movie and borrowed the name Raisuli. Could've been in prison, took up with radical Islamists and their Wahhabi ways. Using violence for a cause turns him on, gives him an excuse to use guns and explosives." Billy paused. "Besides being a hard-ass, does this kid have a sense of humor? Using a name was Sean Connery's in the desert movie? Or did somebody give it to him? They let me board the gas ship I might've found out."

"He isn't on the ship now," Dara said. "Idris and Harry grabbed him, and the other one, Qasim, and right now are on their way to Djibouti. Five SUVs, black ones, with armed guards. They'll be there in two days."

"They don't run into a warlord," Billy said, "with SAMs."

"The chances are," Dara said, "Idris will know the warlord and give him a Toyota."

Billy looked out at the gas ship. "Those two al Qaedas can be replaced in a day, put two other guys aboard. Where's the *Aphrodite* suppose to be heading? I'd like to know that."

"A port in the U.S.," Dara said.

"Maybe," Billy said, staring at the gas ship. "Run into it and those five tanks blow up. The ship's so obviously a bomb it must be a decoy. Bin Laden knows we'll see it that way. So he does use the ship as a bomb. Well, it is or it isn't. The only way to find out is keep it in sight. Trail her till I have to call the navy or sink her myself."

Dara said, "You're not worried about the two al Qaedas?"

"If Harry and Idris have them, they're looking to get that Rewards for Justice handout. Only State will hem and haw, want proof of who they've got. The Gold Dust Twins will lose what patience they started with and refuse to give 'em up till they see some green. State in the meantime's keeping an eye on the Twins. They have local police poking through this rat's nest looking for the two Qaedas. After a while the Twins say fuck it, take the two out in the desert and shoot them."

Dara said, "If the State Department takes too long, the Twins lose patience, why wouldn't they let the Qaeda guys go?"

"Because, my dear, for the rest of their lives Jama and Qasim would be gunning for them. The Twins know that."

Xavier said, "Jama and Qasim might even get away, escape from the Twins."

"What do we care?" Billy said. "They won't be coming after us. They're unemployed Mohammedan terrorists. If State wants them, they'll go after them. But I can tell you right now, whatever happens, the Twins won't make a dime on this deal. Even if State agrees to question the two al Qaedas and they find out, Jesus Christ, these guys are terrorists, I can't imagine them paying a reward."

"What if I help Idris and Harry?" Dara said. "I identify Jama and Qasim, tell State what I know about them."

"They'll believe you," Billy said, "before they make a deal with these two Mohammedans. That is, once they look you up, see you haven't been arrested for demonstrating left-wing causes." Billy said, "Have you?"

"What Dara's sayin," Xavier said, "she wants to head off another 9/11."

"I do too," Billy said, "the reason I'm gonna tail the gas ship. Listen, the feds could refuse to take it seriously because the Twins piss them off. Remember, we're talking about a federal system of people with semi-one-track minds. You make a mistake you spend the rest of your career in a third-world country. So they sit on this till the Twins go away. If they're lucky they pick up the Mohammedans."

Billy thought of something else.

"Or what if the Twins we find out are working for bin Laden? They fake the Rewards program out of six mil and it's used to buy rusted-out freighters they load with explosives. Greek commandos stopped a ship that had seven hundred tons of TNT aboard, and eight thousand detonators."

Billy stopped again.

"The question is, are Jama and Qasim willing to spend the rest of their lives, twenty-three hours a day, in a federal prison cell? Qasim al Salah's a live wire—I don't know about Jama—but Qasim's been setting off explosions since the early eighties. Who's watching him, Somali pirates? I'll bet he ducks out."

"Before that happens," Dara said, "I'll get the Twins in to see the Diplomatic Security people."

Billy said, "I'll bet you ten bucks you don't."

CHAPTER SIXTEEN

'VE GOT TWO HOURS of Somali pirates in the can," Dara said, "and it's no longer about them."

They were at the Kempinski dining table again, her Mac-Book Pro and a fifth of cognac in front of them. They'd had supper away from the hotel and now they were at work.

Xavier said, "You still got the main one, Idris Mohammed, and you got his buddy Harry the Sheikh. You don't need any more pirates. The picture takes a turn here to bigger stuff."

"We don't have a transition," Dara said. "We don't see Harry and Idris forcing the two al Qaedas into the SUVs."

"We got the khat-chewer," Xavier said, "wad in his cheek, telling me what happened that morning, the Qaedas trussed up and blindfolded. Cut back and forth between the khat-chewer telling it in his English—and that's good stuff—and some black Toyotas ready to go."

"I'm not going to fake shots," Dara said.

"The khat-chewer says somebody was shootin what was goin

on. He thought it was me at first, 'cause it was a Somali had my same color, the one shootin the pictures."

"We did look for him," Dara said, "and came up empty." She sipped her cognac. "I need a transition."

"It's turnin into a Hollywood movie," Xavier said, and saw Dara, tired of it, shaking her head. "Or the treatment of a picture," Xavier said, "you could sell to a studio for a pile of money, since you don't want to shoot it with movie stars. Cut your two hours down to twenty minutes of pirates doin their number. See 'em at the party wearin their new shoes. See the hijacked ships layin at anchor—mood shots, the party music from up the hill over the ships sittin in the dark. Idris and Harry watchin the news—Somalis take their first American ship and they love it, both of 'em, and we get our first peek at who these boys are. Second act, you follow 'em to Djibouti."

"Hollywood's way ahead of us," Dara said. "Pirate movies are already in preproduction, Samuel Jackson doing one."

"His might be all right. Sam'll have the accent down."

"We've seen the *Alabama* hijacked."

"The one Discovery did? You kiddin me? They mix up a tiny bit of actual footage with quick shots of nothing. Grown men pretending to be Somali boys."

"You're right," Dara said, "it was awful. Discovery ought to be ashamed of themselves."

Xavier said, "That big sailin yacht gets hijacked in a movie coming up. Only the crew aboard. The girls come out of hidin after a couple of days drinkin wine and eatin peanuts. The pirates don't get it. Say why you hidin? You think we gonna jump you? That's what happen, nothin. Hollywood makes it, they have the pirates look 'em over, leerin at them, jihad boners in their pants. You gonna do this movie you don't have to change nothin. You already in it and you sense where it's goin. You say the pirate movie about pirates is over. By Sunday they showin a sign they want to kill us. Mr. Billy Wynn comes along with his elephant gun and saves our ass from their ire. Mr. Billy Wynn knows what he's doin. Keep him in sight and you have your movie."

"If I'd been there," Dara said, "when they drove off with the al Qaedas, I'd be with them. You wouldn't see me till you got to Djibouti."

"Run off in your little shorts and T-shirt?"

"Wouldn't matter, I'd have my secret camera."

"Same underwear the whole trip."

"I'd borrow a pair from Harry."

"Not Idris?"

"Harry's daintier, he'd have a few extra pair. What we don't want to forget," Dara said, "Harry sells guns. Isn't as clean as he looks."

"Well, you didn't get to go with the boys," Xavier said. "So where you are then in your movie, you see yourself on a boat goin six miles an hour for close on seven hundred miles full speed all day, all night?" Xavier paused to sip his cognac. "Took us twelve days to get to Eyl lookin at ships. Take us seven to get back to Djibouti, the sea behaves, we don't take on a monsoon, and the engine don't quit on us. Remember lookin at another week on the *Buster*?"

"Talking about it while we're tied alongside *Pegaso*," Dara said. "I had a feeling I could use Idris and Harry, but we'd have to get to them soon, in a couple of days."

Xavier grinned a little. "And our friend Billy, remember? He come along sayin, 'What's the hurry?'"

"YOU FIGURE HIM OUT?" Xavier said. "First he say we never gonna make it. The Gold Dust Twins be pitchin their deal at the

U.S. Embassy, after a reward, while we still out in the gulf. Then Billy changes his tune. Says, "Less I can get you a ride to Djib.'"

"His chance to show off," Dara said. "Tells Helene to get on the computer and find the positions of navy ships in the gulf, and plot their estimated courses. Helene's in her little bikini looking at dots on the screen that stand for ships—like she's working in a war room. Billy wanted the *Eisenhower* and got Helene to locate it. I remember thinking, He's gonna have an aircraft carrier pick us up? But it turned out to be our old friend CG-66 closer by, the guided missile cruiser with the skipper who likes my docs."

"You always this lucky?"

"When I have to be," Dara said. "As soon as I saw that blunt face of old 66 coming up on us I knew I'd make it."

"Told 'em you had al Qaeda stuff to report."

"Billy said I had to get to the *Eisenhower* to reach Djibouti in a few hours. He said, 'Once you're on the carrier you take the Greyhound.'"

"Like you gonna hop a bus."

"I told the skipper I had information for Diplomatic Security about terrorists. They relayed it to the carrier and the exec said to come on. They sent me in a helicopter, a Seahawk. We land on the flight deck and I step out—"

"To cheers and whistles."

"You weren't there."

"I can see it. You come off the copter in your little outfit, the cool chick with the cute ass in her short pants."

"I had the Canon and all the tapes in my bag, but already uploaded to my server. I had a feeling the CIA would keep my footage, take their time looking at it. The crew greeted me and I waved, that's all."

"Movie star visits the fleet. They give you more noise'n Virginia Mayo ever got."

"I had to decide, take the twin-turboprop Greyhound leaving in an hour, or dine with the captain and take the morning flight, with outgoing mail and a grocery list. I hear he's a savvy guy, but I had to turn him down I was so anxious to get to Djibouti, acting like I had to go to the bathroom. I told you there were newspeople aboard? All of us going back in an hour. They were out five days hoping to see pirates."

"Didn't see a one, did they?"

"Will you let me tell it? They were aboard the *Eisenhower* five days and had dinner with the captain once. No—they had lunch with him. Five men and one woman."

"You talk to them?"

"Of course."

"Tell 'em you know some of the bad boys personally? Have two of 'em makin eyes at you?"

"Harry's not interested, he hasn't given me any kind of look."

"Not while you watchin him. The newspeople want to see your footage?"

"I didn't offer. I shot them with the flip."

"They get angry with you?"

"They had no idea I was filming them."

"I mean not showin your footage?"

"They stopped asking. I didn't say a word about al Qaeda. I went to sleep on the plane."

Xavier said, "You get to Djibouti, now you have all kind of security on you." Xavier waited, watching Dara raise her glass to take a sip. He said, "You got your mind on the Gold Dust Twins, al Qaedas, CIA people . . . You know, you never once ask how me and *Buster* did our time at sea? Alone, so to speak."

Dara placed her glass on the desk and turned in her chair to face Xavier, waiting. She said, "I did, I asked how'd it go. If you missed me."

Xavier shook his head. "Unh-unh. I'm sittin here so I musta made the trip okay."

She thought of saying she didn't want to fly off and leave him. But she did, dying to get off this cute fucking boat. She said, "I knew you'd make it." He was silent now. Hurt? She said, "Xavier, tell me what happened?"

"Nothin. I tied on to old 66 and got towed to Djibouti. How you think I made it in two days?"

"But I'm out of touch by then." Dara finished her cognac. "The plane lands in Djibouti and I'm met by a quiet young guy from the embassy, the car waiting on the strip, a Lincoln."

"Made you feel important."

"It did, at first. The young guy—I forgot his name, Patrick something—said he was CIA station chief there. I thought he'd start in, ask how I happened to know about terrorists. You know what he said?"

"How was the flight?"

"He said, 'Is it hot enough for you?'"

"He's settin you up. Start slow, then blindside you."

"I think he expected me to start running off at the mouth, but I didn't. I said, 'I'm used to it by now.' Neither of us said another word on the way. No, he said something about the embassy being air-cooled for your comfort. Didn't they use to say that about movie theaters?"

"Before you were born."

"It was the only mention of where we were going."

"You musta known you weren't goin to the hotel."

"You're right, he didn't ask where I was staying. We approached the embassy, local police hanging around in front, passed through the gate and got out at the entrance. The marine post, the first one, was just inside. The marine took my passport and entered what he needed to know and handed it to the CIA station chief. The marine wanted to look in my bag but Patrick said, 'Ms. Barr's with me,' and took it off my shoulder. Now we're in the inner lobby—the whole place done in that harmless government décor. I was thinking they could get—what was her name, Billy's yacht decorator? Anne Bonfiglio. See if she could add a 'look' with a bit more life to it. The next marine stepped away from his desk to hand me a visitor's ID badge. Red with a big *V* in white and the words ESCORT REQUIRED. You believe it?"

Xavier said, "They got you now."

CHAPTER SEVENTEEN

THE CIA STATION CHIEF brought Dara by elevator to the third floor and along a hallway of what must be executive offices to the one at the end, double doors open to a view of the gulf at dusk in the windows and a woman in a beige suit coming toward her smiling, telling Dara, "I can't believe I'm actually meeting you. I love *Women of Bosnia,* the way you shot the men lurking about, watching like hyenas, waiting . . . Were you afraid filming those guys?"

"At times, yeah, they made me nervous."

"Dara, I'm hoping I can help you. I'm Suzanne Schmidt, regional security officer." She took Dara's hand and held on to it. "I love the way you do your hair."

"I don't really *do* it," Dara said.

"It shows your independence. I should have mine cut and quit getting my roots done every month. I blow it dry and by midday in this humidity and I have to go out . . . ? My pageboy begins to go limp." She brought Dara into her office, the CIA man and her bag no longer with them.

"Dara, I've loved all of your documentaries," Suzanne said, "but *Women of Bosnia* is my favorite—the way you kept your eye on the men without ever featuring them, and yet we know what they're about, especially what they did to the women. My favorite character is Amelia. You tell her story after the men had repeatedly raped her."

"Months later," Dara said.

"Amelia explains in simple words, 'Because I am Muslim.' She feels indelibly soiled. 'Because I am Muslim.' What the conflict was all about, really. Her husband leaves and she thinks of throwing herself in front of a train."

It was a tram, a streetcar, but Dara didn't interrupt.

"The men eye you with speculation. Can we do what we want to this American alone in our country, making herself a nuisance? They're not sure if we'll come to your aid. Americans sometimes put themselves in a fix we're unable to resolve."

"I'm not in a fix," Dara said.

"Well, Amelia certainly was," Suzanne said. "In the depths of her despair thinking of killing herself. But she's the mother of a two-year-old boy and her husband has abandoned them. Amelia's in quite a fix, isn't she?"

"She finally took off her *hajab*," Dara said, "brightened her hair to quite a blaze of red, remember? And managed to get on with her life."

"I thought it was more a shade of henna," Suzanne said. "Anyway," she said, "more to the point, I'd like to show you what we've been up to."

THEY SAT IN BROWN-LEATHER swivel chairs somewhat grouped around a coffee table where a laptop computer sat waiting. Suzanne turned it to face them and took the chair next to Dara's.

"So, for the past month you've been filming Somalis hijacking merchant ships. A departure from what you normally set out to document. More like the real thing?"

"They're all the real thing. *Katrina* was my one departure," Dara said, "from what I normally shoot. I seem to be attracted to men I feel acting against their nature, showing off, getting together as thugs in *Whites Only*, the one about white supremacists. Or Somali fishermen enjoying themselves as pirates, and making a lot of money. But now piracy is attracting commercial interest, Hollywood," Dara said. "Several movies about pirates are in preproduction right now. Or, if you're interested and can afford it, you can rent a yacht for five thousand a day, seven-fifty for each AK-47 you think you'll need, and ten bucks for a hundred rounds of ammo. You slip along the coast toward Mogadishu hoping to attract pirates. But once the shooting starts, they'll put an RPG through your hull and you're sunk."

"It's a Russian enterprise," Suzanne said, "operating right here in Djibouti. Entrepreneurs, you might call them, looking for a quick buck."

"RPGs will put the Russians out of business," Dara said, "and the Somalis, once they begin taking lives."

"You sympathize with them?" Suzanne said. "The poor Somalis trying to make a living?"

"I did," Dara said, "until I saw a skiff flying a 'Kill Americans' banner. Since then I've been losing interest in their cause."

"You like the idea of putting yourself in danger."

"I've never been shot at," Dara said. "I've been yelled at, cursed in different languages. *Jebo te Bog, govno jedno.*"

"What does that mean?"

"May God fuck you, you piece of shit."

"It sounds as though you have the accent down," Suzanne said. "Do you always learn the language?"

"Never more than a few words."

"I understand you met a number of pirates in Eyl. One of them threw a party for you?"

"They were celebrating something else."

"But socializing with them—it must take nerve."

"At the time we had nothing against each other," Dara said. "One of them bought his mates new wingtips at Tricker's in London, two hundred dollars a pair."

"Really."

"They're generous, and usually fun-loving."

"Until some cleric or Imam of the radical Shabaab," Suzanne said, "begins lopping off a hand and a foot of each pirate they seize. You know the Shabaab are Wahhabi Islamists, the same sect as al Qaeda."

"They'd be cutting off the hand that feeds them," Dara said. "The Shabaab are on the take." She said, "Are we getting close to it now?"

"We're closing in," Suzanne said. "I have photographs I'd like to show you. They were taken the morning after the party." She reached toward the computer but didn't touch it and sat back in brown leather again. "You say the party wasn't in your honor."

"It turned out they were celebrating the attack on the *Alabama*."

"Don't tell me you were with them, cheering."

"I was there."

"I know you met a few pirates in Eyl, fairly well known, moderately wealthy. One of them had the party at his home. I wouldn't be surprised to hear of some warlord swooping down to clean him out."

"Warlords are also on the take."

"You know who I'm referring to."

"Yes, I do," Dara said. She took out a cigarette and lighted it, Suzanne watching. It was the last cigarette in the pack. Suzanne didn't say a word. There was no ashtray on the coffee table. Su-

zanne made no effort to get one. There might not be an ashtray
in this entire building. Dara decided not to ask for one. She'd
smoke her cigarette and use the empty pack, once she got an
ash worth flicking into it. If this security person thinks you're
nervous, let her. She knows everything about you. Where you've
been, what you've been doing. Who you know . . . Dara thought,
If it doesn't matter, since she's way ahead of you, why do you
sound like you're trying to hide something?

She said, "Is your husband in the foreign service?"

Suzanne had the rings.

"He's down the road in Kenya, my counterpart."

"That's why they can't put you together?"

"As a matter of fact we've both been posted to Nigeria, on the
other side of Africa. We'll be together, not counting holidays, for
the first time in two years."

"Aren't you anxious?"

"Of course I am, I can't wait."

"But as long as you're here," Dara said, "you have to keep
your eye on the ball."

"Yes, I do," Suzanne said, smiling for a moment, giving Dara
a look that had nothing to do with African affairs, until she
said, "The morning after the party"—she pressed a key on the
computer—"these Toyotas left Eyl."

There they were on the screen, in a series of cut long shots,
now seen from several points of view, the Toyotas standing on
a road that would lead to the coast, Somalis with AKs waiting
to board. "There's your friend Idris Mohammed," Suzanne said,
"and his prisoners, two Qaeda operatives, secured, sacks over
their heads. They were placed in separate SUVs. Do you know
who they are?"

"We think one's American," Dara said, "Jama Raisuli. The
other one's Qasim al Salah."

"They've taken part in several bombings," Suzanne said, "but obviously not as martyrs. One in Riyadh killed or injured over a hundred and fifty, nine Americans murdered. They destroyed the compounds where employees live, the ones working for U.S. and British corporations. More recently Jama and Qasim were crew members on *Aphrodite,* an LNG tanker. That's liquefied natural gas, extremely combustible. Ignited, I'm told, it will melt steel within a thousand feet or so."

"And only five ports in the U.S.," Dara said, "equipped to offload the gas."

It got Suzanne's attention. "How do you know that?"

"Helene told me, Billy Wynn's girlfriend. Billy has photos of wanted al Qaedas and I picked out Jama and Qasim."

"Does Billy know Jama's real name?"

"If he doesn't I bet he could find out."

"Maybe. No one in the Middle East seems to know it. Run African Americans with Muslim names, you know how many hits you'd get?"

"Billy would make a phone call and have it," Dara said. "He has a list of people he pays. Helene says for anything you want to know. Most of them in the shipping business. When you look at my footage you'll see Jama and Qasim on the *Aphrodite,* the only ones in the crew who aren't Filipino. Billy said the two of them, turned in for the rewards, are worth over five million. Is that true?"

"One five million, the other possibly a million."

"Billy said the State Department would try to weasel out of paying."

"I know, he told me," Suzanne said, "but without using the term *weasel.* That must be your thought," Suzanne giving Dara something of a smile. "But let's put Billy aside for the time being, all right? I'd like to know who invited Jama and Qasim to the party."

Dara hesitated. She remembered asking Idris the same question and his answer, *"They're Harry's Saudis. He invited them."*

"Idris Mohammed," Suzanne said, "is what he is, a pirate. I met him once. I thought he was fun, in his own way. Did Idris invite them, or was it Ari Ahmed Sheikh Bakar? The one you won't admit you know."

Suzanne looked at the computer screen.

"Those are satellite shots from our Eye in the Sky. We have coverage of just about their entire trip to Djibouti. One SUV conked out, four made it. Idris and Harry, as he's called, brought along the Qaeda operatives who were on the LNG tanker. What I don't understand, why you won't admit you know Harry? You suspect him of illegal activities? Possibly selling arms to warlords?"

Dara said, "I'll tell you how I see it if you'll get me an ashtray."

Suzanne said, "Let me have it," and walked off taking a long drag before butting the cigarette in a planter. She returned and sat down and Dara said, "The way I see it, selling guns in the desert is another way of socializing, getting along with your neighbor, the warlord. It's probably been going on at least a thousand years. Now Ethiopians come over to raise hell and the Shabaabs go around picking fights. Billy calls them 'the lads.' Billy knows the names and numbers of all the players. I won't tell you what he calls our embassies."

"Bureaucracies," Suzanne said. "Billy e-mails us from time to time. You're right, he seems to have exceptional knowledge of what's going on. He's warned us about the LNG tanker. We already have it under investigation."

"It seems too obvious," Dara said. "Terrorists discovered aboard a highly combustible tanker? One of them a well-known pyromaniac with five million on his head? But if the ship's a decoy, what's Qasim doing on it?"

"What I'm enormously curious about," Suzanne said, "is who invited the al Qaedas to the party."

"Harry," Dara said.

"Why were you trying to protect him?"

"I'm like you," Dara said, getting a girl-to-girl feeling, "I'm not a hundred percent sure about Harry. But, if he's turning in al Qaedas he deserves the reward."

"But you don't trust him."

"I think he's more Brit than Saudi."

"His mother's English, isn't she?"

"I hope I'm entirely wrong about Harry, he's a good guy and really not that much of a snob, and I'll be sorry I told you." Dara said, "But if the ship's a decoy, because it's so fucking obvious and likely to be stopped, what happens to Qasim and Jama? I mean even if they hadn't been snatched by the Gold Dust Twins."

Suzanne gave her a look but didn't interrupt.

"They'd be arrested and go to prison. I've been thinking about it," Dara said. "Why would a terrorist like Qasim, one of their heroes, agree to a phony scheme and risk going to prison? He's one of bin Laden's stars."

Suzanne said, "They didn't tell him the ship was possibly a decoy."

"Yeah, but why not? If he knew, he wouldn't have joined the crew."

"Unless he's tired of it," Suzanne said.

"A guy like that, I think he'd kill himself before he'd risk getting locked up."

"I'm not sure of that," Suzanne said.

"I've talked to enough Arabs—it seems like half my life. They'll take the virgins before prison any day," Dara said. "You know where they are now, the caravan of Toyotas?"

Suzanne touched her computer to show more satellite shots of the SUVs on the road in their own dust, evening now.

"At sundown," Suzanne said, "they were less than a hundred miles from Djibouti. A few minutes later I'm told we lost them."

"Did you find any black Toyota SUVs in Djibouti?"

"You're joking, aren't you?" Suzanne said, going to her desk. She picked up a printout of a telephone recording. "They actually called. One of them did. He asked if Rewards for Justice was still offered and I told him it was." She looked at the printout. "The caller said, 'My dear, if I cannot trust you'"—Suzanne hinting at an African speaking English—"'we will take these Qaedas into the desert and bury them.' I said, 'Come in and show us who you have.' I told him we'd already paid out thirty million in rewards."

Dara said, "That isn't much if some guys are worth twenty-five."

"You'd think they'd be breaking down the door," Suzanne said. "Try to get them to come in and rat out someone they know. It's not easy."

Dara said, "They didn't come in, did they?"

"Or phone," Suzanne said. "We put in a request to National Police, see if they can locate them. They might or might not. You never know whose side they're on. We can't nose around ourselves, search apartments in someone else's country. We do have people keeping their eyes open."

"Billy's right, you have to go by the book," Dara said. "I'll find them."

CHAPTER EIGHTEEN

BEFORE HE WAS JAMA Raisuli or Jama al Amriki he was James Russell, pronounced Rus*sell:* picked up twice on suspicion of armed robbery and released; arrested in Miami Beach with controlled substances and sent to the Stockade to await a court date. James said to the lawyer appointed for him, "Do I look like a drug dealer to you? I'm a college student happen to have some blow on me I'm picked up, some weed for my depressed state of mind. I don't sell my medications."

The federal prosecutor asked James's lawyer, "What'd he have, a few ounces?"

The lawyer said, "A pound or so of weed. The boy has a smart mouth. I'll plead him on possession, you offer us three to five and we'll take it, skip the trial."

This was how James Russell came to Coleman FCI in the middle of inland Florida to hang with Muslims, a means of surviving in here, twenty years old doing his first fall. He told the Muslims he was a member of the Nation of Islam, having seen the movie *Malcolm X* and remembered how the brothers addressed one another. Have some serious Muslims around him and not get used by skinheads for their immoral purposes. Jamming a broom handle up his butt.

James caught the eye of a three-timer who talked up Allah in the Muslim part of the yard and went by the name Tariq, an African American Sunni Muslim. He said to James, "You in the Nation of what? Islam? Those people no more Islamic than the white fools call theirselves Shriners, wear a fez on their heads. The Nation say they black and play to it. All right, but me and you . . . are we black? We more a mellow shade of tan, like our Arab brothers the Wahhabi, spreading the word of Allah with explosive devices. You know how else we different? We don't have woolly heads. We have hair we can comb, let grow long if we want."

"I notice that," James said. "I'm looking at Islam as the way to go. But what do I get out of it?"

Tariq had to grin, showing what teeth he had. He loved this boy. He said, "You quiet, you show respect. What is it you hope to become in your life?"

"Famous," James said. "I been looking at ways."

"Become a prophet?"

"I don't tell what will happen, I do it."

"Dedicate yourself to *jihad*?"

"That's a way to go, yeah."

Tariq said, "Do you know what you talking about?"

"I have the gift to remember every word I read," James said. "Everything you people tell me."

"There is a verse," Tariq said, " 'Oh ye who believe, fear Allah and make your utterance straightforward.' "

James said, " 'He that obeys Allah and his messenger has already attained a great victory.' "

"It's 'attained *the* great victory.' But you close. You know the Koran?"

"I read it in the Stockade."

HE KNEW THEY WERE watching him: see if he was a punk or the kind wanted his own way. He was a restless age but seemed at peace with himself. The only time he was hostile, he'd stand away from them in the yard and stare at the skinheads, James with one hand holding his package, and motion to the skins to come over and try him.

He cleaned the kitchen with one of them found stabbed to death with his own knife that said FOR NIGGERS scratched into the wood hilt.

Tariq said, "Don't the guards know you did it?"

"Me?" James said. "I don't cause commotions, I read. It's skinheads always being thrown in the hole. Musta been another skin done it." He could go back and forth from intelligence to street.

A time came Tariq said, "You don't talk much or make noise. But I see you with the one doing time for molesting boys . . ."

James said, "Don't worry about it."

Tariq took his time. "Listen, I ask around of my brothers, if they think you could learn to speak Arabic. I don't mean 'Can you direct me please to the Mosque,' but as we speak and swear at one another. They say no, he can't do it. They say they would always hear your American sound. Your black American sound in our words. No, he can never speak as we do."

"How much you bet I can?"

"If I believe you can learn to speak our language in, what, six months?"

"Three," James said, "having the gift. I'll be speaking like a camel jockey in three months. You can lay three to one I'll do it and get the population betting against me. They'll hear me say Allah's making me do it and put me down as a fool."

Tariq said, "In only three months?"

"Three more. I been learning Arabian from Short Eyes since I started hanging with y'all. I know how to recite 'Your mother fucks pigs' and other kinds of Arabian sayings. Get that man reading to be a cleric everybody trusts to judge can I do it or not. But how you gonna collect from people making fourteen cents an hour, the ones working?"

"The women bring it in or they send money. Don't worry, we always get it." Tariq said, "But listen, when you become Muslim we'll give you a name that will please Allah."

James said, "I've already thought of one I like the sound of. Jama Raisuli."

Tariq looked at the name in his mind. "How did it come to you?"

"From Allah," James said.

It took almost a year to collect the entire twenty-three hundred he won speaking Arabian in the test, even the sayings and idioms.

HE WAS RELEASED FROM prison the day he completed three years less two months: released the same day, the same hour, the Twin Towers were destroyed, blown to rubble 9/11, and James said it again, "From Allah." This time believing it was the Lord's personal sign, a gift to him.

Allah told him to leave Florida and take a flight into Egypt using his new James Russell passport good for ten years. Three flights from Miami to Sharm el Sheikh on the tip of the Sinai Peninsula and hopped on a boat to take him down the Red Sea full of ships to Djibouti. Once he was getting the feel of the Arab world and speaking the language, he used letters of introduction from inmates to put him in touch with jihadists. Now he was going by Jama Raisuli and they began calling him Jama al Amriki.

In Djibouti he met another Amriki, Assam the American, charged back home with treason, a Jew converted to Islam who broadcast threats, promised attacks that would leave the streets of America running with blood. Assam wrote powerful shit about hating America, but speaking proper Arabic like he'd learned it in school. Jama spoke street Arab, was accepted as an African and believed he *was*. But couldn't see blowing himself up next to a school bus in Tel Aviv, his life precious to him. He didn't know what he'd say if they asked him to become a martyr. He kept busy translating Assam's speeches to Arabic, making them sound meaner.

He didn't see being a jihadist made him a traitor any more than selling blow or holding up a liquor store did. He let his hair grow to his shoulders, wrapped a scarf around it and wore a saronglike *kikoi* over his trousers, a Walther P38 in his back pocket. Jama had stopped in a shop that sold guns, kept the clerk busy looking for pistols he wanted to see, the clerk distracted as Jama slipped the Walther under his *kikoi* and left the shop.

On the street an Arab dressed as he was stopped him and said, "You need bullets, don't you?"

It was Qasim al Salah, an al Qaeda hero walking around in plain sight in this quarter. Assam, the other Amriki, had shown Jama pictures of him and spoke of Qasim as a saint: the man who perfected the use of vehicles as improvised explosive devices. In '83, still a lad, he helped plan the destruction of the Marine Barracks in Lebanon, a truck bomb carrying twelve thousand pounds of explosives; 246 killed. He planned and directed the bombing of the U.S. Consulate in Karachi; the bombing of the embassy in Mombasa, Kenya; the Air Force Barracks in Dhahran, Saudi Arabia. Now, Assam said, Qasim was planning a radioactive "dirty bomb" for a second attack on America.

Jama said to Qasim on the street, "You spoke and I felt Allah breathing on me. I know who you are and bow my head."

Qasim said, "And you are the American convict who wants to be one of us. I watched you go in a bank and look at it good and then steal a pistol."

"I'm known to rob banks," Jama said, "when I don't have nothing to do."

"Maybe you can be of use to me," Qasim said. "Come to Riyadh with us and we'll see."

THE NIGHT OF 13 MAY 2003, they rode through the city, nineteen men, three of their four vehicles packing explosives, to come up on the British and American compounds and open fire with AKs and rocket grenades. Approaching Riyadh Qasim had said to Jama, "You can drive a bomb car if you wish."

He spoke easily, a man who knew his business, seldom in a hurry, looking at the next step.

"I'm not worthy," Jama said, "to become a saint for Allah this soon, my first shot."

"You don't have the desire to be a martyr," Qasim said. "I don't either. So we see if you have a desire to kill for Allah."

They attacked guard posts on the perimeter of the compounds, a Ford Crown Victoria ramming the Cyclone gate until it became tangled in the wire and the driver detonated the thousand pounds of explosives in the trunk. A Dodge Ram armed with four thousand pounds of TNT crashed a second gate, raced to the employee housing area, two-story apartment buildings on a curved street, and blew itself up, taking off the façade, the entire look of the buildings, and setting the apartments on fire. A GMC Suburban followed by a Toyota sedan crashed a gate to drive into the center of another housing compound and the SUV exploded.

Qasim watched Saudi employees of American companies buried in the rubble, an evening tally of 34 dead and 194 injured: blinded, arms and legs blown off, listed as injuries. Osama bin Laden said if our people work for foreign companies they become our enemies. If they accept money paid them, they become evil. Qasim, older than bin Laden, believed the point could be argued but accepted bin Laden's view. It made him important.

He watched Jama during the assault. Jama firing his AK at people rushing out of burning buildings, emptying a clip and shoving in another. A man stood in an upper room without a wall, the man looking over the edge of his floor. Jama took him with one shot and watched him fall to the street. He turned to the building across the way and shot two more in their apartment without a wall. A woman and a man who fell to the street. He was deliberate about his killing, taking his time to be certain of his shots. He watched the entrance of the building now, waiting for someone to come out.

He loves it, Qasim thought.

A woman came rushing from the entrance and he shot her. A woman with smoke rising from her burka.

Later, Qasim asked Jama, "What was in your mind when you shot the woman?"

He said, "Which one?"

"In the burka."

"She was on fire."

Qasim heard it as compassion, but thought, Would he care if she burned to death? He didn't want him to care, but never asked if he did or not.

CHAPTER NINETEEN

JAMA WAS TWENTY-EIGHT NOW, his birthday coming on the day they left Eyl for Djibouti.

He rode in one of the five Toyotas rocking across the desert, catching the dust and gravel raised by the two in the lead. Qasim would be in the car directly ahead or behind them. Idris, next to Jama in the middle seats, told him, "We will be there in one period of twenty-four hours. Every two hours we stop to stretch our legs and piss. Twice a day we heat the spaghetti for you. Don't worry," Idris said in English, "these Somalis won't know what we're saying. Harry gave them an English test. He called them camel-fuckers and no one rose to cut his throat. He's with Qasim, but we change cars at times, so I talk to Qasim and Harry talks to you."

There were sixteen Somalis with AKs and their provisions in the five cars: a driver and the Somali in front with him pointing in the glare of distance to the road curving toward a pass through the slopes, telling the driver now to slow down, to watch for falling rocks, until Idris told him in Arabic to shut up. A third Somali sat behind Jama and stared at the back of his head while Jama looked out at the land where Arabs lived and went to sea as pirates.

He said to Idris, "You pretty good at hijacking ships, uh? Make enough to buy houses and expensive cars—why you need to turn me in?"

"So I can retire," Idris said. "Move to Paris. I said to Harry, 'Let's give the boys a tip, enough money to buy cigarettes for the rest of their lives.' Harry refuses to give you a quid."

"I quit smoking," Jama said, "during the time we getting payoffs from gangsters have mules smuggling cigarettes from North Africa to Europe, the Qaeda demanding a cut. We calling it the Marlboro Connection. I went up to Egypt and robbed banks for the cause, a few jewelry stores, and we into dealing hashish from Africa. Qasim says it cost ten million a year to keep the Qaeda running. Some of it Osama's laying down, the reason he hates everybody isn't with him. I saw him in Pakistan one time—not the easiest man to get next to. He kept watching me like he wasn't sure of my credentials. You ever hear bin Laden say anything funny? But I like working for Qasim, the man has his shit together. He's cool without knowing how to act it."

"Why is it," Idris said, "if you're devoted to al Qaeda, you don't blow yourself up for Allah?"

"Me and Qasim don't believe in it. We worth more to al Qaeda alive. There enough boys can't wait to go to Paradise."

Idris said, "Qasim won't talk to me."

"Why would he? 'Less he has a reason."

"Harry threatens to shoot him. He tells me when we stop to piss."

"Harry would give up five mil? Bullshit."

"He suggests we shoot both of you in the knees, so you can't run away."

"And have to carry us?"

"Get the Somalis to do it."

"Then he has to pay them extra. Threaten them to keep their mouth shut. All the shit that goes down," Jama said, "you work out when you're planning a jihad. It took three years to put 9/11 together. Any place you want to blow up can take a good year deciding how to do it. You pick a date, find out it falls during Ramadan 'cause you forgot? I can't ever look forward to the fasting. And the serious guys yell at me. I say if we doing it for Allah, what's the difference? They always yelling about something."

"You took part in the Riyadh bombings."

"My first jihad."

"You began working with Qasim, one of the big players, eh? How were you called at that time? Jama, or by your Christian name?"

"I'll tell you something," Jama said. "Only one man in this whole Arabian world knows my real name. He may even have forgot it by now."

"Qasim," Idris said.

"Ask him, see if he tells you."

"He's difficult to talk to."

"The man can be a wall."

"We could shoot him in the knees."

"See what it gets you," Jama said. "You're talking about a man sets off bombs like earthquakes. They become headlines in every paper in the world. He does it for Osama. They have a brother thing going. You can do anything you want to Qasim. Blind him, cut off his hands, like the Imams do you rob something? You never gonna get him to tell my name or anything about me."

"How can you be that sure?"

"I know him as I know myself."

"You kill for him?"

"We call it assassinations."

"Would you die for him?"

IDRIS AND HARRY WERE standing side by side pissing in the road, the sun going down, the guards eating oranges that came from Israel. Idris said, "I ask him if he'd die for Qasim. Do you know what he said?"

Harry turned his head to Idris. "Tell me."

"He said, 'Is the pope Catholic?' "

He saw Harry squinting. Or was he frowning? "It's a saying among that Christian sect," Idris said. "He's telling me yes, he would die for Qasim, not give it another thought."

"I know, but why bring up their pope?"

"Jama is known in the American language," Idris said, "as a smart-ass. Perhaps the Brits don't use the expression." He saw Harry still frowning or squinting and Idris said, "Why are you so serious about it? He was being funny."

Harry had taken a turn with Qasim during the morning drive, asking if he had ever been to America. Asking if he was looking forward to life in an American prison, or perhaps Guantánamo in Cuba. Asking if any of his mates were there, and getting no response.

"The trouble is," Harry said, "he's been questioned countless times, tortured, urged in various ways to speak. Qasim bends over, he has trouble straightening himself again. He wears kid gloves to cover his broken hands, hit with mallets. I can't get him to say one fucking word to me."

"Why do you bother?"

"I want to know how Jama's called in the U.S."

"He won't tell you." Idris was silent for a moment and said,

"If there was a way to bribe him, offer something he'd want desperately in exchange for the name . . ."

Harry said, "You might have something."

HARRY WAS WITH QASIM again later that evening, the Toyota rumbling, bumping along, night inside behind dark-tinted windows, Qasim close beside him. Harry turned his head to him and caught the odor of the Arab's breath, spaghetti and spiced camel, and said to him, "I understand you know Jama's American name."

Qasim stared at him.

Harry held his breath waiting, counting almost to ten.

Qasim said, "Yes . . . ?"

It felt good to be talking again.

"Can I ask, why you want to know?"

He won't tell you, Qasim thought. He has to set you up first. Finally get around to the reason he's talking to you. Then he'll tell you.

"Let me point out," Harry said and took a breath, "you haven't performed much in the past seven years. Let's see, an embassy—"

"Two embassies and a consulate."

"Most of the past decade, though, you've been a Qaeda fundraiser. The American Rewards people are going to say, 'That's all he's done lately?' I'll bet if they don't drop your reward they reduce it considerably." Harry lighted a cigarette.

Qasim took his time, staring in Harry's face before he said, "You have to give me up to find out what I'm worth. Take my word, the Americans can't wait to get hold of me, show me off to the world. They can make what I did two decades ago seem like yesterday."

"Yes, they will," Harry said, "display you to their hearts' content, congratulate themselves and throw you in prison."

Qasim said to this fellow Arab who wanted to be an Englishman, "For what exactly, acts of war or what you call terrorism?"

"For being *you,* you idiot. Do you know how many you've killed?"

"Tell me."

"And mutilated? Many of your own people, Saudis?"

"Some became blind," Qasim said.

"You sound like you don't believe you're going to prison."

"You have me, that's all."

"You'll be our gift to the Americans." Harry dropped the cigarette between his legs to the floor and placed his boot on it. "But your partner, Jama the Amriki? I'm betting the Americans will pay more than 'up to a million,' once they discover he's a traitor. What do you think?"

"Why do you say I'm going to prison," Qasim said, "and not be executed?"

"You'll get life for crimes against humanity," Harry said. "Federal courts in America rarely decide on the death penalty. You'll spend the rest of your years in a prison cell by yourself. One hour a day of recreation, rain or shine. They allow you to walk about in an enclosure about the size of a decent hotel room. Then back to the cell. You know what you'll look forward to each day? Eating the dog food they give you on a tin plate and evacuating your bowels in a bucket. Ahhhh," Harry said, "until one day you die of old age, finally a happy man."

"You say they won't pay anything for me," Qasim said. "Then why turn me in?"

"I like to think of you as a lifer."

Harry opened his window to inhale fresh air rushing past—a bit cool—and closed it again.

"Or," he said, "I decide not to hand you over."

Qasim waited. He said, "Why?"

"We know Jama's an American."

"Tell me how you know."

"You call him Amriki, don't you, for Christ sake? We both heard him speak English in Eyl the time I shot the first officer. Quit fucking with me, please. We both know he's American."

"All right," Qasim said. "Tell me what you want."

"His real name."

"Oh, is that all?"

"And we let you go," Harry said.

Qasim listened to the sound of the car following its head-lights on a road that came to no end.

"If I had a match," Qasim said. "I would strike it and look at your eyes."

Harry took his lighter from a shirt pocket and flicked it on. "You'd like to know," Harry said, "if you can trust me. Look in my eyes, you bugger, and tell me. Can you?"

What did they call this kind? So confident he believed you could see truth in his eyes. Or what would pass for it. Qasim saw nothing to encourage him. He said, "I walk away, you could track me in the desert and shoot me."

"It would be far better than prison, wouldn't it? I'm kidding with you," Harry said. "I give you my word as a gentleman, tell me his name and I'll set you free."

"You'll give up five million dollars?"

"To get at least ten," Harry said. "My offer for the name of a traitor they can look up in five minutes and know who he is, where he went to school or prison and got mixed up with Muslims. Without their knowing his name, he could speak Arabic to them, say he's a former shepherd boy from the Holy Land. Crewed on the LNG tanker to raise money for his family, they're lepers and can't find employment."

You want to listen to him talk? Qasim thought. What difference is it, they have Jama, you tell his name or not? He said, "All right. When we reach Djibouti you will release me?"

Harry waited a bit staring at the endless road in the headlights. He said, "That's fine with me. What's his name?"

"I told you," Qasim said, "when we reach Djibouti."

CHAPTER TWENTY

THE FIRST THING XAVIER did, he got to Djibouti, was rent a Toyota, a white one.

Dara was already back at the Kempinski, Dara in the same suite she had a month ago, with her clothes now, Xavier having cleaned out the *Buster* and had the boy bring up the bags and cases on his gold luggage cart. It was like the last time they'd seen each other was an hour ago, so used to being with each other. Xavier said, "I come off *Buster,* tied her up where we got her and was given back our security deposit, so we can give it to the Kempinski."

Dara, in her shorts and a bra, was lying across the settee with a flute of champagne and a cigarette, barefoot. She said, "We're taking a time-out," looking at her slim buddy Xavier across the room. "It's too bad you're an old man."

Xavier had to grin coming over to her.

"Girl, you either cheeky or horny talkin to me like that, wantin me to prove the state of my manhood. Find out can I give you pleasure at my age or not. Want to put up some money?"

"I was kidding," Dara said.

"Unh-unh, you feelin horny. You have time now to entertain the idea. On the *Buster* you horny once in a while but never remarked about it to me. I'll tell you what," Xavier said, "I'll put up all the back pay you owe me for two months, add to it expenses I've paid out of my pocket. It comes to ten thousand and somethin. You catch your breath and realize I won—sittin up now havin a cigarette—you owe me double, twenty thousand and somethin."

"I've never in my life," Dara said, "heard of a bet like that." She took a moment to say, "What happens when you lose?"

"I let you call it. You keep what you owe me and I go to sea for a year, or into my savings to make up the difference. But either way," Xavier said, "you know we gonna have more fun than a barrel of naked monkeys."

SHE BELIEVED HIM, SHE did, but told herself to say something funny. Not get serious.

She had a buzz, halfway down the bottle of champagne feeling good, but still had to ask herself, Are you nuts? The times he held her and she'd press against him were comforting, his arms around her, but not as lovers.

What would she say after?

You don't have to say anything, he'll say it. He'll be funny and you'll laugh.

Maybe sometime later on he'll want to do it again.

Yeah . . . ? He's seventy-two years old, how long can he keep doing it, if he ever starts? Being with him every day, it isn't like you don't know him. You even know his bathroom smell. How can you be any closer to someone?

◆ ◆ ◆

XAVIER SAID, "YOU A tired little girl, huh? Worn out from dealin with pirates. I tied up at the dock, there's the CIA man waitin for me, Patrick Mackenzie and two of his boys. Patrick tells me he's met you. They come aboard and take two hours searchin the boat. I ask him what he's lookin for, contraband? Illegal shit like drugs? What for? This ain't even your country. Patrick ask me was it hot enough for me. Been here three years, still talkin about the heat. I tell him, stay out of the kitchen. He frowns at me, don't get it. They only talk straight at the embassy. Patrick takes me to meet the head security person, Ms. Suzanne Schmidt. She look at my passport and ask have I ever been arrested. I told her no, not for anything since I was a boy wasn't piddlin. She serve me Turkish coffee without askin did I like it and we started smilin at one another as we talked. I asked her did she ever chew khat. Ms. Suzanne say no, she never tried it, and I said I'd get her some if she wanted. She said, 'Oh, you can get it here?' Sounding innocent. That's my next project."

From living on the *Buster* Dara could go to sleep holding a champagne glass in her hand and not spill any. Xavier eased it from her fingers and finished it. Next he picked Dara up in his arms and laid her in her bra and short pants on the king-size bed and watched her curl on her side and stick her cute butt at him.

Xavier looked at her thinking he'd been like the houseman with this woman long enough. *Miss Dara, you like a cup of hot tea? I be happy to fetch you one.*

It wasn't ever like that, Xavier serving the lady of the house, but it was a way he thought of it now and then. He'd see her spread the hammock on the deck and lie down on her stomach and unhook her bra to get her back tan. One time he said to her, "You leavin your ninnies pure white, huh?" She didn't say a word but it was like she took it as a dare, rolling over to show her girlish breasts to the African sun. He said, "Careful you don't burn your buns." Not a word from her, eyes closed behind her sunglasses, ignoring him while he stared at her. One of Dara's horny times aboard. He threw out a line and fished for supper. Like the houseman who's seen all kinds of behavior and minds his business.

He said to himself, You not thinkin about gettin married and raisin a family, you thinkin about gettin laid. She wants to do it . . . Wants to try it, see if it works out . . . Like once in a while. It couldn't be often anyway, the tank gettin low. He believed he was cool. Don't say nothin, go at it, man. But looking at her on the bed he thought, No, you want to be tender, she's a tender girl you're holdin. Don't say nothin, just be cool with the slow moves. See if you can get Miss Dara to scream and bang her blond head against the headboard. That's all.

After a while the phone rang.

Xavier took it in the sitting room, picked up and said, "Dara Barr's suite," and heard Idris Mohammed's voice.

Idris saying, "That fucking Harry—I think he's become crazy."

XAVIER HAD STUDIED THE Gold Dust Twins, saw Idris as a gentleman, though a wild one, he *was* a pirate. He had to be crazy to board ships, do all that pirate shit. Harry was something else. Idris couldn't put his finger on it but saw him as a man not to trust, even though there wasn't anything not to trust about him, not even his trying to sound like a Brit. Took after his mom. What's wrong with that? What Xavier wanted to do was go home and let the Arabs do their Arab shit and not worry about it. They were all crazy.

Xavier let her sleep for an hour and got a Coke ready for when she opened her eyes and saw him. It wasn't a bad look, but it wasn't horny either.

"Idris called."

Dara said, "Wait," went to the bathroom first, then the sitting room for her cigarettes and dropped on the settee.

"Idris called . . ."

Dara showing her cool now.

"They not gettin along. Idris say Harry's tryin to fuck up the deal. He wants to find out without comin out and askin if the reward's for dead or alive."

"Alive," Dara said. "The feds want to parade them around first. They've got a major terrorist they can use, get him to tell on some of the other al Qaedas."

"If they can't deliver them dead," Xavier said, "Harry wants to give them Jama under his real name and negotiate up his price. Harry believes he's worth at least ten million bein an active traitor and a black man. Thinkin the things they can do with that combination."

Dara lighted a cigarette.

"Where did he get Jama's real name?"

"Qasim's the only one knows it," Xavier said, "but Idris don't think he's told Harry yet. Like Qasim wants to make sure he's out of there before he tells."

"Where are they?"

"Right now they hidin out in the African quarter."

Dara smoked her cigarette.

"Harry's too glib for me. I ask him a question, he always has an answer I'm not expecting."

"All Idris wants you to do," Xavier said, "see if you can settle

Harry down. Idris says he'll take whatever reward they offer and leave town. Harry wants to shoot the moon, see if he can score big off Jama."

"They know what's going on," Dara said, "the embassy people, they've been following this since the Toyotas left Eyl. Remember we tried to find out who was taking pictures?"

"I thought we might've been hasty," Xavier said, "but it didn't matter to us that much. You want to talk to Harry? Or let them fuck up their deal without your help."

"What do you think?"

"It ain't up to me. I'll tell you, though, that boy Jama, I keep thinkin of him. I wouldn't mind chattin with a real terrorist from back home."

"How do we find them?" Dara said.

"Idris give me directions. He's gonna be waitin for us."

CHAPTER TWENTY-ONE

THEY WERE IN XAVIER'S Toyota, feeling their way south through the African quarter.

"Idris say to go down past the circle by Avenue Thirteen and it becomes rue des Issas. We keep straight ahead . . . all right, we on rue des Issas now and we keep goin till we come to Avenue Twenty-six." Now they were looking into the narrow side streets they crept past, sightseers taking in the native quarter: streets full of junk and rubble, chunks of cement worn from walls to lie where they fell. Laundry hung from clotheslines above the decay.

"It's a slum," Dara said. "Maybe the worst slum in the civilized world."

"How you know it is?"

"How could you make it slummier?"

"Some in India bug your eyes out. But their slums don't seem as busted up and put back together, old boards and strips of corrugation from someplace else. There's what looks like a mosque I've seen in this quarter, made of old strips of tin they painted blue. They pray five times a day and make four hundred fifty dollars a year. How come Allah don't listen and give 'em a raise?"

"Or a kick in the ass. Why do they live here, with the rats and the roaches?"

"It's they-all's home."

"They could leave."

"Go where?"

"Those two guys under their umbrellas," Dara said, "what are they talking about?"

"What khat's selling for today."

"I could do an entire documentary," Dara said, "on the African quarter. You know it? Shoot the European section for contrast, an area somewhat less depressing."

"Show the Foreign Legion in their short pants."

"The Eritrean girls," Dara said, "dainty hookers making a few bucks a day."

"If that," Xavier said. "Cover the nightlife you want some contrast."

"I'd have to do another project first," Dara said, "like Eskimos."

"Take your time. Djibouti's always gonna be here."

Xavier said, "We turn left on Avenue Twenty-six, go down a few blocks . . . Look for a place to get a beverage has Arab writing all over it, the front open . . . Hey, and there's Idris raisin a glass to us."

"He doesn't look worried," Dara said.

"No, 'cause he has *you* now."

IDRIS HAD TO HUG Dara and tell her she was a lifesaver for coming. "But we don't want to stand here talking, police driving by. Harry spoke to the chief of police and promised him a reward from the reward we get and the chief said okay, they let us finish our business. We didn't tell the police where we're hiding the two Qaedas, I don't want them following us." Idris said, "What I want to ask you first, do you know Jama Raisuli's real name and where he's from in America?"

Xavier thought she might tell him "Scan Connery" the way she gave him a glance. But then shook her head and asked Idris, "Why?"

"Let's go away from here," Idris said, "and I'll tell you."

Xavier followed Dara and Idris, sometimes single file, into the heart of the African quarter, winding through streets of litter and crumbling walls. No different than it was thirty years ago once Djibouti gained its independence. Who needs fresh cement on the walls when you got fresh khat to graze on? They sat talking to each other with jabs of words. Man sitting under an awning made from his wife's old *hajab*. The man said to them in half-assed English, "What you doing here?" Got no answer but didn't give a shit. They turned a corner and were in front of a home from colonial times, its stucco peeling, a house of rooms with high ceilings, three floors of them, tall shutters hanging on the windows, rickety shutters once a shade of blue.

"Here," Idris said, getting out his keys to unlock the door.

Light filtered through the shutters. Two Somalis sat with their tea and AKs on a formal dining table repainted green. Idris took them past the Somalis and up an aged staircase from another time, telling them, "We kept the Qaedas tied up in separate rooms. They behaved so we let them share a room during the day, so they can talk, think of a way of escaping. I ask them, 'What do you want to be handcuffed to, a chair or the cot?' We let them talk and smoke. I gave them a glass of wine and Harry had a fit. Not the kind you imagine but a Harry fit. He becomes cold and talks to me in a superior way, as though I'm only an assistant. I would never work for him."

Idris reached the top of the stairs where a Somali stood with his AK. Idris turned to Dara and Xavier a few steps below saying, "Harry wants to sell Jama for nothing less than twenty-five million."

Dara said, "Harry's a gambler?"

"I don't know him well enough. We play cards, he doesn't care if he loses. Harry dreams of being known by important people in the world."

"Stuck in Djibouti," Dara said.

"Harry will tell them we want twenty-five million for Jama—why not—and include Qasim, a notorious al Qaeda, throw him in as part of the deal. Harry says he'll wait until they stop laughing in their cultured way and tell them, 'Once you pay the reward, we will give you Jama Raisuli's real name, an American-born black now a traitor.'"

"He has a passport?" Dara said.

"I believe still on *Aphrodite*."

"You're sure Jama doesn't have it?"

"Harry searched him. We tell the Rewards people they can have the terrorists, reveal to the world how they have cracked open al Qaeda. Harry has it all in his head, what they say and what he says in return."

"I can hear him," Dara said. "But does he have Jama's real name?"

"Qasim," Idris said, "is the only one knows what it is, but won't tell Harry until he's sure he can walk away from here. Qasim has been causing terror I believe most of his life."

"What's the problem?" Dara said.

"Harry wants to get the name from Qasim and still turn him in, with Jama. But Qasim wants to be sure he's free and then telephone Harry and give him the name. He swears by Allah any promise he has made in his life he has kept. Harry's trying to think of a way he can work it."

"Follow him," Dara said. "He makes the phone call, bring him back."

"Harry's thinking of something like that. But who brings Qasim back? Harry doesn't trust the Somalis."

Dara said, "Is he here?"

Idris motioned them up the few steps to the second floor saying, "He went out for a stroll, Harry says so he can think with a clear head, without all these Somalis about."

"Do you trust him?" Dara said.

"Of course not. But what can he do? He has to get Jama's name before he can go to the embassy and work his scheme."

Dara said, "And you want me to talk him out of it."

She glanced down the hall, the light dim, but recognized Jama coming along handcuffed, a Somali, apparently unarmed, close behind him. The Somali unlocked the first door they came to—three on each side of the hallway—pushed Jama inside and stepped in the room with him.

"You see him?" Idris said. "That was Jama."

"I've talked to him before," Dara said. "Why don't I look in and say hi?"

Idris said, "You want to go in their room?"

"With Xavier," Dara said.

THE SOMALI'S NAME WAS Datuk Hossa.

Jama sat in a chair made of stout wood with arms and a padded seat of cracked leather. He let Datuk cuff his right hand to the edge of the springs beneath the pad. He said, "Datuk, I am in your debt."

The Somali looked in his face for a moment before turning to Qasim on the cot, his shoulders sagging, his feet on the floor, his right hand cuffed to springs beneath the thin mattress. The

Somali was at the door now, leaving. He looked back as Jama said, "Allah will bless you."

Jama watched him go out and waited until he heard the key turn in the lock.

"He'll do it for six hundred dollars."

"Out of fear," Qasim said.

"Scared to death of al Qaeda," Jama said. "I told him it's good to look scared. I'm holding a piece at your head as we walk out."

"How do you have a gun?"

"Datuk has a semiautomatic holds eight loads. I told him that would be lovely, part of the show. Else why would they let us out? The other boys act suspicious, I told him give 'em each a C-note, you still get six hundred. They're in it with you then, you and your associates."

Qasim said, "But we don't have money to give them. He wants to see it, doesn't he?"

"I told him it's hidden. If I show it too soon, I'm afraid one of the others might grab it and cut him out. Or you get in a fight over it and somebody gets shot. I said Allah told me not to show the money until we're free."

Qasim said, "You trust Datuk?"

Jama said, "He's the one can open doors."

In the same moment he straightened and looked toward the door, the sound of a key turning in the lock.

THEY CAME IN THE room, Xavier's gaze holding on Jama, Dara asking the terrorists how they were doing. She said to Jama, "I hear your price has been raised to twenty-five million. Did you know that?"

Xavier watched him with his beard and long hair, no kinks in it, sitting there like he was making up his mind.

He said to Dara, "You think I'm worth it?"

Dara said, "Ari the Sheikh does."

Xavier said, "I can't see this street kid goin for as much as the higher-ups. Somebody's made a name for himself like Ayman al Zawahiri."

"You're right," Dara said. "Mullah Omar's big, but he's only worth ten million. And I believe Baitullah Mehsud."

"Baitullah's gone to heaven," Xavier said, "taken out by Hell-fire missile in Pakistan. Had CIA's name on it."

"What about the guy," Dara said, "who planned the suicide run on the USS *Cole*? I can't think of his name."

"If I may," Jama said, "Fahd Mohammed Ahmed al Quso, but he's worth only five mil."

"Thank you," Dara said and looked at Xavier. "I guess bin Laden and Zawahiri are the only ones going for twenty-five."

"Unless this boy qualifies," Xavier said.

Dara thought about it. "What's he done?"

Xavier shook his head. "Nothin I know of."

"Harry's a sly one," Dara said. "He must have a scheme to up this guy's price. Get as much as he can and move to London."

Jama said, "That's where he's going? You're right, I detect a love of Blighty in the man's speech. What about the other one, Idris? Where's he going with his dough?"

"He's leaning toward Paris," Dara said.

Jama, nodding his head, said, "They happen to be gone when I leave here, I'll know where to find them."

◆ ◆ ◆

A FEW MINUTES LATER in the hall Dara said, "He was telling us he plans to escape. Confident about it. Isn't that what he was saying?"

"I thought you'd ask how he thinks he's gonna do it," Xavier said. "All you told him was 'Yeah, right.'"

"He'll never find those guys," Dara said.

"Yeah, but he's thinkin about it."

CHAPTER TWENTY-TWO

ONCE THE WOMAN AND her servant were out of the room Qasim said, "You tell them you're going to escape?"

"Both of us," Jama said. "What can she and her nigga do about it, tell Idris? He knows it's all we think about. It's what we do we're locked up. You been in the slam. You forget what it's like? How bad you want to get out?"

"I can't think of doing life," Qasim said.

"We get out you can do what you want. You tired of this shit, make a run with a suicide bomb."

What Jama was tired of was Qasim.

"Coming here from Eyl," Qasim said, "I was thinking of a way to kill myself so I don't go to prison. Idris Mohammed would speak to me, I don't say a word to him. The other one, the sheikh they call Harry, he's with me in the car at night. He says he will allow me to escape if I tell him your Christian name. I ask him how I would escape. He says we think of a way and he watches me walk off."

Jama said, "You told him my name?"

"I thought at first you and I are going to prison for life. What difference is it they know you are Jimmy Russell?"

"Rus*sell*," Jama said, looking down at Qasim on the cot. "You remember it all these years? I said my name only once that time, seven years ago, and never said it again I'm over here."

Jama paused to think for a moment and grinned. "I did mention it to a chick at the Café Las Vegas, right here in Djibouti, but she don't speak any English. I give her euros and cigarettes for the best two days of fucking I ever had in my life. A Ethiopian chick name Celeste Tamene. Twenty years old, man, she was a panther. So I commit her name to my memory."

"I like an Ethiopian girl," Qasim said, "now and then."

"All those years you remember Jimmy Rus*sell*, uh? Only I was never Jimmy, I was James. Which name did you tell him?"

"Listen to me," Qasim said, worming his body around on the cot to look up at Jama in the stout chair. "I did not tell Harry your name. As Allah hears me, I will take it to my grave."

"I believe it," Jama said. "You have never said my name to anyone, James or Jimmy. Is that right?"

"You tell me your secrets," Qasim said, "I keep them here, in my head."

"What secrets you talking about?"

"Things you have told me of your life, your time in prison. Things we do when we are together and can be ourselves."

Jama said, "You never talk about any of that, do you?"

"Of course not, it's a private part of us."

A private part of all these guys who don't treat their women like women, but hide them.

Jama thinking again of the girl at the Las Vegas:

How she liked to fool around with him while she was dancing. Get behind one of the cement pillars on the dance floor and come out shaking her ass at him. Come over close to him and wink and flutter her tongue. Man. He'd get a good whiff of her perfume and want to jump her. It was a while ago, but he remembered her name, 'cause in the Toyota coming here, Idris Mohammed talking—Idris telling him things he'd never have again in prison for life—Idris said her name and he remembered it, Celeste, and his time with her, while Idris was telling him about this girl he saw every month.

"For how long?"

"A night or a few days. I relax with Celeste and tell her about hijacking ships. She loves to listen to me. I have a doctor inspect her before I arrive. I don't want any of that HIV/AIDS contaminating me. Celeste is always clean, twenty years old, a flower waiting for a good plucking. I pay her enough she doesn't have to sell her body. But she loves to dance at the club with her friends, the Las Vegas."

In the Toyota on the way to Djibouti, Jama said to Idris, "She loves to fuck too. Celeste Tamene? Lives on rue de Bir Hakeim?" You bet it was the same one. In that moment Idris was stopped dead, he couldn't speak, and Jama said, "Yeah, I had her. I thought she wasn't bad."

QASIM WAS LOOKING AT the light coming through the shutters.

"Time to put on my shoes. He'll be here soon. Datuk?"

Jama said, "What's the other one's name up here?" He waited and said, "Ibrahim. You remember it?"

"It's of no interest to me," Qasim said, bent over now to tie his shoes. "You have yours on?"

"Always," Jama said. "You never noticed?"

"You're telling me you never take off your shoes?"

"Only when I sleep. It's where I keep my passport."

Qasim straightened, sitting up.

"They don't look in your shoes?"

"You don't see anything. The passport's between the inside of the shoe and the sole, always there all the time. You know why?" Jama said, "Give me scissors and a straight razor," touching his beard. "I can clear off the foliage and be the cool-looking kid in the passport again."

"They have your fingerprints?"

"Where? You mean in America? Who knows I was ever in prison? Over here I got a Djibouti passport, I'm Jama the khat-seller. I have my real self put away for when it's time to leave."

"You tell me more about who you are," Qasim said, "than I ever knew before, in years together."

"You know my name," Jama said, "you know everything about me."

"Maybe, maybe not," Qasim said, "but it's time."

"For what?"

"To give you a phone number. You will remember it?"

"Is Allah God?"

"The number is 44-208-748-1599."

"Whose number is it?"

"The explosives aboard *Aphrodite*."

DATUK CAME IN WITH their supper, a tin bowl in each hand, and passed behind Jama's chair to place them on a card table. He brought two spoons and a saltshaker from under the shirt hanging to his knees.

"Nothing else?" Jama said.

Datuk said, "Wait," and walked out of the room. In a few

minutes he was back with coffee in tin cups and placed them on the table. Now he brought a Walther from under his shirt, smoothed the shirt over his hips and placed the gun on the table.

"You pay me now?"

"As soon as we leave," Jama said, "all right? I have the money in my shoe."

Datuk unlocked him and went to Qasim as Jama picked up the Walther and said, "This is my gun," surprised, "I can tell by the scratches on it." He released the magazine, saw it was loaded and shoved it back in the grip. He couldn't believe it, the same gun he'd lifted from the shop in 2003. Man, his own gun given back to him.

"We should eat this before we leave," Qasim said in English. "We don't know when we will have food again."

Cold spaghetti in tomato juice; no camel this evening.

Jama said, "Are you fucking serious?" He paused, looking at Qasim's eyes, and saw a faint glimpse of hope in his stare. It wasn't food he wanted but time, some more of it.

How did he know it was coming to an end?

He said to Qasim, "Eat if you want," and told Datuk to call Ibrahim.

THEY WENT DOWN THE stairway, Datuk first, Jama with a hand on his shoulder, the other hand pressing the Walther into his back. Ibrahim had banged through the door to the room. Qasim has his AK now, the four of them going down the stairs.

The sitting room was empty, and the dining room with its formal table painted green. Jama motioned Datuk down the hall to the open doorway into the kitchen. Past Datuk's shoulder Jama saw the two downstairs guards at the kitchen table eating what looked like lamb with peppers and beans. He caught the scent of their meal and swallowed. He pushed Datuk into the kitchen and saw the guard sitting at the end of the table look up. Now the other one was looking this way. They could see who had the guns.

Jama said to them, "Where is my friend Idris?"

The one at the end of the table said, "They left, both of them. But they coming back very soon. They should walk in at any moment."

"It's time for tea," Qasim said. "They will be gone two hours or more."

Jama looked at him.

"It's who they are," Qasim said, "being gentlemen."

The man sounding like himself again, knowing what was going on: at Riyadh telling him about Americans running the Saudi companies, telling him to find them and shoot them. Qasim cool in those days.

The one at the end pushed up from the table and spread out his arms. He said in Arabic, "I am not armed, our weapons are over there. You want to escape? Please, go ahead."

The kitchen table was no more than twenty feet from Jama. He moved to Datuk's side raising the Walther and shot the one standing at the end of the table. Jama put the Walther on the other one, still seated, staring at him, and told himself no, turned the Walther on Datuk raising his arm in defense and shot him through the heart. Now the one at the table—but Ibrahim was taking the AK from Qasim, twisting it from his hands, and Jama shot him in the face, turned to the guard who was finally up from the table and shot him as he started to run. He turned to Qasim now holding the AK. Qasim watching him. He said, "You don't have to do it."

Jama said, "You know my name."

"I have always known it."

"But it's different now." Jama wasn't sure what the difference was but could feel it looking at Qasim. He raised the Walther. Qasim turned his head and Jama shot him where you would shoot yourself if you saw it was that time, in the temple.

He still had three rounds. Two for Harry and Idris.

CHAPTER TWENTY-THREE

HARRY HAD FINISHED SEVERAL gins by the time Idris caught up with him in an African market that stocked canned goods and olive oil and—what do you know—khat, left over from yesterday. Harry sipping and chewing in a pleasant frame of mind, said the khat had lost much of its potency, somewhat dry but it still wasn't bad.

"Have a chew."

Idris said, "There is no sense in arguing with you, is there?"

"None," Harry said. "What's bothering you?"

"You leave people worth millions of dollars in the care of boys."

"No," Harry said, "you did. They were securely handcuffed when I left. Were they still handcuffed when you left? Were they eating their spaghetti like good boys? Tell me," Harry said, "what would you do if they tried to escape while you were in the house?"

"How could they?"

"But say they did."

"If I had to, I'd shoot them," Idris said. "You would too, you'd have no choice."

"Very possibly," Harry said, "and it would break my heart."

Idris said, "Giving up all that money."

He had a gin and in a while they became tired of talking, wondering, Harry feeling like himself again, somewhat buzzed— the first time since leaving Eyl. He was thinking he might be a bit stoned and high at the same time. No, the confident feeling would be the work of the gin. The khat made you think of pleasant moments you might experience, but never urged you to make them happen.

They walked back to the fading town house on the African street and stood a moment before Idris said, "Oh, I have a key. I forgot." He looked at his ring of keys, reached in his pocket and brought out the door key.

Harry said, "Are you going to stare at the fucking key? You had only one drink."

"Two," Idris said. "But I haven't eaten today." Idris slipped the key into the keyhole and said, "It's not locked," and turned the knob and pushed the door open.

Harry brushed past him, the PPK in his hand, the one he had used on the first officer in Idris's garage, Idris remembering how surprised he was when Harry shot the young man, but not surprised now by his behavior. He followed Harry to the staircase expecting him to call out, see who was here.

"Datuk, where the devil are you?" Not loud. Harry still with some control. He looked up the staircase now to tell Datuk, "You left the fucking door open. Is everything," Harry said, "as it should be?"

Idris motioned to him and Harry followed along the hall to the kitchen. Idris stopped in the doorway. Harry looked in past him to see Qasim—with absolute certainty their five-million-dollar reward—lying dead on the floor, the four Somalis lying about, and their twenty-five-million-dollar chance of a lifetime nowhere, gone.

"I'm not going to scold you," Harry said to Idris, "for leaving the house."

"You left too," Idris said.

"Yes, but the main thing is Jama's loose. It's no one's fault but the Somalis, the buggers were just not up to it." Harry said, "I suppose I could call the embassy, see if they'll take Qasim as is. They could stuff him, glue his eyes open and photograph him."

Idris said, "You want to carry him down the street?"

"We'll call the embassy, have him picked up. That fucking Qasim . . . At least, thank Allah, we still have Jama."

"Where?" Idris said, "I don't see him."

"You don't suppose," Harry said, "he's still here. Let's take a look," and started up the stairway with his pistol.

Idris called, *"Harry,"* loud enough to stop him. "What are you doing? The man killed five people. He's gone."

Harry turned on the stairs. "Yes, you're right."

Idris could see he was still buzzed, not sure of what he was doing. "There are al Qaeda around here," Idris said, "who can help him."

Harry came down one step at a time saying, "Have you ever looked at Qasim and wondered if he's homosexual?"

Yes, Harry was still buzzed.

"It's always a woman," Idris said, "tells me some man is gay. But Qasim is al Qaeda."

"They're fellows with fellows," Harry said, "nearly all the time, aren't they? The only girls they see are whores."

"Some quite lovely," Idris said. "But why would you think this one is gay?"

"Certain mannerisms, the way he touches his hair. The way he looks at other men. Coming from Eyl," Harry said, "talking to him in the car, I would feel his breath on me in the dark. This was the time he consented to tell me Jama's real name. I could feel he wanted to."

"But he didn't. Listen to me," Idris said, "we should leave here, get off the street, people watching us, and go to my apartment. We can rest, decide what to do."

"About what?" Harry said.

Idris told him not to think anymore.

THIS TIME—IT WAS THE next afternoon—they turned the corner in the African section and found themselves behind a crowd of people watching police coming out of the house with body bags, two policemen to a sagging bag, one at each end. Police cars, a medical truck, the National Police on the scene. Five bags came out of the house.

Xavier counted four guards, two Qaedas and the Twins, eight in the house. If Harry still hadn't returned, that would be seven. Xavier didn't want Idris to be in one of the bags, so he believed Idris had left. Four guards and one Qaeda. Which one in the bag?

Qasim.

Because Xavier saw Jama thinking up this breakout. He wouldn't be shot escaping, he was the man in this deal, working it. Xavier imagined somebody much later on shooting him. It would be unexpected, Jama with a look of surprise on his face.

Dara was talking to a police officer, the two of them speaking French, both laughing now at something she said. Dara put her hand on his arm, thanking him, and came through the crowd to Xavier, the people in the street turning to look at her.

"Five bodies, but not the Twins. That leaves the four Somali guards and one other. Who is it?"

"Qasim."

"I was pretty sure too," Dara said. "The cops know who he is. Shot through the head, four of them, one through the heart. One shot each. The cops think with a pistol. At suppertime. The guard brings in the spaghetti and is overpowered."

"He was paid off," Xavier said. "Where's Jama get a gun? You notice his behavior, we talkin to him?"

"Cool," Dara said. "Confident."

"Made sure we understood he wouldn't be hangin around. Statin it as a fact. I wondered, why's he doin that, the man tippin us off."

"Showing off," Dara said.

"That's all right, he told us he's walkin out and he did. You notice anything else? I believe he's been livin as a homosexual at this time. Years of runnin with the Qaeda boys. Close to Qasim while they're blowin up things. Workin right under him till they alone. Then Jama's on top."

"I don't know," Dara said. "I bet I can get him to come on to me."

"Listen to you. He gets lucky, remembers girls and goes straight?"

"Why do you think he's gay?"

"Just somethin about him."

"He's not at all effeminate."

"No, a man comes out actin girlish over here he can get stoned. I mean get rocks thrown at him. But you've seen Arabs walkin along holdin hands, haven't you? They in a man's world, the women at home lookin out the window. It's like in prison," Xavier said, "you don't have to be in love to get a blow job."

Dara watched a medical truck back up to where the body bags were laid out.

"Why did he shoot everybody?"

"They know him. Can point him out."

"The cop didn't ask if I knew any of them."

"You tell him you know the man that got away?"

"Every word—one of Judy Garland's biggest hits."

"You tell him you know the guy they want or not?" She hesitated and Xavier said, "You messin with police business now."

"Maybe somebody else shot them."

"If I know," Xavier said, "you know. Jama shot his Qaeda boss and four Somalis, the boys just makin a buck. You want to see if you can turn him up. Hopin it keeps goin. It does, you got material for a feature. I told you that before."

"I see myself sitting in a studio exec's office," Dara said. "He's got my screenplay in front of him. Or it might be a treatment."

"What are you callin it?"

"*Djibouti*. They'll want to change it to something else, tell you foreign words don't sell as features."

"Like *Casablanca*," Xavier said. "They don't like *Djibouti*, go indie. Get financin from some rich guy loves you or the story. Billy Wynn. He's on his two-million-dollar boat thinkin of this same movie as we speak. Starrin himself."

"Helene said he's finally in love with her—killing herself acting like a little sailor. I hope she gets him."

"The man loves movies. Take his money and make him the producer."

"You know what I keep thinking," Dara said. "I write a screenplay and show it to a studio exec and he says, 'I had a great time reading this one. It's a howl. It's out there and has legs. But where are the backstories to show motivations?' He'll say something like 'It lacks verisimilitude.'"

"Tell him you don't know what that means and walk out. Get independent financin and a girl like Naomi Watts to play the documentary filmmaker turnin to features."

"You think I look like her?"

"Naomi can look like you. Naomi never overplays her parts. You see her in *Happy Time*? She makes you keep watchin her."

"She's in her underwear half the picture."

"Naomi could dress like a nun, you still be watchin her." Xavier said, "In that picture, the boy that made her take off her clothes? He's homasexual. Else he'd of jumped her. Can you see another star playin that role? One that liked bein in her underwear? She'd make 'em change the ending. Not Naomi," Xavier said. "Put her name above the title, *Djibouti*. You know what it means, Djibouti?"

"I have no idea."

"It means 'my casserole.' No one knows why. Comes from the Afar language. I read someplace Djibouti is 'splendidly seedy . . . Gallic elegance turned shabby.' Look at this building, you see it."

He watched Dara staring at the house where five men were found shot to death, one bullet each. Xavier said, "You want to find the boy playin he's more African than American, huh? Wouldn't mind runnin into him."

"I'll bet we could," Dara said.

"Labor Day one time," Xavier said, "I was in Atlantic City and called a girl I know lived there with her sister. The sister tells me, oh, she's gone to play the slot machines. I stepped out on the Boardwalk and five minutes later who do I see coming toward me in the Labor Day crowd of people? LaDonna. The girl lit up, she's so glad to see me back from seafarin. She'd just won seventeen hundred dollars playin a quarter machine and we celebrated it together. LaDonna always liked me."

"Don't tell me," Dara said, "you expected to run into her."

"I didn't expect not to," Xavier said. "I always keep it open. It happens, it happens. When it don't, what are you out? It's best never be anxious."

Dara took his arm and they walked away from the house.

She said, "All right, I'll leave it up to you. We keep at it or quit and go home."

"Just a minute ago you talkin about makin a feature with Naomi Watts. All we need to know is what happens next. Now you just as soon go home?"

Dara said, "I think we'd have a better chance of finding the Gold Dust Twins than Jama. Now he's free he's gonna hide out or change his looks."

"They still hijackin ships," Xavier said. "The world navies not shuttin 'em down any."

They came to the white rental car. He opened the door for her, walked around and got in.

"The latest hijack," Xavier said, "they want a million for a Finnish ship, the *Arctic Sea,* with fifteen Russian crewmen on board. Flies a Maltese flag. They think it might have a 'secret cargo' they callin it. They tested it in Finland for nuclear shit aboard and musta scored positive. But now the ship's gone and disappeared."

Dara said, "Where was it last seen?"

"In the English Channel, two weeks ago."

"It's not around here?" Dara surprised.

"In the channel on its way to Algeria, but never arrived. You want to know more," Xavier said, "you have to call Billy. I bet he can tell where the ship's at."

Dara said, "I keep thinking about Jama. He could still be around here."

"But the Twins'll be easier to locate," Xavier said. "Give Idris a call. Find out what they're up to. Talk to Harry. Ask him how come he blew his big chance."

"If he wasn't at the house," Dara said, "he'll blame Idris."

"You think they know what they doin?"

"I think they have no idea," Dara said.

CHAPTER TWENTY-FOUR

THEY MET AT THE Club ZuZu and before long the young gentleman named Hunter was telling Jama where he lived.

"In a residential hotel on rue de Marseille. Sort of an upscale Frenchified joint done in Gallic moderne. My digs are on the top floor. A stairway takes one to the roof—it's quite nice—with a French-blue awning that rolls out to shade the deck, or rolls back to reveal as much sun as you'd ever want. Widows, I suppose well off enough, have suites there, but never venture topside."

The next afternoon they were on the roof, several floors above the surroundings, Jama lying naked. Hunter said, "I'm surprised you have tan lines."

Jama said, "You never kept house with a black man before?"

"Keeping house," Hunter said, "that's what we're doing?"

"Giving shelter to a seaman down on his luck. Hit over the head by a man stepped out of an alley. Robbed while I'm lying dazed and my ship is gone without me," Jama said, his black snake exposed for Hunter to admire.

"You want to touch it, don't you?"

Hunter said, "You mind?"

HE WAS TWENTY-FIVE, AN American in this god-awful place to learn the shipping business. "I sit before a computer all day looking at figures and schedules. I'd rather be scraping hulls." He said, "I'm kidding. I'm bored. Maybe I should go to sea. Is it fun?"

Hunter was from New York, the grandson of a man who owned and ran a half-dozen shipping terminals, "practically with a whip," Hunter said. "Dad slipped away ages ago to sell debentures, and my dear mother, who swears she loves me more than her clothes, offered me up to her father, a dedicated scoundrel."

Another night at ZuZu's, Hunter watching the sailors on the dance floor, Jama's eyes on the slim chicks rolling their asses to the music, he said to Hunter, "When I missed my ship and got waylaid, I was following a boy down the alley."

Hunter said, "A boy?"

"A young man like yourself. And I've been punished for it, losing my ship and getting in trouble."

Hunter took Jama's hand, a candle burning between them on the table at ZuZu's, Hunter telling him, "No, you haven't, you've found what you're looking for," and Jama saw his luck turning.

The third day with Hunter, Jama telling him sea stories about incredibly ugly men finding each other and getting it on. "I saw two miserable dogs, both desperately in need of basic hygiene, kissing each other on the mouth. I did, one night when I walked in the head, I see these two hounds in each other's arms."

Hunter said, "Awww, the poor guys."

"Their grubby look reminded me, I'm shaving off my beard today."

"No! I love your beard."

"It smells old."

"It does *not*."

"I'm letting you shave it off," Jama said, "since you have a tender feeling for it. Use your scissors to cut it down to where you can use your straightedge to finish."

He seemed to like it, running his fingers through Jama's beard as he snipped, his eyes moist, sniffling at first. Jesus. Never said a word. Lathered Jama's face and became intent on shaving it clean. Hunter grinning by then, touching his work, surprising himself as he said, "Why, Mr. Bushy, you're more beautiful without it."

Jama said, "Is that right?" looking at himself in the mirror.

Hunter started on his hair with a comb and scissors till Jama told him he didn't need the comb. "Get to it, cut it down." There was no way to hurry him. Finally, turning his head from side to side in the mirror, Jama said, "Hunter, my boy, you did it."

Jama sat on a high stool in the bathroom, naked. Hunter stood between his legs, taller, head raised just a bit, still fooling with Jama's hair. Hunter said, "Hand me the scissors, the comb too, please, if you don't mind." He said, "Have you ever been referred to as a chic sheikh?" His head still raised.

Jama picked up the straightedge from the counter and sliced the blade across Hunter's throat.

He saw Hunter's eyes taking on a dreamy look, and brought him against his chest to bleed on him, wondering at what moment Hunter would know he was dead and Jama could let the boy slide down his body to the tiles. He'd take a shower and then look through Hunter's closet. Find something casual to wear, something maybe collegiate. He thought of Hunter looking even younger in his T-shirt and jeans and decided it was the way to go. Become Jama the college boy.

Or maybe James Rus*sell,* from Brown.

Wear this brown T-shirt with BROWN on the front of it big, in white. Coming out of the drawer it became BROWN UNIVERSITY with a coat of arms between the names, some red in it.

Jama slipped it over his head and looked in the mirror to see brown on brown, the shirt darker than his bare arms. The size an extra-large that hung straight on him to cover his biceps and flat stomach. He'd be lying naked on the bed and Hunter would pretend to play his ribs, saying if he could plug Jama in he could play him like an instrument. Jama told him he wanted to play music there was an instrument standing right next to him. They did a lot of that kind of shit, saying cute things to each other. This boy, a graduate of Brown University, would use words Jama had never heard people say, like *sardonic* and *saturnine,* and he'd have to look them up. He thought of a saturnine person as mostly cool. Hunter's style was acting like a child, begging Jama to tell him his real name and wanting to know why he'd changed it. All the time asking things like that. He said to Jama, "To be intimate is to know each other's secrets." He said, "God, to be the only person in the entire world to know your mysterious past."

The time came in bed, Jama spent and having a smoke, he told Hunter, "It's James." Tired of him begging in homosexual ways, some cute, some woeful.

"James Rus*sell.* All right? My name while I was doing time. My name before I turned to Islam and became an al Qaeda gunman."

Hunter said, "Oh, my God," spacing the words, and Jama had to hold him for a minute and got him to sit on the bed. He was all right after, by the time Jama got his shave. Full of questions till Jama told him, "Let's wait till we finish here." He didn't

mind being called beautiful, but the guy beat it to death. Said he
was Rus*sell*'s love slave. This grown man who could have all the
cooze he wanted, anywhere, turns it down as the way to go. But
when he cranked up his homo shit with the gestures, he'd let it
come out, knowing he was secure with a lover, and Jama would
feel himself getting semihard. But no comparison to the ones he
got thinking of Red Sea chicks and the number one, Celeste, his
Ethiopian. The one Idris thought was his girl, set her up nice.
Two days with Hunter were okay. The third day he couldn't take
any more and ended the relationship.

Jama wedged his passport into a pair of Hunter's Reebok
sneakers. By now it was hard to tell it was a passport, though it
was readable inside. He'd make up a story how it got this way
for Customs and Immigration when he got home. Tell them a
Nile croc ate it and he had to cut the passport out of the croc's
tummy.

He put on a pair of hundred-dollar jeans, the cuffs folding
on the sneakers just right. He put other stuff, T-shirts and some
of Hunter's panties and some aftershave, in a black flight bag,
plain, no writing on it. He slipped on a pair of Hunter's shades
that didn't fuck up his vision too much, ones he'd been wearing.
Hunter had all kinds of glasses, all the cases here in his desk
drawer. Jama brought them out looking at different styles. He
picked up a case and this one was fat and soft with bills Jama
pulled out, fifty, sixty new hundred-dollar bills. Six grand plus
the three hundred he got from Hunter's billfold, sixty-three hundred, man. Where do you want to go?

There were a couple of things he would do first because he
wanted to and had made up his mind.

Find the two Arab snobs, Idris and Lord Harry, and shoot
them each in the head.

Then locate *Aphrodite,* loaded with frozen natural gas and—
according to Qasim—C4 explosives, shape charges among the

tanks, and watch the ship blow up Djibouti, the gateway to Islam. Or the back door to the West, the dividing line between God and Allah. Watch the city burn, people running for their lives. Qasim showed him how you could blow up the city with a cell phone from a safe distance. They had taken Qasim's cell days ago. But didn't Hunter have one? He believed so.

He had Hunter's car. Use it later tonight to dump his body. This afternoon he would stroll down the rue de Marseille to the Djibouti Airlines office and see about flights south to Nairobi, take it easy for a time, spend some of the money Allah had given him for being a good boy. Then come back . . . No, he should do it first. Kill anyone who knew his name.

CHAPTER TWENTY-FIVE

THIS TIME DARA AND Xavier came to Idris's apartment on rue de Marseille. Idris had Harry staying with him, the shutters closed tight.

"You haven't been here before?" Idris said. "I thought you had. I leased this place when we were paid for the *Faina,* the Ukrainian ship with the Russian tanks. I took home, as you say, two hundred thousand. I'll tell you the truth, I never got less than a hundred thousand as my cut on any ship we hijacked. One three hundred thousand, that giant tanker sat out in the water with a price tag we kept knocking down. The *Sirius Star* was a serious pain in the ass. Dara, excuse the nasty reference, but that's where the pain was, the anxiety giving me the trots."

"Too bad you're out of it," Dara said. "Pirates are still working. I think they've taken over seventy ships by now, the gulf full of the world's navies trying to find them."

"The boys in the skiffs," Idris said. "Oh, it was a time. Being half drunk to hijack a ship and earn a hundred thousand dollars, often dropped from a plane. I had friends among the men in the middle, lawyers, fellows doing nothing for their money, making a few phone calls. They took care of me because they knew I could provide them with ships."

Dara said, "You wish you were still at it?"

"No, I've had enough. Fourteen ships." He said to Dara, "You like another glass?"

"Maybe half," Dara said.

"Lemme do it," Xavier said, picking up the martini pitcher. "I know what Miss Dara means she say a half." He had the reach to top off their stem glasses without getting up. He said to Dara, "You recognize the stone slab cocktail table and the bamboo furniture? Same as down at Eyl."

"I'm selling that house," Idris said. "Why would I want to go to Eyl? I have offers. Booyah Abdulahi, you remember him? He's still doing quite well. Booyah will give me two hundred thousand for the house. Everything in it, I told him it's worth three times that. We'll see."

Dara said, "You couldn't need money."

"No, I have it in banks I don't worry about."

"Then why are you and Harry still together?"

"He's a good friend."

"No, he isn't."

They heard a toilet flush.

Idris said, "He's always in the bathroom grooming himself. Always takes a pistol with him. All right, I thought he was a good friend at one time. I bought four hundred machine guns from him, Uzis, and sold them to warlords for twice what I paid. One of them pompous, I charged three times Harry's price. Harry comes out of the bathroom he's calm, almost himself, but I don't know what he's thinking."

"He has a home here," Dara said, "doesn't he, in the quarter?"

"He's afraid to go home and find Jama waiting for him. He doesn't say it, it's how he acts."

"How does Jama know where either of you lives?"

"Ask and find out. People always watching to see what we do, where we go. They're curious." Idris produced an eight-shot Sig auto from his clothes. "Jama comes, I'll be waiting to shoot him."

"Harry has money?"

"Of course he does. From the sale of arms."

"Then why don't the two of you get out of town?"

"We talk about it. Decide it's better to see it end here. Jama's a fugitive, he can't simply go about as he wants."

They looked up to see Harry come out of the hallway from the bathroom with a Webley revolver, the 1915 British Army model, held in his right hand. He looked quite himself in his starched shirt with epaulets, smiling at Dara, and came over saying, "Our lovely friend Dara," to give her a kiss on the cheek. "I must say we're in dire need of all the friends we can gather." He said, "My friend Xavier," and reached out to take his hand. "By any chance have you a notion of what we might do?"

Xavier said, "You look like you know what you doin."

Dara said, "Why don't you call the cops?"

"Have them sitting around the apartment," Harry said, "drinking tea? We had *paid* guardians before and they proved worthless."

"Well, let's keep in touch," Dara said, "all right? Call if you think Jama's around and you'd like Xavier to give you a hand."

It got Xavier looking at her.

"We ready to go?"

"As soon as I visit the facility," Dara said.

Xavier watched her walk off toward the bathroom while Harry poured himself a martini in Dara's empty glass and topped off Idris's drink.

"Jama comes by," Xavier said, "you fellas gonna be able to shoot him?"

◆ ◆ ◆

IN THE LIFT DESCENDING to the main floor Dara said, "Those guys kill me, sitting around drinking martinis with their guns out."

"You had two," Xavier said. "You all right?"

"I'm fine."

"I never heard you call the toilet a facility before."

"It's a gun room," Dara said, "AKs in the shower stall, one for each of them."

"The boys have their own style of doin things," Xavier said. They stood on the sidewalk along rue de Marseille, Dara getting a cigarette now from her bag and lighting it.

She said, "I noticed Djibouti Airlines down the street when we drove past."

"It's local flights," Xavier said. "Won't get us home if that's what you have in mind."

She said, "I don't know, maybe. We could give Billy a call, find out what he's up to."

"We done here, but you don't want to leave, do you?" He said, "Think about it while I go get the car."

SHE SAW THE BLACK guy in the T-shirt coming along Marseille, the shirt hanging out, too large for him, the guy and his shirt shades of brown. A black flight bag hung from his shoulder.

Dara turned on her spy camera clipped to her shirt pocket and shot him coming straight on with her head turned, not looking at him, the guy in no hurry. Closer now he seemed to hesitate, break his step as he looked at her and said, "You makin it today?" She turned to him.

Passing her his hand went to his sunglasses to slide them down and up, like tipping a hat, and walked past.

Now Dara was shooting him from the rear.

The guy walking toward the Djibouti Airlines office, that direction, about twenty meters past her when she called out:

"James . . . ?"

He stopped. Two, three . . . six beats before he turned around. Now he came back, almost to her, Dara saying, "I mean Jama. I don't know why I said James, you never told me your name. You know what? I think I started to say Jama and it came out James because I know you're American, you tell everybody."

"Yeah, but you recognize me."

"I've photographed you, I know what you look like," Dara said. "You're a much younger Jama—I almost said James again—without the beard."

"I don't recognize myself. I been al Qaeda gunhand too long."

"I doubt anyone else would recognize you. You have to remember, I shoot faces." She said, "What's the story that goes with Brown University?"

"That was a while ago."

"What hall were you in? I bet Harambee, with the black radicals. I had a friend went to Brown. He said the school motto was 'In God We Trust' because it's printed on money."

"Oh, you looking at my shirt. It's a friend of mine's."

"A classmate?" Dara said. "I can't believe you're still around, being on the dodge. I've got quite a few shots of you I'd like to use, with your permission. List your name among the credits. I would say you have the confidence of a movie star, walking around with police after you."

"You were filming me, weren't you, with that bitty thing? I recognize it, from you shooting us on the ship."

Dara said, "I would love to hear how you killed five people at the same time, one of them your leader." She kept talking, giving Xavier time to arrive on the scene. "I'd like to hear about that, too, why you felt you had to shoot him. I could film you telling about it, telling anything you want, your adventures with bin Laden . . . You'd get a credit up front."

"You saying this to me," Jama said, "you don't think you're taking a risk?"

Dara was shaking her head saying no—Jama heard that much before raising his eyes to Xavier appearing behind her, Xavier coming to stand a foot above her head.

He said, "Jama, how you doin? You stayin out of jail?"

Dara said, "It doesn't look like he's giving himself up."

Xavier said, "No, he's got a new thing. Gone college boy on us."

Jama, standing as erect as he could make himself, said, "You want to let it be or take some kind of action?"

Xavier said, "There wasn't a lady present I'd have your neck broke by now. Have it done before you pull the piece you done those people with. Gun you stuck in your jeans but didn't feel right, so you put it in your bag." Xavier said, "On second thought, I don't need to shoot you. We gonna give you to the police."

"You want, we can let it be," Jama said. "Couple of brothers run into each other—why not? And I'm on my way. Tell your grandkids you met me one time."

"Let you go?" Xavier said. "You too scary. First thing, I want you to slip the bag from your shoulder and hand it to me." Xavier took a step to stand in Jama's face. "Try to run, I'll bust your head on the pavement. Mess up your nice haircut." They stared in each other's faces till Xavier pulled the bag from Jama's shoulder and handed it to Dara.

She zipped it open and brought out the Walther first, held it as she looked in the bag. "T-shirts," Dara said, "and girls' panties," bringing out a pair and going into the bag again.

Xavier didn't look at the panties, he was watching Jama, Jama going for the gun, had hold of it as Xavier stepped in to hit him with his big left hand balled up, threw it hard against Jama's clean-shaved face to turn him around stumbling, almost going down. Now he was running away from them, glancing around once, but not running as fast, Xavier judged, as he could.

Xavier said, "Gimme it," took the Walther from Dara, aimed at Jama sprinting up the rue de Marseille, fired three rounds at him, the gunshots loud in the street of buildings, and the Walther clicked empty.

A half block away Jama the college boy stopped and yelled something at them Xavier couldn't make out. He started to run off again, stopped and yelled something else and took off past the Djibouti Airlines office.

"Isn't flyin anyplace today," Xavier said, "is he? I missed some of what he was tellin us."

"He pointed at us and said, 'You two are next.' Like he has an agenda," Dara said, "for killing people. Why do bad guys take themselves so seriously?"

" 'Cause they dumb."

"Jama's not dumb. Sometimes he sounds street, but I think he's putting it on."

"What else he say?"

"Before, when he walked past me, I said, 'James . . . ?' I don't know why. Because he's American? I don't know. He hesitated then and we started talking, but pretty soon it got edgy and you showed up."

"James," Xavier said. "We know that much. He made Jama out of James when he went Arab. Have to figure what name Raisuli came from." He stepped out to the street where Dara was looking up at Harry and Idris in separate third-floor windows, shutters wide open.

Harry's voice came to them. "Did you get him?"

"I ran out of ammo," Xavier said. "I should've had one of your machine guns."

"Do you want to come up for a drink?"

"I think we gonna wait for the police," Xavier said. "Somebody must've called them."

"I did," Harry said. "The chief happens to be a friend of mine. They should be here shortly. They'll want to ask you about Jama," Harry said, "since you were shooting at him. That was Jama, wasn't it?"

Xavier looked at Dara.

"How'd he know that?"

"His AMERICAN NEGRO ACCENT," Harry said.

They were in the Twins' apartment again.

"I could hear it clearly. That 'Yessuh boss' way they have. But he didn't call you boss, did he? I said to Idris—we went to the window—'Who is that guy?' Idris didn't hesitate, he said, 'Jama?' We both knew he would try to disguise himself. It's curious, when he speaks Arabic you don't hear the American Negro sound."

The police arrived. The police chief in a suit and tie, a big man, heavy, said, "Yes, I will have one of your cocktails." His aide in uniform stayed with him to listen to Miss Dara Barr's story and take notes. The police chief said, "So this is the one murdered five people a few days ago. Now has us believe he's the student of a university."

"There's a reward if he's taken alive," Harry said, "and I deliver him to the American embassy."

"I catch him," the police chief said, "I can deliver this one."

Harry said, "Yes, but I've already spoken to them about it. He's on their list."

"If I don't have to shoot him," the police chief said. "This is a desperate man we looking for."

Idris mixed cocktails, raising his eyes to Dara, and seemed to shake his head. Dara would have one drink, that's all, as Harry explained that Jama was not wanted dead or alive. "They made it clear he has to be taken alive if we expect to collect a reward, possibly in the neighborhood of a million dollars."

"You told me before," the police chief said, accepting the cocktail from Idris, "it would be something less than that."

"Dara Barr, in the meantime," Harry said, "has had meetings with the embassy's regional security officer. Ms. Schmidt has agreed to our delivering Jama into their custody."

The police chief of Djibouti said, "Yes, Miss Suzanne Schmidt? Yes, I know her well. I see her from time to time at the Racquet Club."

Dara said in her pleasant voice, "You play tennis?"

"Why?" the police chief said. "You think I'm too heavy?"

Xavier said, "Chief, you got the size to play anythin you want." Xavier got up from his chair and produced the Walther from the back of his waist.

"What you lookin at here is the murder weapon, the one Jama used on the five people." He held the pistol by the barrel offering it to the police chief, who took the grip in his hand. "It had my prints on it," Xavier said. "Now it has yours on top of mine. But me and you never killed anybody with it, have we?"

ON THE WAY TO the Kempinski Dara said, "Poor Harry, he wanted to scream at the cop, '*He's mine*. Keep your fucking hands off him.' While he's trying to maintain his Brit cool."

They were following the Avenue Admiral Bernard now in the dusk, the blanket of Djibouti's lights behind them.

"What we'd like to know," Xavier said, "is Jama gonna hang around or go on home, tired of this Arab shit."

"I don't know," Dara said, "he's been shooting anybody he wants for the past seven years. I think he's the kind keeps score. He told Idris he shot a man for selling cans of soda the man kept on shaved ice. You know why? They didn't have shaved ice in Mohammed's time. It was Qasim told him to do it. Jama said to him, 'There weren't any AKs around in Mohammed's time either.' Qasim told him the AKs were Allah's gift to them to cleanse the world of nonbelievers, and Jama said okay then. But I don't think he's going home, not just yet."

"How about us," Xavier said, "we goin or stayin?"

Dara said, "If I'd been shooting what's going on . . ."

At the hotel desk a phone message was waiting.

"From Billy," Dara said. "He wants us to call him tomorrow."

Xavier said, "One thing after another, huh?"

Dara said, "Let's stop in the bar and talk about it."

CHAPTER TWENTY-SIX

ILLY KEPT *PEGASO* TRAILING the gas ship by a mile, follow-ing its lights at night, the thousand-foot tanker making ten knots all day and through the night. The wind would stir up behind *Pegaso* and Billy would tack to hold the distance between them, Billy searching his memory for the time an LNG accident happened in the U.S. A major disaster. He believed it was in Cleveland.

Helene, with him in the cockpit, sat perched in a tall direc-tor's chair, so far this morning wearing shorts and a T-shirt. She was looking at an issue of *Architectural Digest* from two years ago that featured the pages of Billy Wynn's home on Galveston Island overlooking miles of gasworks. The spread opened with: "Billy Wynn, the whirlwind Texas entrepreneur with countless commercial irons in the fire—" Helene stopped.

"I thought you were an oil man."

"Basically," Billy said. "I keep my hand in for the family, bunch of old farts—God bless 'em—still living in the past. My decorator, Anne Bonfiglio, calls the house Texas Tudor. Has a bowling alley and two swimming pools, one inside." Billy said, "How come it took you so long to find the magazine?"

"I don't usually look at *Architectural Digest* unless I'm waiting like to get a Pap smear, at a doctor's office. I didn't have to find it, you've got at least thirty copies."

Billy said, "The most destructive LNG accident I think was at Cleveland in '44. Look it up for me, okay? Blow up an LNG tanker I imagine would be a terrorist's wet dream."

Helene opened her notebook and turned pages, looking at headings over transcripts and handwritten notes. MISSING SHIP LOCATED, only one page. HOW RANSOM IS DIVIDED, three pages.

Billy was watching the gas ship again, dead ahead, not more than a mile. A man on the fantail was looking at Billy through binoculars.

DETAINEE WENT FROM GITMO TO AL QAEDA, three pages.

Billy picked up his glasses and was eye to eye with the man on the fantail. "He's a Mohammedan," Billy said.

EXPLOSION DEVASTATES A SQUARE MILE OF CLEVELAND.

"I've got it," Helene said, "LNG blast in Cleveland. You're right, 1944. What do you want to know?"

"How big was it?"

"A hundred and thirty-one fatalities, two hundred and a quarter injured. Let's see, two hundred and seventeen cars demolished, six hundred and eighty left homeless."

"Not as big as 9/11."

"Not even close."

"What I'd like to know," Billy said, "is that tanker going all the way up the Red Sea or stopping off?"

"It's stopping off," Helene said.

"Not to refuel. The ship was sitting at Eyl two weeks, its engine shut down."

"But the crew's been eating," Helene said. "I think they'll have to stop for groceries."

"You're right," Billy said. "I imagine the pirates took everything that wasn't screwed down." He turned to Helene, forgetting the eyes watching them. "You know how many times I've said 'you're right' to a girl I'm thinking of having a relationship with?"

"The Forty-Eight-Hour Test," Helene said. "She passes or goes home."

"You can kid about it, you scored high. Most of those girls, they get to take the test 'cause they have possibilities. I start telling her something, I could be speaking Arabic for all the sense it makes. She listens to every word, nods, smiles when I smile and gets rejected. But every once in a while—not too often—the girl says, 'What . . . ?' paying attention, trying to follow me. You know what you said?"

" 'Are you fucking nuts?' "

"You asked if I was serious."

"And that won your heart?"

"You were yourself. I don't mean you don't have tricks, how you put on certain looks. Finally it dawned on me, Hell, you're having fun being a girl. It was the first time in my life I realized it. A girl could be pleased with herself enough she didn't need a guy spending money on her. She's told herself she's a big girl, can make her own decisions."

"And because of that," Helene said, "it was love at first sight?"

"Yeah, well close to it, there're certain conditions. If I'm a sailor, you have to be a sailor. You have to love pitting yourself against the sea. You get seasick? So what? Clean it up. Long as you don't have to keep to your bunk the whole trip." Billy said to her, "Lady, I have to admit I saw almost right off the bat you're a keeper." He left the wheel, came over and hugged her and gave her a kiss.

Helene believed it was time to express herself and be serious about it. He'd already said he liked her standing up to him. Now she said, "Don't I have anything to say about it?"

Let him think she might have some mysterious reason she'd turn down a billionaire's proposal. Or, he might think she wanted to talk about the prenup first.

Billy said, "My Lord, of course you have a say in this, Muffin. Tell me what's on your mind."

Helene said, "You're Billy the Kid, aren't you?"

"I've always felt like a kid in my ways," Billy said, "but guided by a whole lot of good sense, and some learning."

Helene said, "Do you love me?"

"You know I do, Muff, with my whole heart."

"And you want us to get married?"

Helene, looking him in the eye, waited for him to grin and begin making up a story. But he didn't.

"Of course I want to get married, make you Mrs. Billy Wynn. The first and only one I've ever met to go all the way with."

Helene put her head down long enough to get her eyes wet and looked up with happy tears, saying, "Billy, I must be the luckiest girl in the whole fucking world."

Billy said, "Being smart and good-looking didn't hurt. You can be sassy but cute about it, so it didn't blow your chances." He said, "Listen, Muff . . . I have to call Buck Bethards, see if he's gonna help me out here. Okay?"

Helene wiped her eyes, the romantic interlude over. She slipped off the director's chair saying, "I'll go below while you two do your man-thing."

"No, stay here. I told you Buck's a former SEAL? When I

get different opposing stories from my contacts, I like to play my ace. Buck will charge me an arm and a leg, but he most always comes up with the goods. No charge if he doesn't deliver. I'll put him on the speaker so you can listen."

Helene found the sheet on Buck, a printout from CNN with Buck's head-shot on it, his cold eyes staring at her. Billy was looking at the twelve-digit phone number written across the top of the page, and the phone rang.

"HI, IT'S DARA. WHAT'RE you doing?"

"I'm tailing the gas ship, hon. What you think I'm doing?"

"Helene still with you?"

"We get to India I'm gonna have a Jesuit missionary marry us. Here, say hi to Muff."

Dara said, "Muff? You must be the happiest girl in the whole world."

"I told Billy I'm gonna love being rich. Things just seem to work out," Helene said, "if you let them. Here's Billy."

Dara said, "Billy, you remember Jama Raisuli? One of the al Qaedas, not Sean Connery."

Billy said, "Yeah, the Gold Dust Twins were holding him for ransom, and the other one, Qasim."

"Jama killed Qasim and four Somalis guarding them and got away."

"Why would he kill his boss?"

"I don't know," Dara said. "That was three days ago. Yesterday we see him coming along rue de Marseille. We were visiting Idris. Harry's with him. I'll e-mail you about the Twins. I see him coming toward me and I put my spy camera on him. He's had a haircut, lost his beard and he's wearing a Brown University T-shirt, a bag over his shoulder."

"The murder weapon in it," Billy said. "Wait till I light my cigar. Paid fifty bucks for the son of a bitch and it keeps going out on me. So now he's disguised. How'd you know it was Jama?"

"I've shot him enough," Dara said. "You're right, the gun he used on Qasim and the guards was in the bag. He tried to hang on to it and Xavier hit him. Jama took off and Xavier shot at him but missed, only three bullets in the gun."

"What was it, what kind?"

"A Walther P38."

"Holds eight loads," Billy said. "He must've killed the five execution-style, one shot each. Had three left and Xavier wasted them on him. So now Jama's unarmed till he gets another piece. I wonder, is he African American or American African? Tell me what you're doing about him."

"We sat down with the chief of police. I told him what I know about Jama, and Xavier gave him the gun, the murder weapon."

"The cops'll start investigating," Billy said, "and Jama will know you ratted him out and come looking for you."

Dara said, "What he does is out of our hands."

"But you're still in Djib, aren't you? You're not calling from Nawlins. It's good you got Xavier with you, even if he can't shoot straight." Billy said, "The gas ship's scheduled to go to Lake Charles, but I'll bet it's stopping over in Djib for stores. They'll get a few suicide nuts aboard, blow the ship, take out most of Djibouti and whatever navy ships are close by. It won't be an-other 9/11 but it'll make an al Qaeda statement, won't it?"

Dara said, "You think you can do anything about it?"

"Go ashore and talk to the Port Authority, see they keep the gas ship a good twelve miles from town. The time comes I'll call the captain—what's his name, Wassef?—tell him to get all the good guys off the ship before I blow it up."

"Did you ever think, what if you didn't have money?"

"I'd make it," Billy said. "It's not hard."

"You're marrying Helene?"

"You sound like you don't believe it?"

"No, you were meant for each other. Helene's funny, if you listen to her."

"I've noticed that since I let her be herself." Billy said, "Did you hear Osama bin Laden's got a crush on Whitney Houston? They say he's gonna put a *fatwa* out on Bobby Brown for abusing her. Send some true believers to cut his head off. Bin loves Whitney but hates music, says it's evil. Love doesn't have to make sense, does it?"

"That's old stuff, Whitney Houston," Dara said. "Listen, I forgot to mention, when I first saw Jama he said something like 'How you making it?' Like he didn't recognize me, but he had to, I was with him before. He walked past and I said, 'James?' and he stopped and came back."

"You tricked him," Billy said, "and he bit."

"I didn't mean to. He looked so natural in the Brown T-shirt I called him James. And I'll bet anything that's his name."

BILLY HANDED HELENE a color shot of Buck Bethards, the former SEAL, a nice-looking guy, dark hair, forty-one years old, five-eleven, 170 pounds.

"Look at his eyes."

"They're nice."

"They're killer eyes. Look how he's looking at you."

"He's smiling, sort of. Isn't he?"

"Muff, that's called a shit-eatin grin."

Billy reached over and turned the wheel to set *Pegaso* back on the trail of the gas ship, the wog with binoculars still on the fantail. Billy picked up the phone and dialed a number. He heard a voice this time, a live one, and looked surprised.

"Buck . . . ?"

"Billy, how you doing?"

"You know how many numbers I had to try?"

"No more'n I gave you. You start with the last one. It's the newest, what I'm into."

"Where are you, Djib?"

"I believe so. Wait . . . Yeah, I'm still here."

"What's the latest on the LNG tanker?"

"Going to Lake Charles, Louisiana. That was in the paper and confirmed by people who know where ships are going. Those people make so much tipping off pirates they raised their bribe rates. I call those guys the Bribery Pirates."

"That's not bad," Billy said. "You think it's going to Lake Charles but might stop in Djibouti?"

"To take on stores. Arriving a week late after it was held by buccaneers. Man, they fucked up taking a ship al Qaeda wants."

"Even if it wasn't hijacked," Billy said, "I bet a hundred dollars the plan was to stop at Djib. You know what would happen the tanker blew up? I mean anyway near the Gateway to the East."

"That's what I'm talking about," Buck said. "I'm told al Qaeda's getting low on funds. They need to raise money to keep fuckin with us and're looking at the LNG tanker as a way to make some bucks. I got it on authority they're holding up Emirates Transport for fifty million. They don't pay, the Qaedas'll blow the ship to hell."

"Ram it into Djib," Billy said, "turn that town into a pile of mud."

"I doubt they'll let the ship come anywhere near Djibouti."

"Bin wants to blow up the Gateway, how you gonna stop him?"

Buck said, "I'd blow the ship out at sea."

Billy said, "I'll give it some thought. You find out if Emirates Transport wants to bargain with them?"

"They're not talking to me yet."

"Listen," Billy said, "the reason I called you, a guy named Idris Mohammed and his pal Ari Sheikh Bakar had two al Qaedas they wanted to turn in for rewards. They had the two right here in town, under heavy guard."

"I've seen the police reports," Buck said. "One dead with the guards and one absent."

"You knew of them or what?"

"I've followed their careers some. Qasim al Salah's dead and the other one's loose."

"Jama Raisuli," Billy said, "born in the U.S. He's in Djib somewhere hiding out. If there's a reward for him, you can have it. I want to know his real name and where he's from."

"He's American, huh?"

"At one time was called James or Jimmy."

"He never told anybody his name?"

"How would I know?"

"That's all you want, his name?"

"If you can get it."

Buck said, "You don't think I can?"

Billy said, "He kills people who get close to him."

CHAPTER TWENTY-SEVEN

BILLY CALLED THE NEXT morning early, 6 A.M., the blinds closed, the hotel bedroom still dark. She heard him saying they had a terrific tailwind pushing them toward Djibouti, Billy sounding breathless telling her they'd be in by midafternoon if it kept blowing.

Dara said, "What time is it?" half asleep. "You can't wait till morning?" She had to reach for the phone and was on her side, turned away from Xavier.

"It is morning," Billy said. "You out carousing last night? I wanted to get to you before this guy gives you a call, Buck Bethards, my ace. He was a SEAL nine years, a soldier of fortune with Blackwater till they messed up in Baghdad and he quit." Billy said, "Wait a minute," and Dara could hear his voice calling out away from the phone, "Muff, hold her dead-on, for Christ sake. You're losing sail." On the phone again he said, "My mate's still learning the ways of the sea. Listen, Buck's a pro, a good guy. Tell him whatever you can about Jama. You said you have him on your spy pen—I gotta get one of those. Show Buck what a traitor looks like." He said, "Dara, I'm signing off. See you in a while."

Dara reached to the night table to replace the phone. Behind her Xavier's voice said, "Billy's havin trouble?"

"They'll get in this afternoon sometime."

Dara rolled over and was looking at Xavier's face on a white pillow, his eyes watching. Less than two feet from her. He said, "How you feelin?"

"Not bad. I'm still tired."

LAST NIGHT THEY HAD stopped in the lounge for a cognac and were talkative, feeling good, tried Black Russians wondering what Billy would tell them when he called. They came up to her suite . . .

She said now, "You were holding me last night."

"Yes, I was."

"In bed."

"Right here."

"We were naked."

"We were buck naked. We still are, 'less you got up and dressed."

"You were holding me and I fell asleep."

"I did too, since nothin was goin on." He said, "That's the closest we ever come."

"You're so easy about it. You let things happen."

"If they gonna."

"I mean you don't get serious about it."

"Serious?" Xavier said. "Girl, it's the most enjoyment there is in life."

Dara tried to think of something profound. She said, "I

guess you're right. Now I've got the guy on my mind who's gonna call me."

"I could hear Billy. Wants you to talk to his spy?"

"His name's Buck. I think I'll tell him to meet me for coffee somewhere. It shouldn't take long."

"I'll drop you off. I'm gonna see a doctor, then come pick you up."

Dara said, "You have a doctor here?"

"All my years passin through? I got a dentist too, just in case. Gives you gas while he fools with your teeth."

"You have a pain somewhere?"

"Heartburn," Xavier said. "I'm waitin to see you get out of bed. The movies, the girl takes all the covers wrapped around her."

"This is real life," Dara said.

Xavier watched her roll out of bed bare-ass and walk to the bathroom. Watched her put her hand high on the doorframe and look over her shoulder at him. He said, "You havin fun now, aren't you?"

Did she wink at him as she stepped inside and closed the door? He couldn't tell. For some reason he thought of the song about life being a bowl of cherries, the song telling us "The sweet things in life to you were just loaned. So how can you lose what you never owned?"

CELESTE, THE ETHIOPIAN FROM the club Las Vegas, could not believe this guy coming in her apartment, this Negro American college boy. How could he have a key? She had only given two keys to money clients, one very rich, the other very satisfying. This guy opened the door and was smiling at her coming to the bed.

"You know me, don't you?"

Said it in Arabic and it opened her sleepy eyes. She had not had a college boy since last spring.

He said it again, "Do you know my name?"

"Let me think," Celeste said, in her Arabic. She didn't want to say she had never seen him before. Don't tell that to a man. Now he was asking if he had ever told her his name. An American name.

This meant he believed he had.

Celeste said, "Oh . . . ?"

She said, "Tell me what it is and I will let you know."

Jama looked into her eyes. He said, "James Rus*sell.*"

Her expression didn't change.

Her eyes didn't show a memory of his name. The times before he had spoken only English to her, wanting her to know he was American but talking too much. It's why he was back to see her, find out if she knew his name. She didn't. But he was here, he was thinking he should give her a jump. The first time with her, at the Las Vegas, she said, "Why don't you fuck me crazy, big boy?" Said it in English. This morning he said it to her, "Why don't you fuck me crazy? No, you said cra*zee,* didn't you?"

Celeste came alive hearing the only English she had bothered to learn because she loved the word, cra*zee.* This man knew it. He had a key. He was important, but she couldn't remember his name. Well, she knew what it was now.

She said, "James Rus*sell,*" and in Arabic told him, "I was joking with you. Of course I remember loving you so much, James."

She watched his expression change.

"What's the matter with you?"

She waved her hand in front of his face.

"You keep staring."

"I'm all right," Jama said. "Let's get in the bed." Showing a tired smile now. He watched her pull off her shirt and lie down. Now she held her arms out to him, this little Ethiopian chick, this little pro. Jama took off Hunter's drip-dry sport coat, a couple of sizes too large, dropped it on a chair and got on top of Celeste. He pulled the pillow from behind her head, Celeste trying to unzip his fly. Jama said, "No need to let out Godzilla, we gonna be through here in a minute. I'll rest this pillow on your face." She started to fidget. "Don't worry, you can breathe. I got a surprise for you."

He pulled a Walther P38 from a holster on the back of his jeans. He picked up this one in the same gun shop he had robbed in 2003. This time he took the Walther, a box of rounds and the holster. That big nigga with Dara was right, it hurt you shove it in your pants with nothing to pad it. Now he got down close to the pillow and lifted up the edge to see part of her face, her nose, her mouth. He said in Arabic, "Sweet girl, open your mouth for me." She did, she opened her mouth. Jama shoved the barrel of the Walther into her throat, tilted it up a speck, pressed his left hand down on the pillow hard and shot Celeste through her brain.

THE ONLY OTHER ONE Jama could think of knew his name was the movie girl Dara and the big-ass nigga who followed her around. He'd start calling hotels from here, beginning with the Kempinski. It seemed the movie girl's style. He'd ask was she registered.

The hotel voice said he would connect Jama with the room. Jama said, "No, I'll call back," and heard the voice tell him sorry, the line was busy.

She was there, talking to somebody on the phone six in the morning. The movie girl making plans.

Jama left the apartment, went out to the street and got in Hunter's BMW convertible, silver with a black top that was never down since Jama started driving the car. Man, there was a lot had to be done. Four this morning he'd got rid of Hunter. Took him out to the pier used for yachts and dumped him in the bay, a twenty-inch TV set tied to Hunter's legs, the TV the only thing in the apartment Jama could manage that was heavy enough to keep Hunter down.

He told himself he wouldn't be sitting around watching TV anyway, not with all the things had to be done. First, go back to Hunter's place for his binoculars. Then drive up to the Kempinski to watch the entrance from a spot in the trees. Being a terrorist was a pain in the ass when you weren't spreading terror.

It was going on 10 A.M. before he saw them come out.

CARS CAME AROUND TO take different streets off the Place Verdun, circling past the statue of Marshal Ferdinand Foch, 1851–1929, on a pedestal in the center of the plaza, the single word *J'Attaque* below his name.

Xavier said, "Ferdinand was asked what he'd do if surrounded by Germans and he said he'd attack. I believe it was at Verdun he lost somethin like eighty thousand men j'attackin." He said, "There's your man there."

The onetime SEAL and professional soldier for hire looked like any other forty-year-old in pretty good shape; nothing that told he had special tricks for fighting a war. Getting out of the car Xavier watched Dara and Buck Bethards shake hands and sit down at a table on the sidewalk. It looked like he was drinking coffee. He was, black as it comes. Xavier met him and said, "You're doing this job for Billy, huh?" so they'd get right to it. It wasn't going to take Xavier long at the doctor's.

He shook hands with the spy again, got back in the car and turned into a street east of the Central Market, turned a few corners finding his way and pulled up in front of Dr. Chin's medical practice and drugstore.

The sign in Chinese characters didn't mean a thing to Xavier, but there was Dr. Chin himself in the doorway, the little doctor of traditional medicine reaching up now to put his arms partway around Xavier saying, "What's new?" With just a bit of an accent. "I hear you in the movie business." Dr. Chin smiling in his wispy white beard and eyes that were slits. They chatted a few minutes until Xavier said, "You know what I want."

"Horny Goat Weed, of course. How you doing with it?"

"I ran out a while ago."

"You had I believe three hundred capsules of my special blend?"

"That's right, five bottles."

"How long they last?"

"I been out of 'em most of a year."

"But you stay active until a year?"

"If 'active' means a lot of action, you have to remember I'm seventy-two."

"I'm eighty-four," Dr. Chin said. "So . . . ? What do numbers mean? I remain as active as I wish to be. Get ten bottles for a year, I make you a deal, hundred fifty dollar."

Xavier said, "I never tried the Rowdy Lamb Herb."

"It's Horny Goat Weed with a different name."

"How about Fairy Wings?"

"Same thing. It's all epimedium, the same plant, maybe a different variety. It's the name gives you ideas. Use for two thousand years, no complaints."

"What about rhino horn?"

"Stop it. You know it's a myth."

"But maybe it works," Xavier said, "you set your mind on it givin you a donkey can be rode."

"Maybe sometime only. They killing all the rhinos for the horns, shave it to a powder you take. It will cost you a fortune, as much as fifteen thousand for a small one, but gives no life to your waning desire."

"I'll tell you what," Xavier said. "Let me have ten bottles of your Horny Goat Weed."

"Now you talking," Dr. Chin said. "Six hundred capsules. Write to me you need more."

DARA WAS TELLING BUCK, "I remember how confident he was. Jama said he'd take care of Idris and Harry once he walked out. We believed his tone of voice, but not what he was saying. If that makes sense. Idris said, 'Of course he thinks of getting away. For Jama, what else is there of importance?'" Dara giving her thoughts on Jama Raisuli. She said, "Did you know Raisuli was Sean Connery's name in *The Wind and the Lion*?"

Buck said, "You see that as significant?"

"It means he has a sense of humor. Don't you think it's funny?"

"Yeah, but does Jama think it is?"

"You're right. He's American, but according to Idris speaks street Arabic."

"And you think his first name is James."

"I'm pretty sure, from his reaction when I said it."

"The name Jama," Buck said, "looks like James. What does Raisuli look like? You come up with an Italian name, don't you. Like James Ravioli."

Dara said, "You know what I thought it might be? James Russell."

Buck looked up from the photos of Jama on the table. He said, "James Russell, that's good. Russell, Raisuli. Is that how he's thinking, wanting the same sound?" He picked up a photo. "Let me run his name, see how many James Russells are in the system. Say in the past ten years."

"In ten years," Dara said, "there could be a thousand James Russells."

"Not that many with his profile. What surprises me," Buck said, "he doesn't seem to have told anybody his real name. I know a few al Qaedas who can be bought, but that doesn't mean they'd know his name. Yet this boy likes to talk and brag on himself. I would think if he told you he told anybody."

"Why?"

"Wasn't he attracted to you?"

"You mean, did he try anything?"

"Come on, the guy go for you or not?"

"I think he did," Dara said, "but ran out of time."

"Tried to impress you, didn't he? Worth a million dollars to the United States government?"

"Idris and Harry," Dara said, "were going for twenty-five million."

"They might get it for bin Laden, but not some kid learned Arabic in prison."

"How do you know that?"

"It's where black kids become Muslims."

He looked out toward Marshal Foch in the middle of the plaza.

"Who do you know," Buck said, "drives a silver BMW drop-head, has a black top?"

Now Dara was looking for a BMW in the light traffic, a few cars coming around to slip off into connecting streets.

"Directly across from us," Buck said. "It crept past once. Now it's coming around again. Tell me if you know the car."

There it was, silver shining hot in the sun. She said, "I've never seen it before."

She watched it drive past them, the windows dark, she couldn't see the driver. She watched it make a wide turn toward Marshal Foch, taking its time. She glanced at Buck drawing a nickel-plated Mag revolver from under his jacket.

Buck said, "I tell you to hit the deck, hit it."

The BMW got almost to Marshal Foch before it began to come around in a slow right turn, back this way but closer to the curb, approaching the Café Verdun and the sidewalk tables and she heard Buck yell at her and saw him pull the table over on its side, Dara going down behind it seconds before gunfire came from the car. She didn't see Buck. She looked past the table and saw Jama in the car, the window down, Jama holding his Walther and firing point-blank at the table, the rounds splintering wood and she went down to press herself against the pavement, thinking, Where's Buck? Thinking, Jesus Christ, please shoot him. And it stopped. The ringing in her ears faded. She looked over the table and saw Jama still in the car window, still pointing his gun at her. She could say she didn't know what his name was, he'd never told her. But thought, Take a chance, and said, "I bet your name's James Russell, isn't it?"

"Rus*sell*," Jama said. "The idea was a tease, see if law people could figure it out. You know how many knew it? Two. No, three down, four to go."

Past him she saw the white Toyota enter the plaza. Dara gave the white Toyota time to get over here, saying to Jama, "Who cares what your name is. You'll either be shot down or go to prison—" She stopped, was going to say "for life" but never got to say any of it. Jama was aiming at her and Xavier was ramming the white Toyota straight into the right side of the BMW, banging in the door and some of the fender.

Xavier said after, "Jama didn't know what hit him. Fired

three out his right side window, nothin to shoot at, and ran. Fired three times through the table. That leaves him two shots in the gun."

"One," Buck said.

He was standing a few yards from them brushing at his knees.

"He hit me with his first shot." Buck opened his coat to show his white shirt bloody beneath his arm. "He got me right here in my love handle, through and through."

Dara said, "We'll take you to a hospital."

"I can manage," Buck said. "I know where I can have it fixed up."

Dara said, "Did you hear him say his name?"

"I did, but you're the one got him to tell it. I'd say it's your score."

Dara said, "I wouldn't feel right about it."

"It's worth five grand easy," Buck said. "More, you hunt down where he did time and get a positive ID."

Dara said, "Oh . . . ?" She said, "But it would look like I'm doing it for the money."

Buck said, "Yeah . . . ?"

CHAPTER TWENTY-EIGHT

H E WASN'T SURE HE hit the movie girl. Talking too much, not tending to business. He hit the suit was with her but not in a good spot. Saw him grab his side twisting around and go down. Not a cop, a white man with a bright-metal piece. But the one rammed into him could be cops, the reason Jama gunned it out of there, tires screaming on the pavement, and thanked Allah for saving his ass. Jama didn't look back till he was out past Marshal Foch and saw in his rearview it was a white Toyota had plowed into him. Saw the tall nigga outside the car. Saw him standing, hands on his hips, watching him drive away. Saw Dara the movie girl and the suit on his feet now raising his piece, sun flashing on it. Then lowered it, cars passing in front of him. Jama remembered the suit scooting away from Dara and aiming the piece to fire when Jama shot him. Was he drawing gunfire away from her? It looked like it. What was he, the suit, a boyfriend? Jama asked himself what woman he knew, any of them, he'd stand up to draw fire away from. And saw Dara looking out from behind the table, her shirt wet from coffee spilled on her. He saw her at Idris's party at Eyl and aboard *Aphrodite* the time she visited. *She knew his name.* He came to realizing it, he didn't start with it. He saw her by the table and shot holes in it to scare her. He wanted to hit her he'd of done it. Then why didn't he?

He turned north on to rue d'Éthiopie and thought of Celeste and knew she'd lied to him. He didn't know it in her room but did now, sure of it. She didn't know his name, even after he told her. Saying she pretended not to know it. Lying was the girl's business.

He pictured Dara again on the tanker, while they were anchored off Eyl. On *Aphrodite,* full of liquefied natural gas. He thought of the phone number that would set off the C4 in the hold. Saw the numbers in his mind, 44-208-748-1599. He had another number Qasim had given him, an al Qaeda contact. Someone with the latest word. And saw Dara again in the room where he was handcuffed to the chair. She never put on different looks, she used the same one all the time. Show she was interested in him. He believed they could sit down and have a conversation and keep each other thinking. He wondered if she was fucking that tall nigga. If he wasn't too old. He could be her grandfather. Mean. Told you he can break your neck and you believe him. Dara, he couldn't see her going to him to fuck her. Dara could take her pick. No, there was nothing going on with Xavier. Maybe she'd let him see her naked once in a while, that's all. The old fucker stares thinking of the old days. Jama knew he had to kill her. She knew his name. Except he'd like to get to know her better first.

He could be running out of time, once she gave the FBI his name. If she did. Or if she was in no hurry, he believed Dara would like to sit down with him, too. She was cool, but not how she talked, told you things. She talked eye to eye with you and could put you on doing it. That was cool, asking did he want to be in the movie she's making. Was she fucking with him or was she serious? Find that out if you want, then shoot her.

He'd put the car in the alley behind Hunter's digs—what he liked to call his apartment—and make some plans for the next couple days or so. See if he could pull off something with *Aphrodite* he needed to do. That big fat LNG tanker waiting in the stream to blow up. When he wanted to see Dara again for some reason—he might feel a need to do that—he'd go to her hotel. Right now he had to phone his al Qaeda connection, find out if they were still fucked up, couldn't make up their mind, and tell his guy what he was going to do. Take it out of their hands. Get it done.

He called the number of his contact.

THE VOICE ON THE cell repeated the numbers Jama called and said in Arabic, "Allah is God. He hears us and watches over us."

Jama said, "Why, I believe that's Assam Amriki I'm speaking to. My old buddy, is that you?"

The voice said, "Don't use names."

"It's been seven years, man, I still recognize your voice, your proper way with the Arabian, showing you cultured. Assam, my brother, where you at?"

"Don't ask that."

"You still the propaganda man, doing recruitment videos?"

"I'm hanging up the phone you talk to me like that."

"How you want me to talk to you?"

"Tell me why you called."

"I want to know about the tanker, where it's at."

"The mission is no more."

"Delayed? Postponed?"

"It's *off*. We don't touch the ship."

"It's got explosives on it."

"The *ship* is explosive. It makes no difference, we don't touch it."

"Once they took us off, Qasim thought you'd put two more Qaedas aboard and get it done."

"I'm telling you it's been called *off*," Assam's voice rising as he said it. "We have other work to consider. We are losing people in Pakistan, this week in Somalia, our brothers being killed one after another by their planes with no pilots, their drones."

"Where you located these days? I want to see you."

"Impossible."

"I saw you on CNN one time," Jama said. "Had like before and after shots of you. Back in '02 when you still looking Jewish, they call you a computer geek then. Now with your turban and your beard grown out, you running the news for al Qaeda. They calling you their media director. Another time I saw you, I believe on a Shabaab Web site, you showing Palestinian children all blown to hell on a bus, an Israeli bomb set off under it. It don't bother you being a Jew most of your life? You know you the first American charged with treason in fifty-eight years? I haven't seen they put any money on you yet. There was a picture of you with Khalid Sheikh Kiss-My-Ass Mohammed they calling a 9/11 mastermind. You hanging out with the big boys, huh?"

Assam's voice in the cell phone said, "I'm going to warn you, you have been marked for death."

"No shit," Jama said. "Tell me about it."

"See? You show no respect. Listen to what I say, as a former American to another who has my sympathy. You tried perhaps, at least at first, but you failed. Now there is a *fatwa* on you, condemned to death for the murder of Qasim al Salah."

"You talking about?" Jama said. "Was a Somali they hired as a guard plugged Qasim and I plugged the Somali. Understand, Qasim was my boss, my teacher, my best friend in the al Qaeda world for seven years, the most dedicated motherfucker I ever knew, and I say that with respect for the man. I want to know who's saying I shot him."

He heard Assam's voice in the cell telling him, "There is no more I can say to you. I leave you with regret that knowing you I never felt like a brother to you."

"I can't say I give a shit," Jama said. "What I want to know is where the ship is now."

"It is of no concern to you. The ship will take on supplies and continue to the U.S."

Jama knew he was lying. He said, "Assam . . . ?"

He was gone.

It didn't matter. He could pick up a boat and cruise around till he found the tanker. There was no way he could miss it, the ship's structure hanging on to its ass end, the rest of it five tanks of deadly frozen gas reaching to the bow. You couldn't miss spotting a ship looked like *Aphrodite*. It would be off Djibouti, out in the Gulf of Tadjoura ten miles or so. No port wanting a ship sitting close by could blow up on them. He had to make sure of the phone's range, how far it would reach to do the job.

Jama saw himself sitting at an outdoor cocktail lounge in the European quarter having—what would he have?—a rum and Coca-Cola, once he sent it back for more ice. Like they were saving their fucking ice, never put enough in the drink. Hunter's cell in his pocket. At some time, after he'd had a couple of Cuba Libres, he'd take out the phone and dial the 700 number Qasim had given him. Look up and hear the explosion, a terrific thundering *BOOM* coming from some miles away but loud, man, everybody in the place looking up, the glasses on the bar shaking, all the white people in there asking each other what was that. Some would go out in the street. Jama would sip his drink. Somebody would say to him, "Jesus Christ, you hear it?" And he'd say, "Hear what?"

Cool.

But wouldn't he like to see the tanker explode?

Else why go to all the trouble.

CHAPTER TWENTY-NINE

BIN LADEN SAYS IN his speech, we ever quit being nice to the Israelis, clean up our intentions elsewhere, we could be friends. The only reason they ran the suicide flights into the Twin Towers, bin says, was to pay us back for supporting the Jews."

The *Pegaso* was about two hours out of Djibouti still trailing the gas tanker, Helene at the wheel in a cotton sweater and skimpy shorts, Billy watching Fox news.

"Is bin serious? The Israelis may be heavy hitters the way they do their paybacks, but they're still the good guys. You never see 'em taking any shit from Hamas. Why should they give back land they won fair and square?"

"I wouldn't," Helene said.

"What I don't understand," Billy said, "is how bin's still alive, all the smart bombs we've laid on his hooches."

"I'll bet he's dead," Helene said. "And it's what's his name, al Zawahiri doing the talking. They all sound alike." Helene said, "It's scary how a drone flies to a target in Pakistan, a guy in a trailer in California looks at it on his screen, presses a button while he's having a cup of coffee, and blows up the al Qaeda hideout in Pakistan with a Hellfire missile."

"You have a military-type mind," Billy said, "and a cute butt peeking out of your shorts."

"I could fire one from home," Helene said. "Turn from the range where I'm fixing supper for us and blast one off."

"I swear you learn faster than any girl I ever met. I sensed that when I chose you."

Billy went out on deck with his binoculars to spot drones, the UAVs crossing the sky at a few thousand feet in a glare of sun. "I see one," Billy said, "way up there, taking pictures of us and the gas tanker." Billy talking with the glasses at his face. "It's a Mariner, the navy version of the Reaper, the one belongs to the air force. She can stay up looking around for two days at two hundred and thirty knots packed full of sensors, plenty of fuel and weaponry. Six hardpoints, they call them, your Hellfire missiles. Muff, I'd like you to commit that to your memory."

"Six hardpoints," Helene said. "Got it, Chief."

It was fun sounding military. "Aye, aye, sir." Billy would drop into the cockpit and she'd say, "Captain on the bridge," and get him grinning at her.

"The drone can read a license plate from two miles away," Billy said. "What else you want to know?"

"Why are you grouchy?"

"I'm not grouchy. I'm telling about the MQ-9, a bust-ass hunter-killer and its firepower. We're getting to the point we won't need fighters or bombers no more, we send in the drones. I wonder what Joe Foss would think of that. Joe shot down twenty-six Zekes over the Solomons in his Grumman Wildcat and later on became governor of South Dakota. Major Bing Bang Bong flying a P38 shot down forty during his tour and gave his life testing a jet. Another ace, Pappy Boyington, a Sioux Indian, shot down his twenty-sixth Zeke over Rabaul. Later that same day some Nip sent Pappy down in flames." Billy said, "I forgot the name of the navy pilot in a Dauntless crashed his plane into a Jap cruiser after he'd been hit. Another hero giving his life for his country. All Medal of Honor winners."

Helene said, "Can you imagine doing something like that?"

"I'd love to see what it's like," Billy said.

He had his glasses on *Aphrodite* now, on her tall decks aft, the gas ship moping along toward Djibouti.

"We're gonna waste time wanting proof the ship's a bogey till it blows up a port in the U.S."

"But you aren't absolutely sure," Helene said, "are you?"

"If I believe that ship's gonna blow up at an appointed hour, and I see evidence of it, that's good enough for me. You might ask, 'You mean evidence you can prove?' Maybe not. I don't believe in wasting time on the horns of dilemmas, I go with my gut."

Billy paused and Helene said, "Yeah . . . ?"

"My gut told me this morning the LNG tanker's gonna blow up right here. It's as good a place as any east-west-wise. Al Zawahiri makes a bullshit statement about al Qaeda drawing the line to cut us off. What he doesn't know hiding out in the hills, Djib's gonna get bigger, it's in the plans to become a major port in the east-west passage. Like Singapore. And if I'm convinced it's gonna blow up," Billy said, "I've got to do something about it, don't I?"

Beginning to sound like Sterling Hayden doing Jack D. Ripper again. No Communist plot or precious bodily fluids to deal with this time, but the destruction of a city.

He was serious.

Helene said, "Have you any idea what you'll do, Skipper?"

"Warn Harbor Security of the clear and present danger," Billy said. "Do that first, while the LNG tanker's still out in the Gulf of Tadjoura. If they're too dumb or set in their ways to take me seriously . . ."

Helene said, "Yeah . . . ?"

"I'll address the risk of the ship directly. I'm thinking of doing it anyway. Hire a gook and send him out there in a skiff with a bullhorn. He tells them in Tagalog, English and Arabic to get your ass off the ship before she blows."

"They have to swim for it?" Helene said.

"Swim or get in the lifeboat. They got one like the *Alabama* the captain was in and snipers shot the three wogs. I hear they're making a movie about that. Some action picture, three Mohammedans are shot. The al Qaedas still aboard the gas ship want to die for bin, go ahead."

"That is so cool," Helene said. "You save all the gooks and the ship too."

"I don't save the ship," Billy said. "Once the decks are clear, I'll put a six-hundred-caliber Nitro Express round in her sweet spot and blow her up myself. Before, you understand, they can use it on Djib."

"That is so fucking smart of you."

"It's tricky, though, messing with liquid gas all frozen, twenty-seven hundred million cubic feet of natural gas aboard. You'll forget this if I tell you, but just one cubic meter—that's three of the twenty-seven hundred million—spill it, you got twelve thousand four hundred cubic meters of a flammable gas-air mix."

"You sound like you're reading it."

"I memorized it. You might want to look at it. My red notebook."

"I will when I have time, Skipper."

"If, say, nine, ten percent of the natural gas leaks out and spills in the water it will boil to gas in about five minutes. Because the water is at least two hundred twenty-eight degrees hotter than the frozen gas. It comes out and flows in a vaporous cloud close to the water until I hit it with a high-explosive Nitro Express round. It goes up, burning itself back to the ship, fireballs shooting up. That's a hundred times bigger than the Hindenburg disaster. Remember I showed you that news footage?"

"The German zeppelin," Helene said. "People running out of the fire . . ."

"Listen. The heat from this fireball, this inferno can cause third-degree burns and start fires miles away."

"Wow, really?"

"That's why I have to do it ten, twelve miles from Djib. But we have to be in position," Billy said, "where I can take the shots and still get us out of there in a hurry."

Helene said, "We might not get away fast enough?"

Billy said, "I'll make sure we do."

"We stay out here till you blow it up?"

Billy said, "I wish we could, Muff, but I've got to go to Djib to set up where the gas ship anchors. Then later on you can help me write the book, *Ship Killer,* that's the title. Under it: *How We Lit or Lighted the World's Largest Natural Gas Conflagration.* Something like that."

"I'll call the Kempinski."

"Or we tie up at the pier and stay aboard."

"We'll get a suite so you can walk around and think, and make calls."

Billy said, "You mean so you can see Dara and sound like a girl for a change."

"It's scary," Helene said, "the way you read my mind." She thought she'd better add, "But I was thinking of you, you need room to roam around in."

"That's good," Billy said. "'Room to roam.'"

"Around in," Helene said.

THEY WERE IN BILLY'S suite, Helene and Dara having martinis with anchovy olives, talking, catching up. Billy was off to see people, Xavier went to see the police to tell what he knew about Jama.

"Billy started calling me Muffin," Helene said. "I don't know why. A person's face is either a bird, a horse or a muffin, right? What am I?"

"A bird."

"See, he didn't start with Muff. I was Muffin till he short-ened it to Muff, but I don't think it has anything to do with mine. He's smoking a cigar and gets the urge to go down on me?"

"Disturbs your reading?"

"I could be doing the wash. Especially doing the wash and I'm a mess. My crotch smells like a fifty-dollar Havana."

"It must turn him on."

"Yesterday, he was General Jack D. Ripper again, but no pre-cious bodily fluids, he was talking about drones, nobody has to fly the planes anymore. Grouched about that for a while. I think he wants to be a hero. Loves to talk about guys doing heroic things in the war. I asked Billy if he could imagine doing it and he said, 'I'd like to see what it's like.' What does that mean?"

"I'm guessing," Dara said. "He'd like to be known as a war hero who got the Medal of Honor posthumously without dying."

"Or," Helene said, "he wants to get the medal for making a phone call that saves some important guy's life. But now he's talking about doing it. Blow up the gas ship and get away before the gas fire catches up with us. He says he isn't worried."

"But you are."

"He says he may get a cigarette boat for the job, a Donzi."

"If you'd rather not go with him," Dara said, "don't."

"We're shipmates, and shipmates stand together," Helene said. "He's the captain and I'm the fucking crew. 'Bogey off the port bow, Skipper.' When I'm on watch. You don't go down to the galley, you lay below."

"It sounds like fun," Dara said.

"He's serious about it."

Dara said, "With a six-hundred-caliber rifle. You think he knows what he's doing?"

"He sure sounds like it."

"You two must be getting along."

"He loves it when I aye-aye him."

Helene sipped her martini. Put an olive in her mouth, took another sip and bit into the olive.

"God, this is good after champagne every day. I told you it's all he has?"

"But you don't have to drink it."

"My body requires alcohol to get through this."

"It must be a fine line," Dara said, "between keeping up your appeal and staying high enough to see it through."

"It gets tricky," Helene said. "I have to watch I don't fall overboard."

IDRIS STOPPED BY THE hotel in the afternoon, smiling at Dara and Helene having their party.

"The turn of events does not give you pause?"

Dara said, "What turn of events?"

"Jama being loose," Idris said. "You not concerned about him?"

"Xavier's turning it over to the police," Dara said, "giving them Jama's real name. He's their case now."

"So we don't worry about him, good," Idris said. "I'm going to Paris for a few days to catch my breath. Come back and take up piracy again. I miss boarding ships."

Dara said, "If I had the energy I'd be right behind you, make you a movie star."

Idris said, "Yes, thank you," accepting the martini Helene offered him. He sipped it and closed his eyes knowing he'd have another one. Dara lighted a cigarette and gave it to him and he said, "Why do I want to go to heaven? I'm experiencing my reward here."

"I hate to tell you," Helene said, "but it's been a while since we were virgins."

"You are women of the world, and we don't see many of that kind here." Idris said, "Am I crazy to go to the gulf? More than thirty warships there bumping into each other? Over one hundred freedom fighters"—giving Dara a nod—"have been put in jail in Kenya. Most of them waiting for trial and go to prison for ten years. But," Idris said, "I believe pirating is still a good business. At least for someone knows what he's doing. I believe when I get boats with motors of a high power, I will make another fortune."

Dara said, "What's Harry doing?"

"He's drinking, but not too much," Idris said, "and taking methamphetamines. It makes him feel like Superman. He makes sudden moves. Turns holding his pistol."

"Riding on tweek," Helene said.

"He drums on chair arms," Idris said, "to music in his head."

"Does he have a little dance step?"

"He tells me with all the details of shooting a tiger in Bengal, from his seat on an elephant. He tells me he has local blokes, like they're his beaters, lookin for Jama. Scare him out of where he's hiding. Harry tells me he'll shoot the bothersome bugger and that will be the bloody end of it."

"He'll fuck up," Helene said.

"He can't do it alone," Dara said.

"He tells me he has help."

"They'd better be armed and dangerous."

"Two leftover Somalis," Idris said, "guards on the trip from Eyl. They're related to the four he killed to escape. They both want to shoot Jama."

Dara said, "Or is he James now?"

CHAPTER THIRTY

A TAXI DRIVER EVER TRIED to charge him too much, Jama would place the barrel of the Walther against the man's neck and ask him in Arabic, "Again, please. How much is the fare?" The driver would say, oh, he made a mistake and sometimes wouldn't charge for the ride. One time the driver was slow, maybe wondering if he should jump out, but first asking, "Is this a robbery?"

What's the matter with him? Of course it was a robbery. Jama took his money, drove off in the taxi a few blocks and left it in the street.

He used taxis because he'd left Hunter's banged-up car back of his building, through with it, he believed, and through with his Ivy League outfits. He wore a *kikoi*, a white one that fell past his knees, a scarf he knotted around his head, and had stopped shaving. He dirtied up Hunter's white sneakers, needing fast shoes he ever had to make a run. He hung out in the African quarter till people started asking where he was from, if he was selling khat. That wasn't a bad idea. He bought up a clump a khat-seller had and went around peddling it marked up some. He believed he was being watched. He didn't know it for a fact, but believing it was enough. Each night he changed where he stayed, holes in the walls called hotels.

He talked to sailors hanging around the docks. One of them told him the LNG tanker was out there in the Gulf of Tadjoura waiting for stores. He heard the crew, the Filipinos, had quit and were looking for ships.

Jama was thinking he should have stayed at Hunter's. Have booze, all the ice he wanted. Food in the freezer. He was sorry he had been hasty about Celeste. Have her stay with him at Hunter's place, back in the saddle again out where a friend was a friend. Wherever that was. If the phone rang he'd say, "Hunter? He went to Egypt. Me? I'm taking care of his cat Putie." Give the caller shit like that in a nice voice.

He still had a key.

HARRY WAS CLOSE TO biting his nails, tempted, feeling a need to get it done. He said to his Somalis, "Come on, let's stay on it, for Christ sake. Check the African quarter, you know what he looks like. You drove all the way from Eyl with him. He could be dressed like an American or he's gone back to being Arab."

One of the Somali lads said, "I know the back of his head, his hair. I sat behind him two days looking at it."

The other Somali said he was never in the same car with Jama. "But I know he has hair on his face, a beard."

Finally they had traced Jama to the rue de Marseille, Harry out of his car wanting to pace, move around, but managed to hold on to himself. His two Somalis stood waiting, smoking cigarettes. In the dusk, the sky losing its light, the street of apart-ment houses was already dark. Harry's Bentley, delivered today from Eyl, stood at the curb waiting.

"You're sure he's in that building, staying there."

"The car is in back, one side of it destroyed."

"And he was seen driving it."

"People on the street say yes, he is the one, but not with a beard. Wearing a shirt from a university. But they have not seen him in two days."

"Then why," Harry said, "do they think he's there?"

"A woman said she saw him leave and return, leave again and return, two times."

"How did she know who it was?"

"I told you," the Somali said, "the one who wears the univer-sity shirt appears. He leaves. Now she doesn't see him. But when the same one returns now he is in traditional clothes. He goes out, he comes back."

Harry said, "How does she know he's the same one who left?"

The Somali said, "He returns to drive away in the car with its side destroyed."

"Are you sure it's the same BMW?"

"Yes, and the one who lives in this place and owns the car has disappeared."

"Why is talking to you," Harry said, "like trying to solve a fucking puzzle?"

His boys had taken a look at the apartment house mailboxes in the foyer and came back with ten names of Frenchwomen, two Frenchmen they said they had heard of, and one American or Englishman by the name of Hunter Newhouse on the third floor, 303. Harry imagined Jama meeting Hunter in a bar, they talk, get along, Jama desperately needing a place to stay. Hunter, a gentleman and scholar, offers his flat and soon thereafter disappears. If Harry alerted the police to a missing person, he would complicate the ultimate solution, shooting Jama.

He wished he had a bunch of khat to graze on. And told himself *no*. Stay up to the task with another snort of crystal meth.

Harry had made up his mind, the moment he set eyes on Jama he would shoot him. Place the Somalis on each side of the door. One of them raps on it and moves out of the way. Harry would stand facing the door. Jama opens it half asleep . . . Or stand back from it. He thought it might be a wide hall in a building as old as this one.

The PPK in his hand, the safety off. The door opens . . .

He could say something to him.

You know why I'm here, old sport.

But Jama could be holding a pistol, couldn't he? Awakened in the middle of the night . . .

You don't say a fucking word, Harry told himself. You see him and shoot him. That's it.

"What if when I knock on the door," one of the Somalis said, "he doesn't open it? He asks who is it, what do I want?"

He heard four raps on the door in the living room, loud, and opened his eyes. No voice came following the raps, like the custom of police at home. Announce themselves and bust down the door. If it wasn't cops it could be al Qaeda.

Jama rolled out of bed in his Levi's and sneakers, the way he slept now, and brought out his Walther from under the sheet. He shoved four 9-mm magazines into his jeans from the night table. Slipped a shirt on over his head and picked up his flight bag from the foot of the bed. He was in the living room when they banged on the door again, Jama sure there'd be a few of them in the hall packing AKs or Uzis, al Qaeda deadheads serving the contract on him.

He opened the door, swung it open and caught the edge of it in his left hand. He put the Walther on the Somalis and shot each one and shot them again, seeing only one other one left. Jesus Christ, Harry. Harry fired, Jama fired. Both missed. They weren't ten feet apart. Both in a hurry fired again, both moving this time. Jama backed into the room and swung the door closed. He released the Walther's magazine, two left, and shoved a full load into the grip. He looked through the door's peephole and saw Harry standing against the opposite wall holding his gun out in both hands to shoot. Jama believed if he swung open the door Harry would fire and he'd step in the doorway and shoot him. Jama felt the trigger-pressure of his means of staying alive. He looked through the peephole again but didn't see Harry, or know which way he'd gone, right or left. He had a fifty-fifty chance of seeing him or getting shot in the back.

Jama said, "Shit," and opened the door. He'd of been right: there was Harry, only down at the end of the hall by the EXIT sign. So Jama went in the bedroom with his gun and his bag, stepped out the window to the fire escape and ran down it, riding that bottom section as it swung down. He went around to the front of the building and watched the entrance. After a few minutes he stepped into shadow and watched the street. Pretty soon he saw headlights pop on. Then off. A few minutes went by and they popped on again. Now the car was coming from the next block, picking up speed. Jama held the Walther in one hand, stepped out to stand in profile to the Bentley coming at him and fired four shots through the windshield and got to the sidewalk to see the car still coming, Harry firing from his window right-handed. The car swerved to miss trash cans and kept going, Jama watching it, wondering, Jesus, what's Harry on?

"I had my beaters out," Harry told Idris the next morning, "scouring Djib for the scoundrel, and he's not two streets away from us all the time. You didn't hear the shooting last night?"

"I was out," Idris said, laying clothes on the bed to be packed. "I took Dara and Helene to dinner."

"This was two in the morning," Harry said.

"We went to a club for dancing, after."

Harry said, "I had every intention of running him down with the Bentley."

"It arrived?"

"Yesterday morning. I started for him, I wanted to run over him, and he put four nines with that German gun of his through my windscreen, but into the left side, forgetting the Bentley is a right-hand-drive motorcar."

Idris said, "So you failed to shoot him."

"You have to imagine," Harry said, "how quickly this was happening. He did shoot the Somali lads with me, upstairs at his door."

"You shot at him?"

"Of course," Harry said. "We both seemed a bit anxious, exchanging shots in the hall. He went down the fire escape while I was hurrying to get the car. I saw him come out of the building and drove directly at him, flooring the Bentley and shooting from the window. When I missed again I kept going. It was that or stop to reload. But I did have him on the run."

"Now what?" Idris said.

"This isn't really my game," Harry said, "I'll probably leave for England in the next couple of days." He sat down to watch Idris packing.

"How was Dara, in good spirits?"

"She's always herself," Idris said.

"Which is to say what?"

"She keeps her eyes open, knows what's going on."

"I'm reasonably certain I could have got on with her," Harry the Sheikh said, "had my mind not been occupied by Jimmy Jama."

"You mean the price on his head."

"Well, that too."

CHAPTER THIRTY-ONE

I DON'T RECALL," BILLY SAID to Xavier, "if I told you I'm blowing up the gas ship tomorrow."

"I heard you were thinkin about it but nobody had an idea of when. You must have a good reason you want to get to it."

Billy said, "I'd like to hit the fucker while she's sitting there in the stream."

The two were stretched out in lounges on the hotel's sea-level pool deck, watching ships pass in the distance barely moving. Billy had on blue bikini briefs, his stomach trying to hide them, his hair a month wilder than when they'd met. Xavier thought Billy was cool in his way, how he knew everything and believed he could shoot up a highly combustible ship and not worry about getting away.

Xavier had on his silk-looking skimpy green trunks.

Billy had his binoculars resting on his stomach and a local map of the Golfo de Tadjoura, both of them smoking Billy's Havanas. Xavier liked the way Billy made judgments, cool about it in a way Xavier didn't understand, but most often was right how he saw it.

"So you think you'll do it tomorrow," Xavier said.

"I'll light up the sky tonight about dusk. Hit her in her sweet spots and take off. The weather's suppose to be like it is today."

"Hit it with your double-barrel rifle?"

"Firing armor-piercing incendiary rounds. You'll see a sight you won't forget."

"I can watch," Xavier said, "without leavin my lounge?"

Billy raised his binoculars.

"*Aphrodite* is sitting about twelve miles off, the other side of those islands, the Mouchas, I always thought a good place for pirates to lay in wait. Not anymore. There thirty, forty navy ships in these waters now."

"I was talkin to Idris," Xavier said, "after Dara spoke to him. He called to say good-bye. Said he wasn't sure what he would do now. Pirates shot and killed the Syrian captain of a Panama-flagged ship off Mogadishu. Idris thinks it'll bring enough heat to put the pirates out of business before long."

"He's hanging on by his fingernails," Billy said, "waiting for somebody to offer him a job."

"I told him," Xavier said, "he could always go back to sellin guns to warlords, once he does his R & R in Paris. I'm not gonna worry about Idris."

"He called Dara this morning?"

"Around nine," Xavier said.

"You had something you wanted to say to him, so she handed you the phone?"

Xavier turned his head to look at Billy staring at the gas ship through his binoculars. Xavier said, "Dara put the phone on the table and got back in bed." Xavier paused. "See, then I picked up the phone and talked to him."

Billy said, "You were staying there?"

"In the same suite?" Xavier said. "No, I had my own." He let a few moments pass. "But happened to be with her when Idris called. You got it straight now?"

"I had an interesting call," Billy said, "from the other Gold Dust Twin. Harry said he was wondering could he hitch a ride with us, we happened by any chance to be going up the Red Sea. You understand what he's doing?"

Xavier said, "Jama could be waitin for him at the airport. Harry wants to slip away in your boat."

"He said he'd get off at Suez. That is, unless I'm going on to Great Britain. That's what he called it. I told him we won't know where we'll be for a few days. I'm assuming," Billy said, "we'll be delayed. But once we're free to go we'll be heading toward the rising sun."

"Keep on round the world," Xavier said. "That takes pluck, man."

"Well, I've never been accused of lacking it."

He was quiet for a few minutes.

"Dara learned about the shooting last night from Idris."

"That's right."

"Then you talked to him."

"What you doin," Xavier said, "is beatin around to find out did I spend the night with Dara. You think I did?"

"It's none of my business," Billy said. "I'm only trying to get your story straight in my mind."

Xavier said, "It's best you don't try too hard."

THE FIRST THING DARA said was, "You win," once she settled down and was herself again. "Boy, did you."

"But I'm not takin your money, even if it was a bet. I'm not a paid escort," Xavier said, up on his elbow so he could look at her next to him, the room light still on, no time being wasted when they came in. "I had some help from my friend Horny Goat Weed. I'm admittin to you it wasn't all me."

Dara said in her drowsy voice, "You have any left?"

THEY WERE OUT ON the sea twenty-seven days alone and had flirted with each other some. They were in the hotel three days and did it with the light on.

Xavier went back to his suite thinking, Man, like he was ten years younger. Or even twenty years to the easy-does-it times. *Girl, what's your hurry? You heatin up on me? Take and put my fire hose on the job.* Breathing all that kind of cute shit in her ear.

He could not hear himself saying these things to Dara.

She'd had a few out clubbing, came back to the hotel to bang on his door and he knew looking at her it was gonna happen. She said, "Let's go to my room, okay?" Like she'd been thinking about it, seeing them doing it in her bed. It was fine with Xavier, feeling Horny Weed stirring in him. She was more girlish than he'd ever seen her, using moves on him, high—course she was high—but feeling good about it and being herself, he could tell.

This was the time and they let it happen, grooving to a big finish, and he thought, Now what? She gonna hide on me? No, she said, "You win."

After she came out of the bathroom, no longer girlish, she said, "I have to go back to bed, okay?" Putting on a face like she expected him to object. That's all it was, Dara being a tired little girl. Course she could come back to bed.

He wondered how it would work the next time.

You start thinkin about the future now, the first time in your life?

She looked around the bedroom for her nightgown talking about Idris and Harry's experience, Xavier staring at her naked, knowing she wasn't showing herself on purpose, for any reason, she was just letting herself show in a natural way.

That was a good sign.

Don't think about the next time. It would happen when it happened. Xavier, seventy-two years old thinking like a boy.

XAVIER AND BILLY HADN'T moved from the hotel pool.

"What I was wondering," Billy said, resting his glasses on his stomach, "if you ever served on an LNG tanker."

"I tell you I have," Xavier said, "I know the next question. I served almost a year on a LNG tanker called *Methane Princess* when I was a boy. Drove me crazy waitin to off-load, waitin for escorts, waitin for inspectors lookin for cracks in the tanks full of deadly gas sleepin there. I was a kid, I didn't like crewin on a ship wasn't movin."

Billy said, "The tanks sleeping, I like that," and said right away, "You know how a ship like that works?"

"We get to Lake Charles and tie into the lines suck the gas off. That's all I know. You let it leak, the air turns it to vapor. Water makes it a kind of mist you can see. Somethin touches it off and you got the biggest maritime explosion in history."

"I've been thinking," Billy said, "of asking you to join my crew."

"Who's your crew, Helene? You don't need a seaman, you aren't goin no place after."

"I shoot holes in the five tanks and say '*Go,*'" Billy said, "I want a seaman at the helm of a Donzi to get us out of there."

"While they shootin at you, all the surveillin they have around a gas ship?" Xavier said, "A Donzi, huh?"

"One day's work. Tell me what you want."

"You pay my bail?"

"You're making a movie with no clue I'm gonna blow the fucker out of the water. The networks hear about it, you make a fortune."

"I could film you," Xavier said, "tellin why you think you can blow up a two-hundred-fifty-million-dollar gas ship and get away with it."

"My man," Billy said, "I've got lawyers up the ying-yang. They'll show I acted with purely heroic intentions, took the only means to prevent a major catastrophe, sunk the ship while it's out of harm's way."

"You don't care if you kill the crew?"

"I'll give anybody still aboard ten minutes to abandon ship. We have fatalities other than al Qaeda, my lawyers will meet with the next of kin."

"How 'bout gettin brought up for murder, even if they bad guys?"

"Don't worry about it," Billy said.

"I won't, you say so," Xavier said. "I believe what you doin is workin through me to get to Dara, huh?"

Billy said, "You think she'll do it?"

Xavier knew she'd jump at it. He said, "I don't know, I'll talk to Dara, see if she thinks gettin put in irons'd be worth it. I'll find out how much she charges extra for goin to jail, keepin her from workin."

"Nobody's getting locked up," Billy said. "You're innocent bystanders making a buck. Tell her that. But I better tell her how I'll pierce the double hull with my high-potency rounds. Get the gas leaking out to pool, the ship's hull losing eighty percent of its tensile strength in five minutes and starts to come apart."

Xavier said, "Yeah . . ." like he understood what Billy was saying. It didn't matter, long as he knew the ship was gonna blow.

"We're upwind," Billy said, "the gas vapor seeping out away from us and the ship. I set it off with another explosive round, light it up and the fire gushes back to the ship."

Xavier said, "All hell break loose?"

"Like you've never seen in your life. The ship goes up with flames reaching six hundred feet into burning air. Makes the Hindenburg disaster look like a weenie roast. But don't tell Helene that. She cries every time she watches the zeppelin burn up."

Xavier said, "You seen this happen to a gas ship?"

"My information," Billy said, "comes from studies of LNG fire hazards, thermal radiation damage, impact scenarios, all by guys with PhDs in chemical engineering, the top names in the liquefied natural gas field."

"But you haven't," Xavier said, "actually seen a LNG gas ship set afire."

"It's never happened at sea. TV will be all over this one, but I'm not looking for credit. I squeeze the trigger, chemistry does the rest."

"All we do," Xavier said, "is watch, huh?"

"You're gonna see an explosion with a force of energy," Billy said, "fifty-five times more powerful than the bomb we dropped on Hiroshima."

BILLY GOT READY TO leave the pool, picked up all his papers and handed the binoculars to Xavier to keep an eye on the gas ship out on the horizon. "You see it move, call me. I'm having a Donzi 26ZF brought to the hotel pier, five hundred horsepower. Ready to go tomorrow." He said, "I'm gonna get some room service and take a nap."

Xavier watched him walk off, going to the glass doors to the hotel. He opened one and stepped back and now Xavier saw

Dara appear to stand talking to Billy, Billy doing the talking at first, Dara listening. Now Dara was talking, Xavier would bet setting him straight about something in her nice way. She even reached up to give Billy's cheek a pat. She came over to Xavier taking off the robe. Now he was looking at her in her yellow bikini showing her tan. Xavier remembered her tan lines last night, the light on. Now as she reached him he said, "That's the most clothes I've seen on you lately."

Dara bent over and kissed Xavier's mouth, Xavier looking at her lollies right there in the tiny bikini top. She stood up adjusting the bra, telling Xavier, "You know what Billy was doing? Hinting around, trying to get me to say we slept together last night. I *know* he thought I'd make up something, so I said, 'Yeah, we got it on and then went to sleep. What else you want to know?'"

"And you gave his cheek a pat."

"Did you like that?"

"Loved it," Xavier said. "Billy wants you on his go-fast boat when he blows up the gas ship. Wants you right there filmin it."

"Perfect," Dara said. "We won't have to rent *Buster* again."

CHAPTER THIRTY-TWO

Ubu Kalid, an assistant at Djibouti Marine, drove Jama in a golf cart out to the pier where several trawler yachts were tied up. He said, "This first one we see is the *Coaster 40*. It has two staterooms and is designed for comfort and not paying too much money."

Jama said, "How you know I speak English?"

"From words you use with Arabic. You say you don't want a fucking dhow, you want a small vessel with a cabin. I think *fucking* is a good word you can use different ways in speech, angry, being critical, or simply to say it. Or you want to show you have surprise, you say, 'What the fuck am I doing?' I know French since I was a boy. My boss say I have to learn English too, for doing business with Americans."

"I see you wear a white shirt and a necktie," Jama said, "dressed for business. Your glasses, good. Make sure your fingernails are always clean too." He said, "What's that one down there has orange trim on it?"

"Oh, *Buster 30*," Ubu said, on the pier now. "*Buster* is one tough little power cruiser. It has a Saab engine that will produce two thousand five hundred rpms a minute."

"What's that get you," Jama said, "ten knots?"

"If I tell you six and a half," Ubu said, "will you be disappointed? Two travelers were out in *Buster* for a month and return very happy with her."

"Tall black dude and a white chick name Dara? They friends of mine," Jama said. "Told me, take her out for a shakedown, she's all the boat you need."

Ubu said, "A shakedown?"

"A trial run. See she behaves, easy to maneuver around."

"But you want her only one day. This is for pleasure?"

"I'm taking my girlfriend out for a night cruise. See if we can set off some fireworks."

Ubu didn't like the sound of that.

"You mean explosions?"

Jama said, "No, man, like in the movies. Grace Kelly and Cary Grant are fuckin on the sofa and out the window you see the fireworks goin off, the same as what's happening in the room."

Ubu said, "They have fireworks, Grace and Cary?"

Ubu staring at him, trying to get it.

"Fireworks," Jama said, "you shoot off Roman candles, rockets that burst in the air, it's meant to be the same as fuckin, what the two major stars are doin the same moment. Does Grace get up and go in the bathroom? You know Cary Grant ain't wearin a slick. See, what should be the real part ain't even real."

Ubu frowning now, trying hard to understand.

Jama said, "Forget it," and went aboard with his bag over his shoulder. He wore his *kikoi* in the streets, his head scarf. He had on his jeans and a cotton jacket now, visiting Djibouti Marine. He stood on *Buster*'s deck watching Ubu coming from the golf cart with life jackets and Jama's cardboard box of provisions.

Jama went below to look around. He didn't care about any of it, the galley, the head; he'd be on the boat twenty-four hours, no more than that. Still, he kept looking. The mattress in the bow . . . He tried to see the two sleeping together. Couldn't do it. Not with that high-ass nigga, that old man. She was polite, didn't use any tone of voice on you. She'd give the old man some shit how he was her best friend, her buddy, her protector . . . her employee. He was pretty sure they'd cleaned the boat. He started looking in drawers. There were papers in one they'd missed, a pamphlet had her picture on it . . . He closed the drawer as Ubu came below wearing a yellow life jacket and the box of provisions he placed on the counter.

He said, "You know the rental charge for *Buster* is four hundred dollars a day."

"Let's get going. I'll pay when we get back."

"You have the rental fee?"

Jama reached in a back pocket and brought out his roll of bills. "You want your money?" He peeled off four hundred, said, "Here," and handed the bills to Ubu.

Ubu said, "Thank you, sir, for the fucking money," grinning at Jama.

THEY WERE OUT IN the Gulf of Tadjoura now, *Buster* chugging along. Jama said, "I want to see how close we can come to that ship." Jama had the wheel, pointing *Buster* toward the LNG tanker now.

Ubu had come in from the deck using his shirttail to wipe his glasses. He put them on and said, "No, you get close they tell you to give way, get away from the ship."

"You think we're being watched?"

"Yes, of course, from the sky. Soon a boat or a helicopter approaches you don't turn away."

Jama cocked the wheel and they headed off to starboard.

He said, "I don't have to be too close. I phone a cell number and the ship blows up like that, *boom*. Becomes the biggest fire you ever saw in your Arabian life." He saw Ubu thinking but didn't know if he got it.

Yeah, he did. All eyes now.

"You going to blow up the LNG ship?"

"And haul ass out, man, fast as this love boat'll go."

"You don't return *Buster* to us?"

"If I have time."

"I become fired from my job."

Jama saw panic setting in and cut the engine. He said, "Let's go out on deck while it's quiet," and pushed the young guy in his shirt and tie, his clean glasses, saying, "Go on. I'm right behind you." Ubu stepped out of the wheelhouse and Jama came after him, taking his Walther from the bag hanging on his shoulder.

Ubu stood on deck looking toward the LNG tanker, more than a mile to port now, Jama waiting for him to see the gun pointing at him.

"I'm taking the boat," Jama said, "but I don't need a deckhand. Nothing for you to do."

Ubu turned as Jama began talking and now had his eyes fixed on the gun, Jama thinking he'd start pleading for his life. No, he held on, this boy learning English, pushing his glasses up on his nose. He said, "I don't know why you want to shoot me. I don't do nothing to you. Are you a robber? Take the boat. There is nothing the company would expect me to do about it."

"You're doing good," Jama said. "Standing up 'stead of crawling on the deck to kiss my shoes, these Adidas given to me by a buddy of mine." He said, "You want to get off the boat, go ahead."

Ubu Kalid looked at the sea lying almost still in the fierce glare of the sun, and looked at Jama.

"I don't know how to swim."

"You don't have to, you float ashore on the tide."

"I don't know how to float."

"Lay your head back and relax your body," Jama said. "I never told you my name, did I?"

"Yes, Mr. Jama Raisuli."

"That's what I been going by. My real name's James Rus-*sell*."

"Rus*sell*," Ubu said, "that's a good fucking name."

Jama pushed him over the side. He watched him fighting the water and yelled at him, "Be cool, Ubu. Take it easy." He saw the boy looking up at him, eyes staring in his glasses, trying to calm himself now, Jama realizing, *Shit,* he'll never sink wearing the life jacket. He put the Walther on the jacket, right below the kid's face, and shot him twice.

He'd use the boat hook to pull him alongside. Get the jacket and the four bills he'd paid him.

HE HAD TO SHOOT him. Couldn't let him drift off. He wanted to say something like, Don't take this personally. You're a witness, that's all. It had nothing to do with the kid knowing his real name. *Then why'd you tell him?* He thought the kid ought to change his. Ubu. That wasn't a name for a man spoke pretty good English. *Why'd you tell him?* Jama told himself. Because he knew he'd have to shoot Ubu and wanted to have a good reason. Man, everybody knew his name by now. He'd have to change it. Get it done while he was still in Djibouti, passport with a different name, like Hunter. He knew of people in town forged things like that.

Find Dara next. Settle with her.

After. Once he blew the ship. He was here to blow it and he would. Said, *You can write that down,* to himself. See to Dara after. He didn't know yet how he'd find her but he would. Right now he was heading the *Buster* toward that big hump of coral sticking up out of the gulf, the main Moucha, the daddy.

HE'D BROUGHT BANANAS AND a sack of dates, a gallon jug of water, cheese, pita bread and a fresh bunch of khat he chewed to stir up scenes of Celeste loving him all over his body. He fell asleep and opened his eyes to sunlight. But by the time he'd eaten the same things for breakfast—dates, he'd never had one before he was over here—clouds were coming in low, streaks of clouds, parts of them gray. He wanted to look around, see where he was.

Buster was tied to a branch in a cove full of mangrove on the south side of Big Moucha. He'd seen outboards along the beach, people standing in water up to their ankles. Jama pulled the dinghy off *Buster* and paddled through an aisle in the mangrove that took him to a strip of beach and a view of the other side: a row of cabanas on the beach, people sitting under thatched palm umbrellas, looking at the sky. He knew this Moucha was popular with scuba divers. Get in the water and mess with reef sharks and manta rays. There was a gang of dive boats, tarps shading the decks and dive platforms on the stern, the ones on deck looking down through clear water, Jama believed, at divers fucking with the fish. Now he watched a girl step off the platform and thought if he was a shark, man, he'd nip off her rack for appetizers. He could hear their voices, words coming in

French and some English, now they were laughing. Jama wondered for four seconds could he make up a story and join them, *How y'all doin?*

And one turns out to be a scuba-lovin cop never forgets a face from a poster.

Best follow this beach around and look for the highest part of the island. Least thirty feet off the sea. Then go on back to *Buster*. Chew some khat and see if he could get Dara to show some life. He'd sleep till it started to get dark.

What woke him up at four thirty in the afternoon, got him standing to look out past the mangrove, was the sound of a big outboard coming this way.

CHAPTER THIRTY-THREE

XAVIER REMEMBERED DONZIS FROM offshore powerboat
racing. Cowes to Torquay along the south coast of England.
He saw a race one time waiting on a ship. The Donzi Billy
got hold of was different than the racing Donzis, this one an
open-cockpit twenty-six-foot speedboat with two big Mercury
outboards turning out 225 horsepower each. It reared up and
flew when Billy let it out; Billy and Helene at the controls behind
the high windscreen; Dara and Xavier in the bow with their
camera.

Dara felt the trip starting out like a midweek excursion.
Helene brought a hamper of hotel appetizers, dozens of oysters
on ice, fruit and cheese, pastries—napoleons, Billy's favorite—
Cokes and a half-dozen bottles of champagne. A snack, for the
few hours they'd be on Île Moucha.

Billy heading them out of Djibouti straight for the island's
southeast corner, Pointe Noire, the *Aphrodite* at anchor less than
five miles from the island. Billy said, "Muff, why don't we break
out a bottle for the trip, drink a toast to our destiny."

Dara and Xavier gave each other a look but kept quiet.

Once they were in sight of the island Billy said, "What you see is a big pile of coral less than two miles wide but with a weird shape to it. Picture a wolverine in profile biting a seal standing straight up, in the crotch."

Helene said, "A wolverine . . . ?"

"That's the shape of Big Moucha I see on my map," Billy said. "Bends around on itself with a bay taking up the center of the island." Billy said, "Muff, let me have that one for the cockpit and open another bottle for all hands, the drinking lamp is on." He swigged from the bottle and said, "Any green you see is mostly mangrove. Xavier, you know what those stunted trees are?"

Xavier said, "I believe they bushes tryin to act like trees."

"We're advised to bring our own water," Billy said. "Tourists pay forty-five bucks to come out here and sit under a thatched umbrella, have a few drinks and fall asleep. They wake up and go back to Djib." Billy raised his glasses to scope the beach. "Not many out today, or they've gone home. Army people come out and stay forty-eight hours."

Xavier said to Dara, "The man could be a tour guide."

"Talkative," Dara said. "On his second bottle already."

THEY CIRCLED BIG MOUCHA to see what it was all about, up the east side and around north to Pointe du Scorpion, Billy reading from his map, Xavier shooting landscapes and thatched umbrellas along the beach. They passed the mouth of a bay to Plateau du Grand Signal and around to the south side of the island, not much to see but a few cabanas, until they approached a cove full of mangrove, the big Mercury outboards rumbling on low power.

Something white caught Dara's eye and she said, "Billy, stop," Dara standing now in the bow, her hand on Xavier's shoulder.

Billy said, "You want me to come about?"

"I swear I just saw the *Buster*," Dara looking back toward the cove.

Billy raised his voice circling out to come around, saying, "I imagine you'd know her after a month aboard. But there a bunch of those little trawlers come out of Djib."

"White with orange trim," Xavier said. "It sure looks like her." Xavier was shooting the boat now, tucked in among the mangrove.

"This is the closest I can get," Billy said. "You want to get out and look at her?"

Dara thought about it and shook her head. "I was surprised, that's all. It could be the *Buster,* but so what. It's somebody scuba diving."

Xavier said, "In a mangrove swamp?"

JAMA'S SISTER TOLD HIM when she was a little girl, a good ten years before she turned to prostitution, "You pray for what you want, and if God likes the idea of you havin it, he gives it to you." He remembered thinking it might be true. The thing was, Jama never prayed for anything and always got what he wanted.

It was Dara standing up in that speedboat, wasn't it? See, he didn't have to pray to find her again. There she was.

He said to his sister that time when she was a child, "If God knows everything, what's he do when you pray for something, have to change his mind sometimes?"

His sister said, "God knows everything all at the same time. Knows you gonna pray and knows if you getting it or not. But when you pray and you get it, it makes you feel good, God wanting you to have it from the beginning of eternity." His little sister who turned to hookin.

He believed she was right. Jama got everything he wanted and thanked Allah for it after. Least most of the time.

There was Dara out cruising.

He'd bet money they saw the boat and recognized it. They might even've caught a glimpse of him in the wheelhouse. If any of them did, it would be Dara. He believed they both wouldn't mind getting next to each other for a time. Right now he'd best take his gear and the rubber boat and go someplace else.

THEY WERE STILL IN the Donzi, sucking oysters off the half shells now, Billy swigging champagne from the bottle, Dara having a Coke. Xavier helped himself to the champagne, have a glass or two.

Billy said, "I'm not going near the target till I'm ready. Sneak up with the wind behind us—what there is of it—and put a round each into her five tanks. In other words I'm gonna shoot the ship." He gave his crew time to grin or say something. No one did. Billy said he would put hot rounds in her from close on a thousand yards. Get the gas seeping out to thaw in pools. In a few minutes there'd be the biggest fireball ever seen by man. He raised his bottle of champagne and took a good swig.

Helene said, "Hon, I think our guests would like some too."

"I'm sharing with my man Xavier," sounding offended. "Muff, you know I'm a dead shot, even with a glow on." He said, "Aren't I?"

Helene hesitated but said, "You sure are, Skip."

Billy went back to sit low in the cockpit and Dara said to Xavier, "You haven't said anything funny since we got here."

Xavier said, "Billy looked at me, gave me time to ask him, 'You say shoot the ship or shoot the shit?'"

"But you didn't."

"I don't need a straight man. What I been wonderin is how I feel about bein here."

"You don't see it as a big finish?"

"What of?"

"My documentary. I'm starting to get ideas."

"You don't see any holes?"

"This setting," Dara said, "it's a world where we fill holes with cuts to the Central Market, the mosque, women pecking out of their burkas, and see if we can build tension. If the explosion comes off anywhere close to Billy's description, we'll have a hot property."

Xavier sat there not saying anything, and Dara said, "What are you thinking?"

"What you're makin of all this. Wonderin could Jama be here with the same idea as Billy."

Dara said, "I'm wondering how he meant to blow it up."

"I thought about it for a while," Xavier said, "but the man's on the dodge. How's he gonna work it?"

"He's still al Qaeda," Dara said. "What else was he doing on the ship?"

Billy stepped into the bow to tell them, "Minutes after I fire, we could have gunboats chasing our wake. What I'm hoping, everybody's off the ship before it turns into a ball of fire. If the gunboats don't know that, they could start looking for survivors, people in the water."

Xavier said, "Or the vapor catches fire and runs off the gunboats." He said, "I'm goin ashore, maybe look up anybody still around."

Dara said, "You're gonna check out the *Buster*, aren't you?"

Xavier said, "I'll let you know if it's ours."

◆ ◆ ◆

BILLY WAS IN THE cockpit on the phone talking to Buck Bethards, telling him what they were up to.

Dara in the bow said to Helene, "Why doesn't he go shoot the fucking ship and quit talking about it?" She was having a glass of champagne, promising herself just one.

"He doesn't think it's dark enough yet." Helene lowered her voice to say, "Listen, I hate to tell you but he isn't a deadeye when he's ripped. I worked up my nerve and told him he can't hit shit and he knows it. Billy goes, 'If I can't hit a tanker a thousand feet long with my eyes closed . . .' He had to stop to think of something. I said, 'Well, if you can't, you gonna quit drinking or shooting?'"

Billy's voice came from the cockpit to tell them, "He hasn't located the guy yet, but he's onto a lead looks good."

"He's got Buck trying to find Jama," Helene said. "Billy thinks it's funny, his ace gets popped by the guy he's looking for."

Dara said, "If Billy's not sober enough to shoot, I mean at the gas ship—"

"I don't know if he wants to now," Helene said. "He'll change his mind, but doesn't want to look like a wimp and it's too late to get out of it. Billy and his big mouth. He's even told me, like during tender moments while we're doing it? He says sometimes he talks too much. I want to tell him, 'Jesus, will you shut up?'"

"Let's see what happens," Dara said.

XAVIER FOLLOWED THE BEACH hiking over coral north but mostly west to the cove they'd seen earlier in the Donzi. He crossed the cove's entrance, water to his waist, worked his way in and there was *Buster* in the mangrove, knowing it was his and Dara's *Buster* once he got close enough to see marks he recognized on the gunnel, the wheelhouse glass discolored, turning yellow. He could tell Dara believed it was the *Buster* the way her hand had gripped his shoulder. It was all right, she had no reason to visit the boat. But he did.

Xavier wanting to look for something he forgot, might still be aboard in a drawer.

He stepped up on the deck, ducked into the wheelhouse and stood looking down the ladder. He raised his voice to ask, "Anybody home?" Waited and said, "Permission to come aboard? This *Buster* is an old friend of mine."

No sound came from below.

Xavier took his time on the few steps of the ladder, ducking his head, then raising it to see all the way to the mattress in the bow, no one aboard, *Buster* didn't look like she'd been cleaned. Xavier said, "Well, let's see if it's here." Something he thought he'd packed but wasn't in his bag at the hotel: literature about Dara and her movies he'd kept right here in a drawer. Opened the drawer and saw pages of Dara's notes, changes she wished she'd made in pictures released years go. Dara looking back when she made those notes. Looking ahead now to make something of these bad boys she'd met.

The literature, a publicity folder with her pictures, wasn't in the drawer. He knew he'd put it there and if the boat hadn't been cleaned, who took it? Djibouti Marine people?

He turned to leave thinking of good times aboard, a month of leading up to their getting to it. He'd experience a feeling for when it was time to become intimate again. Wait for Dara, movie scenes on her mind, to show signs of turning horny. He saw the life jacket on a seat and a box of some groceries on the table. He pulled the seat out and saw two holes in the jacket and bloodstains. Blood all over the inside of the jacket.

Where was the one brought the groceries?

Where was the rubber dinghy?

FROM ACROSS THE COVE in cover, Jama watched Xavier board the trawler and come out after a while and stand on the deck looking around, holding the life jacket Ubu had been wearing.

Man, you plan your moves and somebody comes along to fuck you up. He hadn't seen the life jacket as a problem. Or Ubu. They'd fish him out of the water one of these days . . . Yeah? What did Ubu or the life jacket have to do with him?

He watched the high-ass nigga thirty yards from him going out to the beach, stopping now to look at something, footprints? Showing the Reebok's tread? He could shoot him. Run up calling for him to wait and take him out with one shot. They hear it and say what was that? Come looking for Xavier and he'd have to shoot all three, pick them off or walk up firing at them. Even Dara, without talking to her first. Maybe have to come back and go through this whole fucking drill again. What if the tanker wasn't here? Got moved someplace and he couldn't find it?

Let the high-ass nigga go. Catch up with him later on. More clouds were blowing in, making the look of the island dismal. Be dark early. Another hour, that's all. Make the phone call and watch the ship blow up. Go to all this trouble—he had to see it happen and thought, They'd see it too, wouldn't they?

For the first time he wondered about something should've been on his mind. What were these people doing out here popping champagne corks a few miles from the gas tanker?

◆ ◆ ◆

XAVIER WAS BACK, EVERYBODY ashore now sitting under one of the thatched umbrellas. They had dessert left, no more oysters, and the last bottle of champagne not yet opened. Xavier showed them the vest with bullet holes and the blood. Said he didn't see anybody but he might've been seen.

He said to Dara, "I know what you thinkin."

Dara said, "He's al Qaeda, he blows up ships."

"So does Billy," Xavier said. "He must be with the Republicans' al Qaeda."

Billy said, "You gonna tell me what that means, the whites' al Qaeda?"

"I doubt it means anythin but sounds like it does. The one on the *Buster* saw us or he wouldn't be hidin out now. Has his dinghy , , , I think he forgot his groceries and jug of water."

Billy said, "Or he doesn't want to be seen by anyone on the island. He could be an escaped convict, if they have any around here. Your *Buster* doesn't have a thing to do with our venture. I say let's get the show on the road. Muff, my weapon, please, and my vest with the hot new loads. I mean the new *hot* loads. It could be construed as hot because they're new, and I don't mean that."

Xavier listened and was patient, seeing he'd have to take the man's gun, but at the right time. He still wanted to see the show.

JAMA FOUND HIGH GROUND where it rose on the other side of the bay, inland, the coral getting piled up over thousands of years of tides, maybe thirty feet above the gulf. It should be high enough to make his call. Coming here he saw who had to be army people on the island. Girls with tats coming out of their bikinis, one with a fish jumping up her arm. Girls from pokey towns come over to where everything's the opposite and got their bodies fucked up with drawings. It took him ten minutes to get up to the high ground and he saw *Aphrodite* way out there. A spotlight from the ship's bridge shining down on the five LNG tanks.

Qasim hadn't known what the shape charges would do to frozen gas. Rip it open, thaw it out quick with the heat from the blast? Qasim said if you were closer than three miles it could burn your skin. He said oxygen in the air kept the fire burning. Could blow this way or that. Have to be careful it doesn't come at you.

Any of the GI chicks happen to stroll by, he'd say, "Want to see what the end of the world's gonna be like?" They weren't too bad-looking for girls you run into on an island ten miles from the end of the line. Tattooed white girls drinking Cosmos, checking him out. He'd tell them to look at that ship out there all lit up. "See what happens I point my finger at it, the kind of power I have?" His other hand in his pants touching the cell number committed to his memory. He points at the ship saying, "Be gone," and the motherfucker explodes. The GI chicks freak.

If he tried to pull out tonight he'd be in open water two hours, searchlights swiping at him to pin him down. The best thing was to stay on the island. Wipe *Buster* clean and hang with the GI chicks. Tell them he worked on the base doing translations. Wear his Brown University T-shirt and recall some of Hunter's bullshit about college days. Get the GI chicks on his side, he'd be home.

Jama told himself to pay attention now, looking out at the lit-up ship. You ready to make the call? He believed he was.

◆ ◆ ◆

"LET HER DRIFT NOW," Billy said, "correcting enough to give me clear shots from the port side of the bow. I say go, you cut to starboard in a half circle and we'll be tying up at the Kempinski dock ten minutes later, assuming we get sixty out of these Mercs. The only trouble, ships'll be coming out of Djib and put their spots on us. I'll slow down and wave and ask the officer hanging over the rail what that big explosion was. Muff'll be looking up at the ship and her captain. This officer asks too many questions, I say, 'Lemme talk to your skipper.' Loved destroyers, we called him Tin Can Courtney. Or whatever his name is."

Xavier said, "What if it's Jackabowski?"

"He'd be down in the engine room," Billy said. "We get stopped again, don't worry, I'll handle it."

Xavier said, "You want to steer for a while?"

"No, I'm ready to shoot. The gun's loaded. I fire both barrels, open the breech and the Muffer slips in two more high-explosive rounds. I fire, hit two more pods and that might be plenty." Billy was holding the Holland & Holland in his firing position.

Muff said, "Can we practice doing it, Skipper?"

Billy lowered the rifle and opened the breech. Dara, eye to her camera, tripped and fell against Billy as Muff grabbed the rifle, jacked it closed, put it against her shoulder and fired the six-hundred-caliber Nitro Express rifle at the gas tanker.

IN THIS MOMENT, JAMA holding the cell in front of him, pressed the final digit of the twelve numbers he knew by heart . . .

And the gas ship exploded five times.

Jama, looking right at it, said, "Jesus," awed by the sight and the air-splitting sounds, rocking *boom*s like none he'd ever heard, waves of heat coming at him from the inferno he'd set off.

THE ELEPHANT GUN KICKED Helene hard, slammed her into Billy's arms to see the sky on fire, Helene saying in a murmur, "I hit the ship?"

Billy said, "Who else?"

Her shoulder killing her, she groaned, saying, "Really, I hit it?"

Billy told her, "Look at what you did, Muff."

The fire rising in a fury to sweep over the tanks to the stack of decks in the stern, fire climbing to cover the bridge. Now gas was oozing out of the hull's broken plates to form vapor pools that ignited and burst into fireballs, exploding in the clouds hanging low over the *Aphrodite,* the ship consumed by its cargo, burning to death.

Billy saw the vapor cloud coming toward them on the water and yelled at Xavier, "Go, for Christ sake. *Now.*"

Xavier powered up and kicked the Donzi into the arc of a circle, Dara turning to keep her camera on the fire, and he got the Donzi around to do what Billy wanted: planing out of there at sixty miles an hour to be home in ten minutes.

Being good citizens it took them almost a half hour, slowing down when navy patrol boats came out of the dark to put spotlights on them. They were looked over till Billy got on his bullhorn.

"We have an injured young woman aboard who needs medical attention. In severe pain with a separated shoulder. Hurts like hell."

They took off again and Billy said, "Muff, lemme have a look." He got her in kind of a headlock, Muff screaming, Dara shooting the procedure, and Billy yanked her shoulder back in the socket. "We'll get an X-ray, have you taped up. You'll be left-handed for a while, but I don't think it'll interfere with anything. I'll help you put your clothes on, help you take them off . . ."

Helene was quiet now, smoking a cigarette. She said, "I can't believe I did it."

"You only blew up a thousand-foot tanker with one shot," Billy said, hugging and kissing Helene trying to hold him off. "Only you can't tell anybody you did it, Muff, or we could get thrown in jail."

"Nuts," Helene said.

Dara got close to Xavier in the cockpit, wind whipping past them. She said, "Muff didn't come close to hitting that ship."

"Aimin at the sky when she fired," Xavier said. "Now you gonna say, I told you. They somebody else settin off explosions."

Dara looked like she was thinking about it. "If I use the scene in a feature, does it seem too much of a coincidence? He blows it up as Muff fires?"

"You want to change what happened?"

"No, but I have to make it believable."

"You still aren't sure it was him."

"I know it was," Dara said.

"We don't see him do it."

"But we know he's on the island."

JAMA WOULD STAND HERE watching the fire till it went out, man, the weird shapes it was taking, but an idea hit him and it was a honey. A way to get shuck of the boat. Try to keep it hidden, the navy'd come ashore and find it soon enough. People coming to investigate what happened. He'd push it free of the mangrove to the open sea. Start the engine, aim it at the ship on fire, set the pilot and jump off. Watch *Buster* head out there to get burned up.

CHAPTER THIRTY-FOUR

FROM THE COVE JAMA climbed over the island again to the beach facing east. Five young white folks, three girls and a couple of dudes, were watching the ship out in the dark still burning away. Jama walked up in his Brown University shirt, bag over his shoulder, asking, "Was that the most intense fire you ever saw in your life?" He said, "Hi, I'm Hunter," like a movie star doing an ad on TV. "Man, that fire was burnin crazy, shootin up to the sky . . . What you suppose set it off?"

All these GI people, keyed up but feeling no pain, were still in their swimsuits drinking beer. One of the dudes being cool said, "It was a combustible gas tanker and it combusted. They can do that."

Jama said, "Yeah, but something set it off."

The other dude said, "Sparks, man. Prob'ly some asshole smoking."

A chick with *Jackie* tattooed blue and red on her shoulder said, "I got ten bucks says it was al Qaeda."

Jama liked this Jackie, blond hair and a cute nose. He'd bet she had pure-white titties in there, the rest of her tanned up good. He said, "I come here this afternoon on the water taxi. Took a six-mile hike around Moucha while y'all are havin fun at the beach. If I was to tell you I'm on a undercover assignment for the CIA, would you believe me?"

"And we're missionaries," Jackie said, "out here converting towelheads."

"They become Jesus-loving Christians," the dude thinking he was cool said, "or we shoot them. I don't know why we don't anyway."

"You don't believe I'm CIA?" Jama said. "All right, how about this? I was on a tanker full of gooks I couldn't speak a word to or get what they were saying, so I jumped ship."

"That's more like it," Jackie said. "They looking for you?"

"I doubt they even miss me."

Jackie said, "You poor guy, you want a Cosmo?"

THEY TOOK JAMA HIGHER up on the beach to a thatched-roof shelter, no walls, but beach chairs and all their stuff here: sleeping bags, ice chests half-full of beer, two bottles of vodka left and cranberry juice, Jackie making Cosmopolitans for the group. Jama said, "Y'all know how to live, don't you? You think I could join up, do my basic and get sent to Djibouti?"

"Put in for it," the dude thought he was cool said. "The assignment office goes, 'Jesus Christ, this guy wants duty in the asshole of the world.'"

"Hey," Jama said. "Don't you know I'm putting it on?"

Jackie said, "But you *were* on a ship full of gooks?"

"Learn Tagalog," Jama said, "or keep my mouth shut. I was on it and got off it. Tanker name *Manila Bay*."

By the time they saw lights coming in from the sea, the shelter was quiet, two of the girls asleep in lounge chairs.

Jama said, "I see the U.S. Navy's about to visit. Want to know did any of us happen to blow up that ship." He peeled off his Brown University T-shirt, rolled it up and stuck it in the bag with his pistol.

MARINES WITH SIDEARMS AND flashlights came in first, shining the beams over the group, stopping on bikinis, girls waking up with scowls, then pushing up once they saw the suits—not wearing suits, but that's who they were—no question in Jama's mind—behind the flashlights. One of them back there said, "You people are all air force?"

"Except Hunter," Jackie said. "He's with the CIA."

The invisible suit said, "Is that so? Which one's Hunter?"

Jama said, "I told her"—and got flashlights in his face—"I worked for the CIO, not the CIA, the labor people."

"What's it stand for?"

"Which?"

"CIO."

"Congress of Industrial Opportunists, the higher-ups, living off the sweat of their fellow man, probably never worked a shift in their life."

The suits in shirtsleeves talked among themselves. A voice said, "You're all air force?"

Still in their beach chairs they nodded, said yeah, the 449th, watched the flashlights sweep away to follow the suits leaving.

For a few seconds Jama caught sight of a man wearing a

baseball cap and Hawaiian shirt hanging out of his jeans. Saw him in a beam of light before he turned away. Jama got up and went to the edge of the thatch overhang. He didn't see him now, the beach full of navy people. He hadn't recognized the guy. It wasn't he was familiar, but looked out of place among the gang of investigators.

He thought of *Buster* in the mangrove. He'd better move if he wanted to get rid of her.

JAMA FOLLOWED THE BEACH south ducking patrol boats sweeping their spotlights over the coral with no idea—Jama believed— what they were looking for. He cut across the bend in the island to the south shore of the beach, quiet here, no boats messing up the dark, and came to the cove where he'd left *Buster*. In the wheelhouse when he saw Dara go by in the speedboat. Heard the boat circle back and saw her again. He was in water to his chest by the time he reached *Buster,* threw his flight bag in the wheelhouse and got to work untangling her from the mangrove. Once she was in the channel Jama pulled himself aboard.

The man in the baseball cap was waiting at the mouth of the cove, up on the bank holding a nickel-plate revolver on him. Some kind of tropical white flowers decorating the hem of his Hawaiian shirt, black flowers on the top part, black on black you could hardly make out.

Jama said, "That's a good-looking shirt you got on. How much it set you back?"

Buck Bethards said, "You don't remember me? I'm the guy you shot the other day at Marshal Foch Square."

Jama grinning at him now, slipped his hand inside the flight bag sitting on the wheelhouse table.

"That was you?"

"Gonna take you in this time," Buck said. "The hell you doing out here?"

"I blew up that tanker."

"You did, huh."

"Dialed a phone number and set it off."

"You're a real terror, aren't you?"

"I'm giving it up," Jama said, his hand on the Walther's grip. "You a cop or what?"

"I was military, now I'm on my own."

"You gonna shoot me?"

"I'm taking you to Djib on those homicides. Or I can check, see if there're warrants for a James Russell in the States."

"Rus*sell*," Jama said. "How much you want?"

"What I want is to see your hand come out of that bag."

"I'm getting a cigarette."

"Shame on you."

"Want one?"

"I quit. Listen, I want you to take your hand out of the bag before I count to five. Give you time to make up your mind. You don't, I tell my client you passed away on Gilligan's Island. Last seen taking a stroll."

Jama said, "Lemme tell you again. I blew up that ship with a phone call. I'm the same as you, man. They pay me to do a job, I do it." Jama said, "You mind if I bring out my cigarettes? Man, I have to see can I talk you out of this."

"I'll count to five," Buck said. "One . . ."

Jama let him get to three. He took the bag in his left hand and half-turned to sidearm it at Buck, Jama's right hand coming out with the Walther and shot Buck in the gut to relax him, cause him to sag, and shot him in the chest to kill him, from less than twenty feet. There was life in him for a few moments, his eyes open, looking at something he couldn't believe.

Shit, then had to go in the water again to get under Buck and dump him on the deck, the nickel-plate gone. Once Jama was aboard he started the engine and steered *Buster* deep into the cove and shut her down. Be for the next hour or so. He heard patrol boats out there and saw lights playing through the mangrove; the boats had too much beam to come in the channel. While he was waiting Jama dug Buck's passport and wallet out of his back pocket and dropped them in his bag. Look at them when he had some light. For now he kept the boat pitch-dark and sat there waving at mosquitoes. Finally asked himself, You going or not? Started the engine and putt-putted out of the cove.

It was too late to send *Buster* out to catch fire, *Aphrodite* looking almost burned out. What he did was start his own fire belowdecks, sloshed a can of gasoline around and dropped a match down the ladder, heard it go *wooosh* and *Buster* was on fire, her bow aimed at the hulk burning a few miles off. Jama put on his life jacket and hung his bag of personals against his chest to hold on to it. About a hundred yards out he set *Buster* on autopilot and slipped over the side.

CHAPTER THIRTY-FIVE

XAVIER CHECKED WITH DJIBOUTI Marine wanting to know who it was took out the *Buster,* while Dara met with the chief of police himself to hear what happened to the boat. Now they were in Dara's suite at the Kempinski exchanging what they'd learned.

"One of the young guys workin there, Ubu Kalid," Xavier said, "took this African out for a test run, see if he liked the boat."

Dara said, "Jama?"

"Sounds like Jama, but neither one of 'em came back."

"*Buster* caught fire," Dara said. "The chief thought at first she got too close to the gas tanker. But he said the feds told him no. Whoever stole the boat set it on fire."

"They could tell, huh?"

"They knew it wasn't the dead guy aboard."

"Wasn't Jama?"

"A white guy. The chief likes to make investigations social occasions when he can. We met at Las Vegas for lunch."

"Lunch meaning drinks."

"I had a gimlet, the chief three or four martinis," Dara said. "Would you like something?" He shook his head, Xavier on the settee in the suite's living room, Dara standing, moving around some, smoking a cigarette, looking cool in her white shirt and tan skirt for a change. Looking cool to Xavier anytime.

"The chief said he was white but looked like a colored man where the fire burned him. He smiled saying, 'I understand that's what you call Nigras in America.' No identification on him, but the FBI printed him. They'll find out who he is."

"You sound relieved," Xavier said, "it wasn't Jama? You need him for the movie?"

"He set fire to our boat," Dara said, exhaling a hard stream of smoke. "He shot the white guy twice and left nine-milli-meter casings in the wheelhouse. Police Chief Ali Zahara—I finally learned his name—said it will turn out to be the same weapon that killed Qasim and the four Somalis the time Jama escaped."

"So he's still roamin the land," Xavier said. "Maybe tryin to use the dead guy's ID."

"How can he? The guy's white."

"In a few days he can be black in the passport. If that's what Jama has. Djibouti, man, you can become anybody you want, long as you able to pay for it."

Dara came over and Xavier made room for her next to him.

"If he's in the film I want to know what happens to him."

"Wouldn't mind runnin into him again, huh? If you both still around, I think you can bet on him runnin into you. Find out you're stayin here, if he don't already know it. You want to give him a chance to find you?"

"Why's he after me, 'cause I know his name?"

"Even if you didn't. I think Mr. James Russell Raisuli's got the hots for you, girl. Likes the way you step out on the edge talkin to him," Xavier said. "You ever see *Hiroshima*? You haven't, have you?"

"That TV movie?"

"How we got around to droppin the A-bomb on Japan. The real Harry Truman's in it and you see an actor playin Harry Truman. I mean in key scenes where they don't have the real Harry Truman on film they use the actor. Understand what I'm sayin? The real Harry Truman and the one playin him come in and out of the movie, cuttin from one to the other in different scenes, and it works."

"The actor looks just like Truman?"

"Enough. Plays the piano."

Dara seemed to think about it, frowning some.

She said, "Who do you see playing Jama?"

LATER ON DARA WENT to Billy's suite to see how Helene was doing: Helene in bed, her upper right arm taped to her body, the hand sticking out of her camisole. Dara said it looked like it was growing out of her tummy.

"The room service guy," Helene said, "asks me how my hand's doing. I try to tell him it's not my hand, it's my fucking shoulder. I'm afraid the tape's gonna flatten my boobs. Billy says don't worry about it, we'll have them inflated. Billy doesn't have a doctor here so we're going home. Wait two days for Air France or hire a private jet to get us to Paris. He wants me to see a doctor in Houston he calls his bone guy. Billy separated his shoulder one time playing polo."

Dara said, "Fell off his horse?"

"This Mexican hit him from behind," Helene said, "because Billy was beating him."

"Too bad," Dara said, "you have to interrupt the cruise."

"Till I'm all better. I'll stretch it out as long as I can, see if I can develop complications. Billy said, 'When you fell off your bike, you got right back on, didn't you?' If he thinks I'm gonna fire that gun again, he's out of his fucking mind," Helene said. "He's down at the bar talking to the FBI again. They found out we were on the island, Billy told them yeah, having a picnic. We saw the ship explode and he got us out of there fast. This was the first time the FBI talked to him. They wanted to know why we had a Donzi for the trip instead of his yacht. He said they called *Pegaso* 'your pleasure boat.' Billy said he was thinking of getting a Donzi for fun and wanted to see what it was like. He can buy anything he wants, so they believe him."

"But they're talking to him again?"

"Billy said 'cause we're all they have, the only ones they know were at the scene. This time he's gonna tell them when they identify the guy who was shot, they'll find out he's Rolland Buck Bethards. Billy said they'll ask him how he knows and he'll tell them, because he hired Buck to find James Russell, aka Jama Raisuli. He'll tell them Jama, now, could be using Buck's name."

"Xavier thought the same thing," Dara said. "But how does Billy know the dead guy's Buck?"

"He hired him to find Jama, didn't he?" Helene said. "And I guess he did."

JAMA DID THE SIDESTROKE no more than twenty yards, put his feet down, found the bottom and walked the rest of the way to the beach. He had his bag, had his gun, had money, some he hadn't counted yet, the passport. He believed he could throw it away without looking inside. They'd ID the white dude and put his name on their watch list. He had to get dried off before he joined the gang at the grass house. Wouldn't that be something it was a real grass house? Get high waiting for the taxi. Whisper in Jackie's ear . . . think of something cool this soldier-girl never heard before. Or keep it simple, ask her she wants to fuck. He believed girls having tattoos on their body liked you to be direct.

He imagined taking his clothes off in the grass house and sitting there nekked waiting for the gang to wake up. Shit, leave the clothes on, they be dry soon.

Get to Djibouti and become one more nigga till he became somebody else.

CHAPTER THIRTY-SIX

XAVIER CROSSED THE ROOF to Dara's dining room and kitchen, stuck his head in the door and said, "Billy's on the webcam, and Muffie."

"Why didn't you call me?"

"I want to smell whatever you cookin."

Dara lived on the top floor, had her studio on the second floor, and kept the first floor full of movies, books and music, tapes of almost everything she'd ever seen since she was twelve.

It looked like she was getting ready to fix a trout, court-bouillon it in white wine, some spices. Or she might go meunière with it. No aromas yet, he followed Dara down the wood stairs to the studio, her big desktop Mac with a thirty-inch screen waiting on the worktable. "It's ready," Xavier said. Dara waved him over next to her and clicked the pad. Now Billy's face filled the screen.

"There you are," Billy said. "Xavier told us you cookin. What y'all havin?"

"You get home," Dara said, "you turn up your Texas sound?"

"I'm away from here too long, I start sounding like a Yankee."
He said, "Here's Muff," sat back in the sofa and there she was,
her hand sticking out of her blouse.

"Hey, y'all, I'm pickin it up too, being around this good ole
boy too long. As you can see, I'm still laid up, but nobody here
asks me how my hand's doing. They've all fallen off horses. You
know what he's gonna have me doing next?"

"Lemme guess," Dara said. "Riding?"

"Chasin after hounds. They do that here." Helene ran a hand
over her breasts. "This tape is itching me to death."

Dara watched Billy lean in saying something to her. Helene
punched him in a girlish way. "I think I'm marrying a sex
fiend."

"Where are you, still in Texas?"

"Near Houston. At one of Billy's winter places. The rest are
in other countries."

Dara said, "Xavier and I are trying to find a movie in all the
footage we've shot." She turned to him saying, "He wants me to
write a feature motion picture and make up stuff we don't have.
I still want to do the real thing, a documentary." She said to
Helene, "You remember Jama? I showed you shots of him in his
Brown University T-shirt?"

"Yeah, and I said he looks like Will Smith."

"That's right," Dara said, "you did," remembering it now.

"I bet Will Smith would sell his soul to dress up like an
Arab."

"What are you doing," Dara said, "besides healing?"

"Nothing much. Billy sent a crew to bring *Pegaso* home. But
we're not gonna continue the cruise right away, darn it."

"That's a shame," Dara said.

"He can be a meany sometimes," Helene said. "He knows
how much I love sailing around the entire fucking world."

Dara watched him say something to her again and Helene

hit him with her free elbow. "Billy kids around but he's sick over losing Buck. He says he was a stand-up guy I would have liked a lot."

"And respected," Billy said, "like a brother."

"You know I was talking to Buck," Dara said, "when Jama pulled up in the car and shot him."

"The first time," Billy said, "then shot him on the boat, twice. Xavier's right, you make this a documentary, how you gonna show all the action stuff happened you don't have?"

"Jama takin out five people with five shots," Xavier said, "one each. That's movies. But you have to shoot it. Dara can make a feature anytime she wants."

Billy said, "How much would it cost?"

"Fifteen million," Dara said, "below the line."

"That's like fixed expenses, the ones you know you gonna have," Xavier said. "The camera equipment, all the lights, the best boys and their grips and gaffers, the camera crew . . . What else? The pirate boats and people we use as extras."

Dara said, "We've got pirate boats."

"Not with actors in 'em. We have long shots we can use, the skiffs racin out to board some kind of vessel."

Billy said, "How much for actors?"

Dara said, "How much can you spend?"

Billy said, "I'm in the picture?"

"In this instance," Dara said, "if you put up the cost of the picture, you're the producer."

"What if I want to be in it?"

Xavier said, "Play yourself?"

"I bet I could do it," Billy said. He looked at his watch. "But right now Muff's due for a workout with her trainer. We'll talk at you later."

"He means my therapist," Muff said, rolling her eyes at Dara.

◆ ◆ ◆

DARA HAD A WHEELED cart with a glass top she used as a bar, bottles of different kinds of spirits, even a siphon for zapping the drink with a hit of soda, always on hand in sophisticated 1930s movies, sitting on the bar while William Powell stirred Myrna Loy's martini. Xavier couldn't recall Dara ever using the siphon, but saw it as a cool touch for a bar.

Ever since they got home they'd been talking about their movie, four days now: Xavier pointing out holes where good stuff was missing. Xavier telling her, Girl, you know how to make a feature, you've seen every one ever made.

This evening they were slouched at either end of Dara's tan corduroy-covered couch with its ochre and orange pillows. On the coffee table two glasses of after-supper port, hadn't been touched yet.

"I bet," Xavier said, "you can make a real movie without anyone in it sayin 'besides.'"

"Or waste time with backstories. What you see is what happened. We do have to hire a few stunt people. You know what holds me back, don't you? Making up an ending."

"You'll think of one. Beginnin, the pirates; middle, Djibouti stuff; end, maybe end it on that island, the ship burnin. Say the right words over it, Muffin blows up the tanker and stops al Qaeda from blowin up Djibouti. Lake Charles'd be better, save a port in the U.S."

"We're making a comedy?"

"Get the right girl to play Muff. All her lines she says straight, not puttin on anything. The audience can laugh, it's all right. But Muffin's real."

"I asked her who she saw as Jama."

"Will Smith. I heard her. He's Jama if you can pay him."

"He opens a picture," Dara said, "earns his money. Who do we see as Idris?"

"I was thinkin of a young Omar Sharif for one of them."

"He's too dark."

"Too serious."

"That's what I mean."

"You know who'd kill to play Harry?"

"Harry," Dara said.

"Man loves to act. You wouldn't have to direct him much."

"I'd have to hold him down," Dara said. "But he might not be bad. Harry wants to be known."

"We can get actors from over there, stars. One of the guys in Clooney's picture *Syriana*."

"The ship blowing up," Dara said, "is documentary footage."

"The black Toyotas," Xavier said, "crossin the desert from Eyl to Djibouti, what did Idris tell Jama? Qasim? What did Harry say to 'em. I think that trip can be a trip."

Dara was nodding. "It could move the plot."

"See the boys get out and take a leak."

"Talking to each other now," Dara said, "Idris and Harry."

"Where are they when the boys escaped. I bet they arguin."

"Harry's having a drink."

"They at a bar in the African part. Harry's nerves are showin." Xavier handed Dara a glass of port and picked up the other one. "I bet you go into Jama's backstory some. How he became a Muslim—"

"In prison."

"Most likely. Went over to Djibouti and got into jihads for al Qaeda. He can tell it in two lines."

"But not why."

"He don't even know why. He joined 'cause he's fucked up, likes to show off, fire guns at people, the sound. Loves it. That's as deep as he is," Xavier said. "You still thinkin doc-u-men-tary, start cuttin what you have, wishin you had things you heard about. In Bosnia wishin you had women gettin beat up by their hubbies for gettin raped. You got more of what you don't have in this one, you shoot it documentary."

"All right, let's say we're casting a feature."

"What we been talkin about."

"I write a script—"

"Scenes with Dara and Jama," Xavier said, "somethin stirrin between them. This other nigga's sittin on the sidelines; he wants to go home, but Dara decides to hang around, see what happens. She's reachin too far, gonna hurt herself."

"I fall for Jama?"

"Girl, he falls for *you*. You the star, he tells you everything you want to know about him and al Qaeda. You get me to watch him, he don't disappear on us. We go to that island 'cause he told you it's where he's blowin up the LNG ship from. Helene's the only one could play herself. She's been actin all her life. Billy, you won't have to pay him you let him do Billy. Idris and Harry, get a pair of young Arab stars."

"And who plays Xavier, the old seafarer," Dara getting with it, "some young buck?"

"Not too old, but never heard of Goat Weed."

Xavier got up from the couch with his glass of port. "If I'm spendin the night, you mind I use your shower?"

"I'd be grateful," Dara said.

"Who you see playin you?" He waited for her to tell him. Something she likely hadn't thought of. "You the lead," Xavier said. "There a lot of good women in the business gonna want this part. Watch that movie again, all the Italian chicks goin after Daniel Day Lewis. It's *Eight and a Half* with music and comes out *Nine*."

Going into the bathroom with his port he heard the phone ring.

A few minutes later Dara opened the door to the shower, Xavier filling the tiled space, body soaped, his face raised to the spray.

"That was a friend of Harry's. He's here to read for a part in a zombie picture. Would like to stop by and say hi."

"You have to read to play one of the undead?"

"All I know is Harry told him I make movies. He'll be here in a few minutes."

"What's his name?"

"Hunter Newhouse."

THE FIRST THING JAMA did he got to New Orleans, he phoned Coleman Correctional in Florida and said he was calling about a death in the family of one of their inmates, Tariq Bosaso, and gave them a number for Tariq to call, saying he was Hunter Newhouse, a lawyer representing the family.

Tariq called saying, "Who is this? Who's dead? I don't have no people anymore, all died on me."

Jama said, "You remember a boy read the Koran and could recite it from memory? Don't say my name."

"This is you speaking to me?"

"Home on leave from the *jihad*. You read about a gas ship blowing up off East Africa?"

"Man, it played on TV a week. Was al Qaeda done it?"

"Young fella name of James phoned the ship and she blew. You ever hear anything like that?"

"Come and visit me, I want to hear what you been doing."

"I will I have time. First I got to take care of bidness," James said. "Tell me where I get a piece in this town."

"What kind you need?"

"One I can slide out of my pants."

"Gonna cost you."

"I flew here first-class from Paris. Tell me where to get the gun and I'll tell you who I'm gonna shoot."

DARA'S BUZZER BUZZED AND she pressed the switch to open the door downstairs—two doors on Chartres, one for the first floor and the other for upstairs. She opened the door and looked straight down the stairway she would fall down in dreams until she'd won her first award. She saw a figure come in the same time Xavier called, "Dara . . . ?" She turned from the door, open now, and heard, "Where's my Aqua Velva?" She told him it was in the cabinet, turned back to the door and Jama was a few steps below her looking the same, grinning at her.

"Who's that, your nigga? You live together?"

"Tonight's his sleep-out."

"Likes Aqua Velva means he's got cheap skin. Tell him that, we have time. You gonna invite me in?"

"Yeah, Xavier'll want to see you."

Jama said, "You want to know something? You aren't as different as I thought. You live with that nigga, he contaminates you."

"What did you think I was," Dara said, "a virgin?"

"You were yourself, always you every minute. Different than other women."

"Tell me what you've been up to."

"I blew up that ship."

"I thought Helene did. It doesn't matter." She saw Xavier come out of the bedroom in his white briefs looking right at Jama.

"He says he blew up the gas ship."

"He might think he did," Xavier said. "Was Helene blew that ship up. With a rifle, fired it and the ship blew."

Jama said, "Listen to me. There were explosives with a cell phone we planted. I call the number . . . It was in the newspapers they found it was explosive charges blew open the pods of lethal gas."

"But was Helene must've touched it off," Xavier said.

They were standing in the living room, Jama in front of the coffee table, Dara and Xavier a couple of strides from him.

"You don't combust a combustible ship," Jama said, "with a rifle."

"You do this one. Had steel-cuttin rounds in it. You still usin a Walther?"

Jama unzipped his jacket to show them a new Walther stuck in the waist of his pants.

"You must've got it here," Xavier said. "Don't let it slip down in your pants."

"I can pull it before you move."

"You practice in front of a mirror like Bobby De Niro in that picture?"

Jama said, " 'You talkin to me?' "

"That's the one. You see a lot of movies?"

"In Arabic, with French subtitles, or English."

"Bobby De Niro speakin Arabic."

"It looks real."

Xavier said, "Dara . . . ?" and saw Jama's eyes shift and his hand go to his gun. He didn't pull it. "You want to offer Jama Rus*sell* a glass of port?"

"No, I don't," Dara said. "He comes here to shoot us 'cause we know his name."

"Everybody knows his name," Xavier said. "He's got to think up a new reason to shoot people."

"We have to watch him pose and swagger, act like an asshole," Dara said, "and I want to hit him with something." She turned looking around and picked up a sculpture from a lamp table: two girls sitting on a toadstool back-to-back, a brass piece six and a half inches high, but heavy. Dara raised it looking right at Jama.

And Xavier said, "Why don't you throw it at him?"

It was the same way he pulled it on Buck: drew the Walther as he sailed the flight bag at him like a Frisbee. Only it was aimed at Jama this time. Jama saw the brass statue coming at him and threw up his hand and rolled his shoulder the same way Buck did—giving Jama time to shoot him—giving Xavier the moment he needed to come at him with bare hands and take the Walther by the barrel sliding out of his pants and twist it hard and shove it into him, Jama pulling on the gun and it fired. Xavier held on to him face-to-face and said, "Boy, I think you just killed yourself."

Dara came over as Xavier laid him on the coffee table and pulled on his legs so his head would lie flat on the glass.

She said, "He's still alive."

"Can't believe it happen to him."

"Look at his eyes," Dara said. "He's thinking, But I was holding the gun."

Xavier said, "I didn't mean it to happen this way."

"What do we tell the police," Dara said, "he committed suicide?"

"He's been tryin to all his poor-ass life," Xavier said. "It finally took."

Dara said, "Is this how it ends?"

"What, your movie?"

"Djibouti."

"We must be close to it."